Spinning around, Jake saw a figure standing eight feet away. He could not tell if it was male or female, only that it wore a brown robe with a cowl that masked its features. It stood maybe five and a half feet tall, with stooped shoulders.

Jake's mind raced. No human being had made the shrill sound he had just heard.

The thing shuffled forward, its feet hidden by the robe. The canvas fabric undulated from the waist down, as though the thing moved on legs that lacked a skeletal structure.

Shoving his camera into his pocket, Jake reached for his Glock, holstered beneath his left arm. Before his hand closed around the gun's grip, the thing emitted a loud gurgling sound that chilled his blood, and something shot out at him from beneath the cowl. He ducked to his left, and the protrusion darted onto the space where he had just stood, then retracted into the darkness within the cowl like a tape measure. It must have been four feet long.

That's a tongue!

With his heart hammering, Jake pulled the Glock free, thumbed the safety off, and aimed at the approaching thing. The tongue, as thick as a snake, lanced out again, and he cocked his arm, aiming the Glock at the sky. The tongue wrapped around his forearm several times, its tip shaking in the air inches from his face. A vertical slit opened in the grayish-pink flesh, and Jake jerked his arm away as a stream of yellowish-green fluid sprayed out of the orifice.

Venom!

COSMIC FORCES

THE JAKE HELMAN FILES
COSMIC FORCES

GREGORY
LAMBERSON

MEDALLION
P R E S S
Medallion Press, Inc.
Printed in USA

DEDICATION

Dedicated with love to my daughter, Kaelin, who won't be
allowed to read this for another decade . . . or two.

Published 2011 by Medallion Press, Inc.
The MEDALLION PRESS LOGO
is a registered trademark of Medallion Press, Inc.

Typeset in Adobe Garamond Pro
Printed in the United States of America

ISBN: 9781605424088
10 9 8 7 6 5 4 3 2 1

First Edition

ACKNOWLEDGMENTS

As is often the case, I wish to thank Chris "the cop" Aiello for his advice on matters NYPD, specifically about the mayor's security detail. Thank you also to my wife, Tamar, who served as my advance reader and convinced me to make changes to the narrative. And thank you to author Jeff Strand, the other person I count on to steer me straight when I've gone too far.

As always, thank you to the team at Medallion Media Group (both Medallion Press and Medallion Movies), especially Helen A Rosburg, Adam Mock, Heather Musick, Emily Steele, Ali DeGray, Paul Ohlson, James Tampa, Arturo Delgado, and my editor, Lorie Popp, who now knows the Jake Helman timeline better than I do.

Finally, thank *you*.

PROLOGUE

The man and woman scrambled out of the forest and over the rocky crest overlooking the cliff, their gait disjointed because her left hip had been fused to his right side. They had broken all of their limbs after leaping to the bottom of a canyon months earlier. They had survived, as always, and their unattended bones healed in such a manner that they now resembled some strange hybrid of a spider and a praying mantis more than a pair of human beings.

The tanned animal hides they wore for clothing had become stuck to their open wounds and had become part of them, and flies and other insects nested in the wounds that remained exposed. Scabs and blisters covered them from head to toe, blood just one of several fluids that seeped from their cracked skin. The man had lost an eye in the fall, the woman most of her teeth. To make matters worse, the woman carried a child in her belly, for despite their misery and self-mutilation, they still found each other desirable.

They had been together for more years than either of them could count, their love surviving famine and flood, winter and warfare, pestilence and punishment. But this last year on God's green earth had been the worst. Even before their self-inflicted injuries, hunting for food had become all but impossible, requiring them to subsist on fruits and vegetables and, during their time on the ice, fish. On occasion they had stumbled upon fresh kills abandoned by other people and animals, and they had torn into the carrion with wild abandon, all the while becoming even more dependent upon each other to achieve even the simplest tasks. Things had changed so much since the days when they had been young and beautiful.

Now they crawled and kicked and stumbled along the shale cliff in the odd rhythm that had become normal for them, the mist from the waterfall cooling their tortured flesh in the afternoon sun. A stream of obscenities poured from their mouths, hers more guttural than his; that too had become part of their rhythm. Spasms of pain ripped through their ankles and shins and the bloody fingers they used to stab the ground for balance. Salty tears burned the sores on their cheeks, causing whimpers and drool to slide off their tongues in unison.

At last they reached the cliff's edge, where they stood as erect as possible, man and woman, husband and wife, and gazed across the great lake. The clear blue sky permitted them to discern the hazy shore on the opposite side, some sixty miles away. The man's right hand found the woman's left hand, their fingers interlocking. The lake appeared beautiful, natural, and serene. Seagulls swooped above the choppy waves.

The man turned his head so his good eye focused on his woman. *I love you*, he thought.

And I you, he heard her think.

They each mustered a hopeful smile. Then they stepped off the cliff.

Maybe we'll die even before we strike the water, he hoped. But he knew better and so did she.

They plummeted, their stomachs rising up their throats. The velocity pulled at their flesh and blurred their vision as the water grew closer, the sun's silver reflection on its surface brighter.

Impact.

The water shattered their bodies. The man prayed they would lose consciousness, for it would be impossible to swim to shore in their fleshy sacks of broken bones. But water filled his nostrils and mouth, and he found himself choking and alert.

Husband, his wife cried into his brain, still gripping his hand.

They did not drown.

They did not die.

Sinking deep into the water, they changed.

CHAPTER 1

On a chilly April morning, Jake Helman sat on a dark green wooden bench bolted to the ground in the Tower's shadow, eating a hot dog that bled ketchup and mustard. The narrow stretch of trees, divided by a single asphalt path, was all that remained of the park which had once existed where the modern skyscraper now stood like a corporate monolith. Jake had worked for Nicholas Tower, the reclusive billionaire who had owned Tower International until the man's violent death in his penthouse a year and a half earlier. In fact, Jake had caused Old Nick's death, which hadn't exactly been in his job description.

A lot had changed since then: Jake had set up shop as a private investigator just a block away on East Twenty-third Street, the better to observe the Tower and any suspicious goings-on there. Tower had monopolized the genetics industry and had engaged in secret and illegal genetic experiments. The old man had also hired a serial killer, the Cipher, to steal souls for him. Tower had imprisoned the souls in his Soul Chamber, and after Jake uncovered Tower's plan to strike a Faustian bargain with the demon Cain in exchange for an extra lifetime, the old man ordered the Cipher to kill Jake's estranged wife, Sheryl. In return, Jake killed the Cipher. He had also killed Kira Thorn, Tower's executive assistant, but that had been in self-defense.

Jake often had trouble believing those horrible events had transpired. He had already quit doing drugs shortly before Sheryl's murder, and since then he had stopped drinking and smoking. Exercise had become part of his daily routine, and except for the dark void Sheryl's death had left in his soul and the mind-bending knowledge that supernatural forces existed, he felt physically better than he had in years. He enjoyed working as a private investigator far more than he had as an NYPD homicide detective. One vice he hadn't given up was hot dogs, which he found convenient to eat during his daily vigil outside the Tower. Years earlier, he had watched squirrels race around the park that had been here before the Tower's construction. Now he wondered if Old Nick's man-made park remained in the Tower's penthouse.

His cell phone vibrated in his pocket, and he checked the display screen: *unavailable.* He waited for the call to end and listened to his voice mail. He didn't like surprises.

"This message is for Jake Helman," a distraught-sounding female voice said.

In her forties, Jake estimated.

"I'd rather not give you my real name. Just call me Mrs.

6

White. I'd like to engage your services. Please call me back so we can arrange a meeting."

Duty calls. Jake finished his dog and returned the call.

Sitting in his fourth-floor office, Jake gazed out the sooty window at the Tower with his remaining eye. Dark clouds crept across the sky above the building. A former informant, addicted to a street narcotic called Black Magic, had destroyed Jake's left eye with a knife in an assassination attempt in this very office. In retaliation, Jake had buried a stone replica of the Maltese Falcon in the man's skull. He had worn an eye patch for a while and then switched to a glass eye identical in color to the one he had lost.

One doctor had urged him to file an application to have an experimental new eye grown, but Jake refused to have anything to do with therapeutic cloning, one of the businesses Tower International had monopolized before the government had intervened with an antitrust suit in the wake of Old Nick's death. Jake's right eye had adapted to the change in its depth of field, and Jake had grown accustomed to cleaning his glass eye on a daily basis.

Jake knew he had become obsessed with the Tower, but who could blame him? He had made bringing Tower International down his goal in life. He'd come close, and as a result, the global economy had gone into a tailspin. At least things were starting to rebound on that front; certainly his business prospects had shown improvement. But that didn't let Tower International off the hook.

A man's got to have something to live for, he thought.

Edgar lighted on his desk. Jake had erected a cage wall that ran the length of the office, providing the raven with space to move about, but he seldom secured the door, instead giving Edgar the run of the place. The windows remained closed at all times. Staring at the shiny black feathers of the two-foot raven, Jake found it almost impossible to believe that the bird had once been a human being: Edgar Hopkins, his former partner in the Special Homicide Task Force. Edgar had dated the wrong woman, a voodoo bokor who had transmogrified him into his current state. As a raven, Edgar had sent the woman plummeting to her death at a construction site, extending his feathered state to a life sentence. Not for the first time, Jake wondered how many of Edgar's memories or humanity the raven retained.

As if in answer, the black bird blinked at him.

"You love that bird, don't you?" Carrie stood in the open doorway, all four and a half feet of her. Razor-sharp dark hair, body piercings, tattoos.

Jake held one hand out to Edgar, who pecked at his fingers. "Yes, I do."

Carrie smiled. "That's so sweet. Big, tough private eye with a sentimental streak. I bet you couldn't hurt a fly. Need me to stick around, boss?"

Carrie had cut her grad school schedule in half, so Jake had increased her hours at the office. He allowed her to manage his business, which needed managing since he procrastinated when it came to filling out reports and maintaining records.

"No, take off. I have to meet a client soon, and she wants to keep a low profile."

"Ooooooh . . ."

Now Jake smiled. "Get out of here before Ripper gets suspicious." Carrie had been dating Ripper for as long as Jake had known her. She claimed he was a real badass, but Jake had never met him.

"Okay. See you tomorrow. Good night, Edgar."

The raven watched Carrie leave.

Good kid, Jake thought as he heard Carrie walk through the railroad-style suite and close the front door. Genetics research had all but eliminated dwarfism, so Carrie belonged to the last generation of her kind. *Progress.*

Ten minutes later, he heard the buzzer for the downstairs door. On one of the security monitors recessed into one wall he saw a woman standing in the vestibule. She wore sunglasses and a hat, an obvious attempt at going incognito. Without bothering to ascertain her identity, he buzzed her into the building, then crossed the suite and stood waiting with the office door open.

The woman exited the elevator and approached him, her high heels clacking in the empty hallway, both hands inside the pockets of her belted raincoat. The sunlight shining through the window at the far end of the hall made the tiled floor gleam. Not so long ago, Jake had put a bullet through that window when a hit squad had invaded the building to take him out.

The assassins had failed. More bodies.

The woman walked with the poise and confidence of a movie star. She had removed her sunglasses in the elevator, and now she removed her hat, allowing Jake to discern her sophisticated features. She wore her dark hair pulled back as tight as Botox had left her porcelain skin.

She dyes her hair, Jake thought.

"Mr. Helman?" She enunciated each syllable like someone who had aced charm school. And yet Jake detected an edge in her voice, as if her insides were wrapped as tightly as her face. Her light brown eyes, which reflected light back at Jake, studied the walls behind him.

"Jake." He stepped away from the door. "Please come in." As she passed him, he caught a whiff of her perfume, subtle and expensive. In heels, she stood four inches lower than him. As her shoulder brushed against him, he felt an involuntary tingle of excitement. A year and a half after Sheryl's murder, he had yet to sleep with another woman. His body longed to be touched again even if his soul did not. So far, he had been too busy building his business to act on such impulses.

The woman turned to face him after he closed the door. "Would you mind locking that?"

"I'd planned to." He twisted the three locks on the door.

She scanned the reception area. "Are we alone?"

"As you requested." He gestured toward the open office door beyond the kitchen. "This way."

She walked forward and stopped within the office doorframe. When she removed her hands from her pockets, Jake noted her white gloves. "Would you mind closing those blinds?"

Classy but paranoid, Jake thought. *Or just cautious?*

Moving behind his desk, he closed the blinds, which elicited a mild croak from Edgar. Turning, he saw the woman's gaze settle on his office companion.

The color drained from her face. "Is that a *crow*?"

"Raven," Jake said in a soft voice, feeling compelled to put her at ease. "Though it's part of the crow family. Go to your room, Edgar."

Fluttering his wings, Edgar hopped into the caged area. He landed on the front page of the *New York Times*. Jake always left the paper on the floor for him, even though he had no idea if the raven could read. Jake closed the cage door, which was the size of a standard bedroom door.

"What an unusual pet," the woman said, sitting opposite the desk. She seemed groggy to Jake, who eased into his chair, the slab of mahogany between them.

"You look familiar, Mrs. White."

Glancing over her shoulder at Edgar, she crossed her legs. "I used to be a local TV reporter. Before that, I was Miss New York."

Jake resisted the urge to snap his fingers. As a uniformed cop, he had seen her on TV and in person. He had also seen her in the media many times since then. "And now you're married to the mayor."

"Marla Madigan." She offered him a sympathetic smile, as if embarrassed for his failure to recognize her.

You have my *sympathy*, he thought.

Myron Madigan had built his career as a crime-busting Manhattan district attorney. As a cop in the Street Narcotics Apprehension Program, Jake had only worked with the man's assistant district attorneys, but he knew Madigan's reputation as an opportunist who took all the credit for work done by his underlings, which of course was nothing new in the arena of politics.

Madigan's biography as a crusading mob buster on the order of Eliot Ness was pure modern mythology, and the man had been sworn in as mayor of New York City the same year Jake's life had gone to hell. When the world's economy plummeted after Jake had brought Tower International to its corporate knees, Madigan's popularity also fell to an all-time low, his chances of winning reelection slim at best. The tough, occasionally nasty veneer required to prosecute powerful criminals had not served the new mayor well. With employment down, crime rose, making the man who had campaigned on law and order appear ineffective.

Jake had inadvertently given the mayor a gift when he destroyed the organization behind Black Magic, the deadly narcotic that had ravaged the city. The drug vanished from the streets overnight, and the crime rate decreased by double digits. Because Jake had been forced to cover his tracks, the drug's sudden disappearance went unexplained, and true to form, Madigan seized the credit. At the same time, the nation's economy showed gradual signs of improvement due to federal support, and such signs always manifested themselves in big cities first. Madigan's approval ratings climbed, and now he was a shoo-in to remain in Gracie Mansion.

"Do you mind if I smoke?" Marla's voice conveyed hope and sadness at the same time.

"Not at all."

"Do you have a cigarette?" A muscle in her cheek twitched.

"I'm afraid not."

"Oh." She sighed. "I'm not allowed to smoke anymore. It's bad for Myron's image, so he made me quit when we got married."

Control freak, Jake thought, summoning a mental image of the mayor's sneering features and receding hairline. The man reminded him of Count Orlok in *Nosferatu*, the silent German vampire film. "How can I help you, Mrs. Madigan?"

Marla's face drew tighter. "I want you to spy on my husband."

Jake studied Marla's features. A beautiful woman recognized as the city's first lady and admired for her charitable works, she had sacrificed her career as a popular TV reporter to serve as unofficial hostess to powerful visitors and dignitaries from around the world. "You think he's cheating on you?"

"I'm certain of it. A woman knows these things."

"I'm sorry, but I don't handle spousal cases. It's sort of a code with me."

She uncrossed her legs, drummed her fingers on one knee, then crossed her legs again. "How . . . *manly* of you. It's my understanding that spousal investigations comprise the bulk of a private investigator's caseload."

"Maybe for most investigators . . ."

"But not you."

"I'm not big on busting up marriages."

"My marriage has already been broken for a long time."

"Your husband is very powerful."

"So he should be allowed to do whatever he pleases? I sacrificed a lot for that man. I gave him two beautiful children. And my reward is that I'm *allowed* to be his public face, the warmth he lacks himself, while he lies to me and shows me and our children disrespect."

You sacrificed one career in the public eye for another. "Doesn't that go with the territory?"

"*Touché.* But this is no ordinary cheating husband. Myron is a man who trounces his enemies and gets whatever he wants. He's surrounded himself with yes-men whose careers depend on his success, so they'll do anything to protect him. I'm just a trophy for his mantel, trotted out to smile for the TV cameras."

"Again, I'm sorry. There are plenty of eyes out there who will take this case. I'll be glad to recommend one, if you like."

"You're not the first one I've come to with my problem."

Gee, thanks.

"Three other investigators accepted my retainer, only to tell me I had no case, that my husband is faithful to me."

"You don't believe them?"

"They were bought off or intimidated. I need someone who follows a code."

Her words seeped into his brain like maple syrup. "Have you

confronted your husband with your suspicions?"

"I have. He had me confined to a private medical facility up-state for psychiatric observation for two weeks. He would have kept me there longer, but my disappearance would have raised too many questions. His advisors kept it out of the press and even created a paper trail to show I was vacationing in Europe."

Jake had to wonder if she was pulling his leg. Or maybe she really needed the treatment. She certainly exhibited enough nervous traits to support psychological issues. "They held you against your will?"

"Of course. There was nothing I could do about it. When I made a fuss, they doped me up. To remain clearheaded—to hold on to some part of myself—I had to cooperate. Otherwise I'd still be there, pumped full of God knows what. Those drugs would have made me psychotic for real."

Who said anything about being psychotic? "What did you do when you were released?"

"I told Myron I wanted a divorce."

"And . . . ?"

Marla fixed him with a stare. "He said, 'You know that I can never let you have a divorce. I'll never allow that to happen.' I want you to think about that. In this day and age, what kind of a man believes he has such control over his wife, *especially* a man who's a public figure? But you see, Myron has a big family values base, and they would never accept a divorced mayor as their presidential candidate."

Jake raised one eyebrow.

"My husband has grand ambitions, and I'm one piece of his mosaic."

He felt her tension rising.

"Myron's always secretly admired the gangsters he used to put behind bars. He likes the way they rule with an iron fist and keep their women in line despite their indiscretions. I have no doubt I'll wind up back in that clinic if I try to leave him. He's having me followed; I know it. In the mansion, his 'advisors' always hover around me. When I leave, it's in the company of a security detail, for my 'own good,' and I have my own handlers to make sure I never speak to the press. I can't go anywhere without their eyes on me. I ducked out of a department store and took the subway to meet you now. I'm sure the security detail's going mad.

"This is why I need a private investigator: I need my life back, and to get it, I need evidence to force Myron into letting me go. Nothing else will work. I came here out of desperation. You're my only hope. I'm begging you, for the sake of my children, to take this case. Otherwise, I might as well be dead."

Jake followed the wide path along Carl Schurz Park facing the East River. Moisture hung heavy in the air, and darkness swirled within the clouds blotting the sky. So far, it had been a wet spring. He and Sheryl had lived only a few blocks from here, and this had been one of her favorite places. He had stopped coming months earlier because such trips had become too painful for him. The Cipher had murdered Sheryl beneath the viaduct less than two hundred yards away from where he now stood. She had been helpless, just like Marla Madigan.

He had his doubts about taking Marla's case, though. She exhibited signs of paranoia. It was entirely possible she was delusional. But he sensed genuine fear in her eyes. Still, he had good reason not to touch this case. Myron Madigan had powerful resources at his beck and call.

"Do you know who Karlin Reichard is?" Marla had said in his

office. "He's a kingmaker. A rich old shipping magnate who's bank-rolled the campaigns of dozens of senators and governors all over the country. And all of his boys won their elections. Karlin took an interest in Myron when my husband was a lowly ADA. It's because of him that Myron became district attorney and then mayor. And it's because of him that Myron has his sights set on the Oval Office. It can happen. Men with that much money can't be stopped."

Jake had done some quick research on Karlin Reichard after Marla left his office. The man made millions in the shipping business, then millions more on the stock market. *Forbes* magazine estimated his current net worth at nearly twelve billion dollars, which did indeed make him an attractive figure in political circles, even though he used part of his fortune to remain out of the public eye. Jake knew the type.

Leaning against the metal railing, with his back to the river and Roosevelt Island, he studied Gracie Mansion through the trees. The two-story structure stood nestled in the park, surrounded by a high fence, facing East End Avenue, off Eighty-eighth Street. The main floor served as a museum open to the public, with the mayor and his family residing upstairs. Uniformed police officers manned an outside security booth, while plainclothes cops made up the security detail. Jake knew this because he had spent six months working the security detail between his tours with SNAP and Special Homicide. He had no trouble picturing the layout of the mansion's second floor, at least as it had been maintained by Madigan's two-term predecessor.

Right now, somewhere on the second floor, Marla lived in fear of her husband. Myron Madigan was a vindictive politician who penalized those who opposed him. Entire neighborhoods suffered when their councilmen refused to toe the line.

Powerful men. Powerful forces.

Jake knew he would be risking his livelihood if he stepped into this fire.

Taking out his cell phone, he pressed the number he had saved earlier.

A telephone rang once, followed by a beep. No outgoing message identified the voice mail service's user.

"This is Jake. I've decided to take your case."

CHAPTER 2

"I'm sorry to bother you so late, but I need your help and I couldn't sleep."

Jake glanced at the digital clock beside his bed. He still lived in the small back room behind his office, a situation he hoped to rectify soon. It was just after midnight, and he hadn't fallen asleep yet. "What is it, Joyce? Is Martin all right?"

"Not exactly."

Jake's muscles tightened. Joyce was an ex-girlfriend of Edgar's and the mother of his son, Martin. Jake had vowed to take care of them both after Edgar's transmogrification into a raven. He had made good on that promise for several months, taking an interest in Martin's education and shooting hoops with the boy, as the two of them had done with Edgar for several years. But a well-paying case had interrupted their routine, then another one and another after that. Jake found himself unable to reject needy clients, and now he felt guilty for ignoring Martin. "What's wrong?"

"I got a call from his principal," Joyce said. "He hasn't been to class for over a week. Before that, he missed two days a week for two weeks, and before that one day a week for three weeks."

Six weeks, Jake thought. *Has it been that long?*

No, it's been longer. He stared at the door that separated the room from his office, where Edgar now lived. "What does he have to say for himself?"

"Nothing. He won't talk to me, and when I question him, he throws a fit. I've been making him lunch every day, and every morning he heads off for school. I'm at work when he gets out, but when I come home at six, he's in his bedroom with the door closed. I'm afraid he's getting into some real trouble."

Jake rubbed sleep from his eyes. "What's for breakfast?"

Jake saw Joyce framed within the living room window as he parked his Nissan Maxima in the cracked concrete driveway of the two-story Jackson Heights house. He had bought the vehicle brand-new as a replacement for the Chevy Malibu he had destroyed outside One Police Plaza six months earlier. Trotting up the front steps, he saw the front door open. Joyce stood there dressed in a pastel pantsuit for work.

"Thank you for coming," she said.

He kissed her cheek. "Don't mention it."

Moving inside, Jake regretted that Edgar had never made things work out with Joyce. Maybe things would have turned out differently for him. Jake entered the yellow kitchen and sat at the table.

Joyce served him a plate with fried eggs, sausage, and potatoes. "Welcome to Joyce's Diner."

"It's been too long since I had a home-cooked meal." *How long?* he wondered as he peppered the food. *Months before Sheryl's murder.* He had been too busy in homicide and shaking down his informants for drugs to enjoy a quiet meal at home with his wife. Lost opportunities, just like Edgar and Joyce. But at least Joyce had a son to show for their time together. Sampling the potato, he moaned with pleasure.

"Martin will be down any minute."

Jake cut into his eggs. "Then I'd better hurry."

He had finished half his breakfast when he heard a staccato of footsteps on the stairs. A moment later, Martin appeared in the doorway and froze in his tracks. The boy had grown at least an inch since Jake had last seen him. *Is this what it's like to be a divorced father?*

"Jake . . ." Martin sounded pleasantly surprised. Then he shifted suspicious eyes to his mother.

Jake tried to sound cheerful. "Hi, Martin."

"What are you doing here?"

Jake heard a change in the boy's voice.

"He's here to see you, baby," Joyce said.

"I can guess why. And I'm not your baby."

He's definitely grown a chip on his shoulder, too, Jake thought. "Hey, don't speak to your mother that way."

Martin scrunched up his face. "Who are you to tell me what to do? You aren't my father."

"I never said I was. But I am your friend. I always have been.

And wherever your father is, he'd want you to treat your mother with respect."

"My father's dead. If he isn't, then he's dead to me."

Ouch. Martin had changed almost as much as Edgar had. "He's not dead; I promise you."

"Your promises don't mean shit to me."

Joyce let loose an exasperated sigh. "Martin . . ."

Jake gestured for her to relax. "I hear you're cutting school." "So?" Martin eyed Joyce again. "I guess there's no need to pretend anymore." Pivoting on one sneaker heel, he stomped into the living room.

A moment later, Jake heard the front door slam.

"Teenagers," Joyce said, massaging her temples. "So sure they know more than we do."

"Teenager? Ah, shit. I forgot his birthday."

"That's all right. I know how busy you've been . . ." *Yeah, busy paying off that damned car.*

"Jake, I'm at my wit's end. Please tell me what to do with that child. I'm so frightened that he's running around with the wrong crowd, getting himself into trouble. I don't want him selling drugs, or worse, getting himself killed. He's all I've got."

"Nothing's going to happen to him," Jake said, rising from his chair and entering the living room. "Have you checked his room?"

Joyce followed him. "Yes, of course. No drugs or weapons."

Peering out the window, Jake watched which direction Martin took. "That's good. What does Martin do when he's home?"

"He's on his computer all night. You know, chat rooms, message boards, that sort of thing."

This triggered Jake's radar. The Internet was a wonderful tool for predators seeking children to prey upon. "Check what sites he spends his time on. Can you get off from work today?"

"If you think it's necessary. Aren't you going to stop him? I thought you were going to talk to him."

"Oh, I'll talk to him, all right. After I've seen where he goes."

"You're going to *tail* him? He'll make you for sure in this neighborhood."

Jake offered her a reassuring smile. "Don't count on it."

Raising the Maxima's trunk door, Jake traded his leather jacket for a navy peacoat. Next, he pulled on a knit ski cap and a pair of dark sunglasses. As the pièce de résistance, he dabbed spirit gum onto the silicone backing of a reddish handlebar mustache, which he pressed against his face. Closing the trunk, he glanced over his shoulder at Joyce, who stood wide eyed on the steps.

"Don't worry. I'll get to the bottom of this."

Pocketing the car's remote control, he set off in the direction Martin had gone. He sighted the boy one block later, walking alone with his hands in his pockets and a headset running to his iPod. At Roosevelt Avenue, Martin climbed the stairs to the Flushing line.

Jake swiped his MetroCard through the turnstile slot, then followed his subject up another flight of metal stairs. He joined the crowd on the platform, about twenty-five feet away from Martin, who continued listening to his iPod. Morning rush hour commuters stood shoulder to shoulder, front to back, breathing and sweating on each other.

He's not moving his body, Jake noted. Kids tended to bob their heads or shuffle from side to side when they listened to music. *He's listening to something else.* Martin took no notice of him.

The headlights of a train appeared in the distance, and the Number 7 pulled into the station accompanied by the sound of screeching metal. Commuters filled the train, packing it like canned vegetables. Martin boarded a car in the middle, so Jake pushed his way into the front of the same car. Twenty people separated them, the distance negligible. Like most of the other straphangers, Martin stared straight ahead, not really focusing on anyone as the train left the station. The New Yorkers avoided each other's gazes, averting their eyes whenever they accidentally made contact.

Jake felt liberated behind his shades, free to survey the dense mixture of ethnicities, professionals, blue-collar workers, and students. He swayed from side to side, curious to see where this ride would take him.

Back to Manhattan. Jake always returned to the island city, like salmon swimming upstream to their spawning ground. The train pulled into Forty-second Street, Times Square, and the commuters released a collective sigh as the doors chimed open. Jake allowed the flesh and fabric tide to guide him onto the grimy platform, where he slowed to locate Martin. Bodies rushed around him. A woman bumped him. A man shoved him. Someone stepped on his left foot.

No sign of his quarry. He heard a jazz band playing off to his right and saw the feet of three teenage boys above the crowd as they performed acrobatics.

Where is he?

Jake whipped off his sunglasses to see better and spotted the back of Martin's head forty feet in front of him. Now it was his turn to make his way through the crowd, though he believed he did so with a great deal more grace than his fellow commuters.

Martin, and then Jake, joined a tributary of commuters rushing downstairs to the N and R platform.

West side or downtown, Jake thought as he reached the filthy lower platform. On the other side of a large metal garbage receptacle, Martin glanced in his direction. Jake's body stiffened, but the boy peered down the tunnel, waiting for the next train. When an R train pulled in, they waited for the passengers to disembark. Jake watched Martin board the train and did likewise. Martin sat on a corner bench. Jake remained standing, even though he saw seats available, so he could turn his back to Martin. He observed the boy's reflection in the glass pane of the door at the rear of the car. One stop later, at Thirty-fourth Street, Martin rose.

West side and *downtown.*

Jake exited the train a second after Martin and followed him upstairs, through the turnstiles, and up a flight of steps to street level. The scents of pretzels, salted peanuts, and fresh brewed coffee assailed his senses as he emerged into the daylight. Manhattan never smelled better to him than when he escaped the subway system. Traffic noise filled his ears, and Macy's filled his vision. His heart sped up as he feared he had lost track of Martin again, but he spotted the boy up the block, heading toward Eighth Avenue.

Go west, young man.

At the intersection, Martin crossed Thirty-fourth Street, then Eighth Avenue, passing beneath the shadow of a tall granite building.

Jake followed at a distance, ignoring a young woman in hippie attire who handed out flyers at the corner. A man and two other women, each pushing twenty, distributed flyers on the other corners. *Some kind of sale,* Jake supposed.

"Watch the stars!" the hippie said, holding a flyer out to Jake, who noted small stars tattooed in a circle around her wrist.

Oh, Jesus, Jake thought.

Martin turned left, through the building's revolving door, and Jake stopped in his tracks. With his eyebrows furrowed, he tilted his head back so he could see the top of an Art Deco structure, which rose thirty stories into the air. The Dream Castle, once a grand hotel, had been remodeled into an office building known for decades as the Manhattan Building and then converted into a residential hotel. But the building's reputation had taken an altogether stranger twist over the last three years: the son of a deceased science fiction author had bought it, ostensibly to headquarter a production company and publishing house, Sky Cloud Dreams. Instead, he created a cult with its own worldwide social-networking website. During the last year, Manhattan had become ground zero for the Dreamers, and the Manhattan Building had become known as the Dream Castle.

Jake waited twenty seconds, then bolted across the street and pushed his way through the revolving door and emerged into a dark lobby with polished floors and a high ceiling. Boutique shops lined the walls: a bookstore, a magazine store, a DVD outlet, and a clothing store, all dedicated to the organization that owned and operated the building.

Jake crossed the lobby, his rubber-soled shoes squeaking, to a concierge behind a black marble station.

A pale-looking young man with wispy blond hair looked up at him with a curious expression. "Can I help you, sir?"

"A boy just came in here, thirteen years old. Where did he go?"

"I'm not allowed to share information about our visitors."

Jake picked up a clipboard and ran his right pointer finger to the bottom of the list of signatures. Then he ran his finger sideways from *Martin* to *Orientation*.

"Sir!" The concierge reached for the clipboard, which Jake

allowed him to take.

"Orientation for what?"

"I really can't say."

"Take me to that boy or bring his ass out here."

The concierge cocked one eyebrow. "You don't look like his father. Are you a police officer?"

Not anymore. Jake controlled his temper. "No," he said through clenched teeth.

"Then I'm afraid you'll have to leave. *Now,* before I call security."

Resisting the urge to say, *I'll be back,* Jake turned on one heel and strode outside, where he flipped open his cell phone and struck autodial.

Jake pulled off his cap, peeled away his fake mustache, and stuffed them both into his pockets as a short Hispanic woman with curly brown hair approached him. She wore tight slacks and a short jacket that did little to de-emphasize her figure, and her gold hoop earrings gleamed in the gray morning light. "Okay," Maria Vasquez said with a degree of challenge as she chewed her gum. "Here I am. What's wrong with Martin?"

Jake looked Maria over. She appeared as lovely and as lively as she had been on their one and only dinner date six months earlier. Like Jake, she had been Edgar's partner in NYPD's Special Homicide Task Force. Unlike him, she had no idea what had happened to Edgar and blamed Jake for his disappearance.

Jake nodded at the Castle. "He's in there. The Dreamers have him."

Maria aimed a sideways glance at the building. "Are you

fucking kidding me? How do you know?"

"Joyce called me so I tailed him."

Now she looked him over. "Did you try to pull him out?"

"Tried, failed. I don't carry a shield anymore, remember? That's why I called you."

"Come on." She pushed through the revolving door, Jake following. Inside the lobby, she flashed her gold shield at the concierge. "You got a kid in here named Martin Hopkins. Take me to him now."

The concierge blanched. "Do you have a warrant, Officer?"

"It's detective. And I don't need a goddamned warrant. You got a minor in here somewhere, his mother is worried sick, and if you don't take me to him this minute I'm going to haul your ass to jail."

"But—but I'll get in trouble!"

"More trouble than if I charge you with kidnapping? That's a *federal* crime."

"Right this way." He led them to the elevators and summoned one, then gestured inside it. "You want the auditorium on the fourth floor."

Maria seized his collar and pulled him into the elevator with her. "You're insulting me. Do I look stupid? Get your ass in here."

"I can't leave the lobby unattended!"

"Don't make me pull my gun out of its holster."

Stepping beside them, Jake thumbed the fourth-floor button. As the door closed, he couldn't help but notice the sweet smell of Maria's perfume. "Nice moves."

She shot a sharp look at him. "I'm doing this for Martin."

"Understood."

They exited on the fourth floor, a long, wide corridor that led to double wooden doors. Maria shoved the concierge forward, and he stumbled over his own feet. Jake *really* liked her style. The concierge faced the doors, took a deep breath, and pulled them open, revealing a darkened auditorium with seating for a hundred.

Perhaps two dozen people watched the speaker on the stage, a man in his thirties standing at a lectern, the holographic images of planets, solar systems, and galaxies projected around him. A giant light box in the center of a black void gleamed, *Watch the stars!* The speaker shifted his gaze in their direction and stopped speaking in midsentence.

Maria tapped Jake's arm. "You stay here."

As she strode forward, the concierge tried to slip away, but Jake clamped one hand on his shoulder and the man relented.

"Lights!" Maria waved her shield over her head.

"What is this?" the speaker said in an indignant tone.

"Turn the lights on before I stick a flashlight up your rectum and illuminate your cavities."

The man toggled a switch on the lectern, and the house lights came up. At the same time, the holographic universe winked out.

Scanning the audience, Jake spotted Martin sitting up with his eyes locked on Maria.

"Let me see your ID," Maria told the man.

"I demand to know what you're doing here—"

"I'm ready to call in a strike force if you don't produce some paperwork."

As the man took his wallet from his back pocket, Martin sprang out of his seat and ran up the aisle, freezing when he came face-to-face with Jake, who guided the concierge into a chair.

Maria glanced in his direction, then held the speaker's wallet closer to her face. "You see that young man, Mr. Prewitt?"

The speaker nodded. "Yes, I see him."

"He's a minor. He's got no business being here."

"Our doors are open to everyone."

Maria gestured to the other people seated in the auditorium. "These other idiots are adults. You want to teach them to worship spaceships, or whatever the hell it is you're about, you go right ahead. But you stay away from children." She handed the wallet back to him. "That boy belongs in school. He's truant, and you're contributing to the delinquency of a minor."

Prewitt's face darkened. "This is religious persecution. Maybe I should ask for your ID, Officer—?"

"*Detective* Vasquez." Maria snatched the wallet, then took a business card out of her jacket pocket, inserted it into the wallet, and pressed the leather back into the man's hand. "You want to call my principal, knock yourself out. But I promise, if you try to indoctrinate any other kids into this wacky cult of yours—"

"*Religious order.*"

"—I'll bring a shit storm of trouble raining down on you and this whole organization. You think I'm just a cop? Wrong. I belong to a brotherhood. And that brotherhood has ties to other brotherhoods, like the FBI and the IRS. You like those letters? I got more of them for you, like DOJ. Shall I continue, or do we understand each other?"

Prewitt drew his lips into a tight smile. "We understand each other . . . Detective."

"Good." Maria returned up the aisle. Facing Jake, she slid one hand on Martin's shoulder. "Let's go."

Outside the building, Martin shrugged Maria's hand off. "Let go of me."

Maria looked him in the eye. "You want me to kick your skinny little ass? Because I'll do it."

Martin glared at Jake. "Why'd you have to bring her?"

Before Jake could answer, Maria said, "Because he can't do shit when it comes to the law. He's just a private dick. But me, I carry weight, at least to fuckwads like those losers in there. What the hell's the matter with you, getting involved with those people? Don't you know they're crazy?"

"You don't know what you're talking about. *Either* of you."

Maria glanced at Jake. "Makes you glad you don't have kids, doesn't he? What are you going to do with him now?"

"Joyce is waiting for him at home," Jake said. "How about a lift to Queens?"

"Do I look like a taxi driver?"

"You think he's actually going to take two trains back with me? Like you said, I can't do anything in this situation. I need the long arm of the law at my side."

Maria studied Martin's angry features. "Okay, let's go. I'm parked on the next block."

"Wait a minute." Jake jogged over to the nearest flyer distributor. "Give me a couple of those."

The freckle-faced girl's dark eyes brightened. "Watch the stars, brother!"

"Yeah, yeah. Live long and prosper."

CHAPTER
3

Maria parked her Toyota in front of the Jackson Heights house.

Joyce opened the front door and ran down the steps as Martin got out of the car. The boy had listened to his iPod during the whole drive to Queens, refusing to speak to Jake in the backseat.

"My God, where did you go?"

Ignoring his mother, Martin strutted into the house.

Jake and Maria got out at the same time.

"What happened?" Joyce said.

"It's okay," Jake said. "At least he's not slinging."

With a relieved look, Joyce hurried after her son. "Martin!"

Maria motioned to the Nissan Maxima. "I take it this is yours?"

"Need to see *my* paperwork?"

Maria followed Joyce inside.

"A *cult*?" Joyce stared at Martin.

"It's a religious order," Martin said, looking down at the living room coffee table.

"They worship space aliens," Jake said.

Martin jerked his chin in Jake's direction. "What do *you* know?"

"Enough." Jake handed one of the flyers to Joyce. It depicted childlike drawings of people of different ethnicities holding hands, a giant planet earth behind them. At the top, *Watch the stars.* At the bottom, contact information.

"At least you don't have to worry about him going back there," Maria said. "They won't let him in. I promise you that."

Martin's eyes filled with fury. "I hate you both!"

"That's enough, Martin," Joyce said.

Martin jumped up, knocking his chair over. "I hate you, too!"

"Your father would kick your butt for saying that," Jake said.

"Well, he isn't here, is he? You're the worst one of all, because you've forgotten what it means to *belong* to something. You were a cop until you screwed up." He charged upstairs.

Joyce's voice softened. "Martin . . ."

"Let him go," Jake said. "He needs to work things out."

Martin's bedroom door slammed shut, and they heard him thump across the floor.

Joyce shook her head. "Back onto his computer . . ."

Maria said, "Joyce, the Dreamers communicate through

a social-networking site—"

"He spends his time on a sci-fi forum called HyperSpaceBook."

"Either he's misleading you, or there's a link between them," Jake said. "You need to put a block on that computer. Also, he probably subscribes to a newsgroup of some kind. Make sure he has no way of communicating with these people."

"I don't believe it," Joyce said. "I know he's hurting over Edgar's disappearance, but I had no idea he would do anything like this. I can't watch him around the clock."

Jake's gaze settled on the iPod that Martin had left on the coffee table. He picked it up, positioned the earphones, and switched the player on.

A soothing female voice with a British accent intoned, "Imago will return to earth, and on that day we can all shed our human forms . . ."

Jake pulled the phones out of his ears and set the player before Joyce. "You need to figure out exactly what this wacky cult is all about and what they want from their members."

Joyce stared at the iPod with realization growing in her eyes.

"I'm sorry, Joyce. I should have kept a better eye on him. I didn't expect anything like this to happen."

Joyce refused to touch the player. "There was nothing to see. He was always in his room on his computer or playing video games. Or reading. He's always loved science fiction."

Maybe too much, Jake thought.

Outside, as Jake unlocked the door to his Maxima, Maria said,

"This doesn't change anything between you and me. I'm still watching you."

Jake offered a slight smile. "Good. I like that."

"You may think you're cute, but I don't. I know you know more about Edgar's disappearance than you told Missing Persons and IAB. They may be satisfied with your story, but I'm not. I'm going to find out what happened to my partner and what you had to do with it."

Jake did not respond. Instead, he watched Maria walk to her Toyota. Then he slid behind the Maxima's wheel and keyed the ignition.

Sitting at his office computer, Jake located the website he sought: *Sky Cloud Dreams, Spiritual Enlightenment for the 21st Century*. Stars glowed, quasars pulsed, and galaxies beckoned on the screen. As he tracked over the celestial images, hidden menu buttons appeared for a message board, a social-networking site, current events, teachings, global outreach, and a bookstore.

Navigating the home page, he clicked on the button for "About Sky Cloud Dreams." An image appeared of a smiling, gray-haired man with dark sideburns, who wore a turtleneck and a blazer and stood beside a desk, two fingers touching its surface. A globe on the desk and a library behind him conveyed a friendly, academic demeanor.

His teeth are bleached or the photo's been doctored, Jake thought. So much for sincerity. He read:

Sky Cloud Dreams is the culmination of decades of research, exploration, and development by Benjamin Bradley, son of the late, acclaimed science fiction author Campbell Bradley.

"My father used his fiction to encourage people to question their beliefs, to open their minds to the infinite possibilities of the unknown, and to look within themselves for truth," says Benjamin. "He instilled in me the philosophy of interiorization, the powers of the mind, and mankind's connection to the universe. I've spent my life developing these spiritual principles and scientific methodology into mental technology that can bring you peace and fulfillment. I hope you'll take the time to explore what Sky Cloud Dreams has to offer you. Visit our forums and social-networking site. Speak to our members and find out what you have in common with them and how they can help you discover truth within yourself."

Sky Cloud Dreams is a global network of spiritually minded individuals dedicated to universal truth and enlightenment. *Universal truth.* Jake frowned. *Interiorization. Mental technology.* No reference to space aliens, but buzzwords designed to captivate and mislead people desperate for guidance. *Enlightenment.*

He clicked on *social networking*, and a separate website loaded.

You must register to log on to this site.

"I bet you do."

Click.

The registration page requested all of the usual information: name, address, telephone number, e-mail address, birth date. Jake tapped at the keyboard, and his imagination gave birth to Brian Powers, who lived on West Fourteenth Street in Manhattan. He submitted the information and waited.

This information is incorrect. Please try again.

Jake narrowed his eye at the screen. The Dreamers possessed a sophisticated database. *Who the hell are these people?*

He keyed *HyperSpaceBook* into his browser, and that website loaded. Images from popular science fiction movies and television series morphed into each other on the screen. Jake navigated reviews, news blogs, and a message board. Scanning the forum, he took note of the odd aliases used by the community members: Space Dusted, Kid Nova, Star Rapper. He searched for Martin's name but couldn't find it, and none of the aliases seemed like obvious possibilities.

Then he searched the site for more pertinent information, like its owner: Solar Dreams Entertainment. A quick Google search revealed that Sky Cloud Dreams owned the dummy corporation.

They use the entertainment site as bait to lure people to the primary social-networking site. Without knowing Martin's alias, it was impossible for him to follow the exact method of contact. Clicking on "Registration," he created an alias for himself—Soul Searcher—and posted an introductory message in a section of the forum reserved for that purpose. He identified himself as a New York sci-fi fan looking to befriend people with similar interests.

Within minutes, half a dozen HyperSpaceBookers welcomed him aboard, each asking a different question: *What are your favorite books? What movies do you like? Do you TiVo any shows? What do you think about politics and religion in science fiction? How old are you? Do you like to attend conventions?*

They're probably all the same person, Jake thought, picturing one of the Dreamers sitting at a computer in a Dream Castle office. Using his trusty search engine, he located another science fiction entertainment site, ascertained that Sky Cloud Dreams didn't own it, and drew up a list of recent science fiction movies, novels, and TV shows. He used this list to answer the questions posed to him and waited for additional responses.

It didn't take long: *Hey, you should really check out this forum. It's great!*

Jake clicked on the link posted by Star Warrior and wound up on the Sky Cloud Dreams forum. Switching back to HyperSpace-Book, he saw he had received a private message in his new mailbox.

Would you like a pass to see an advance screening of an exciting new science fiction movie? Just sign up here!

He clicked on the link and again found himself staring at the sign-up page for the Sky Cloud Dreams forum.

Martin had probably perused the entertainment website innocently enough and had then been lured to the Dreamers' board. How long had it taken the cultists to reach him? Surely longer than it took them to contact Jake, who had offered himself as bait.

Using different search engines, he assembled dossiers on Campbell Bradley and his son, Benjamin. The senior Bradley broke into publishing by writing science fiction stories for pulp magazines in the late 1950s. In the 1960s, he wrote a trio of novellas that were ultimately packaged as a single novel, *Celestial Passage.* The book received positive reviews but didn't catch on with the public until it was reprinted in 1970. Bradley capitalized on his "overnight" success by writing three sequels, which became even more popular in the early 1980s. The novels combined political commentary, psychedelic imagery, and enough action to satisfy different groups of readers.

When Hollywood came knocking on Bradley's door, the author refused to license the film rights to his books, which eventually became best sellers. He commented in a *Rolling Stone* interview, "I don't like what the 'dream factory' has done to wonderful books written by Ray Bradbury, Phil Dick, and Jim Herbert. Hollywood is run by accountants, and I don't need any more money. How much dough does one person need?"

Bradley died in 1999, leaving Benjamin the sole beneficiary of his estate. Benjamin had earlier tried his hand as a novelist with no success and had worked as a real estate agent for many years. Upon settling his father's inheritance, Benjamin sold the film rights to the four *Celestial* novels, attaching himself as a producer. Two films were theatrical motion pictures, followed by one TV miniseries and one direct-to-DVD sequel. Jake had heard of the films but hadn't seen them. Benjamin licensed several of Campbell's short stories and other novels as well, though no film adaptations had actually been made.

Unable to reignite Hollywood interest in his father's work, Benjamin formed his own production company, Sky Cloud Dreams. The company announced a slate of features based on different Bradley stories and hired several screenwriters to adapt them, but none of the films got off the ground. The only film produced by the company was a feature-length documentary on Campbell's life, which did well on the film festival circuit but failed to receive theatrical distribution. Sky Cloud released the film on DVD.

When the great recession struck, Benjamin found himself in a fortunate position: he had invested the millions he had earned from the *Celestial* productions wisely, and when the Manhattan Building went on the auction block because its owners had failed to pay their creditors, the former real estate agent seized the opportunity to purchase the building at a fraction of its former value. He kept several floors for his own needs and rented the others. He held *Celestial* conventions in the building, sold DVDs of the documentary in the lobby, and started his own publishing company to keep his father's books in print and cut out the middlemen; Sky Cloud Publications released the first e-book versions of Campbell Bradley's work.

And then, with very little fanfare, Benjamin set himself up as the central figure in a self-help organization that tapped into the science fiction market. Although he never became a recluse, he did avoid the spotlight other than that afforded him through his own media company.

Jake cracked his neck and his knuckles. Campbell Bradley had achieved success as a novelist and had resisted the urge to make a buck off Hollywood. Benjamin could not wait to license the literary properties and had used the money he made to start his own production company and purchase Manhattan real estate. Somewhere along the line, he decided to start a religious order that would appeal to the fans of his father's books. Had Bradley's production company's failure led to that decision, or had it been a front for the operation all along?

Jake returned to the sign-up page and keyed in his real information.

Hi, Jake! Thanks for visiting Sky Cloud Dreams. If you wish to participate in our exclusive forum, there is a $10.00 annual membership fee. Your membership package includes the Space Cloud Dreams handbook, access to the forum, invitations to free movie screenings, news updates, and discounts on Sky Cloud Dreams merchandise.

Jake stared at the screen. *A membership fee.* He tapped the middle finger of his right hand on his computer mouse. *For Martin.* He entered his credit card information and waited.

A prompt informed him that he had received "a special message" in his mailbox, where he found a greeting:

Dear Jake:

Thank you for becoming an Affiliate member of Sky Cloud Dreams. We invite you to visit our forum and interact with our other Affiliate, Associate, and Active members. Your membership package is on the way! In the meantime, we encourage you to click on the following link to download a preliminary version of the Sky Cloud Dreams handbook.

Your new friends,

The Sky Cloud Dreams Membership Committee

How inviting and encouraging. Jake clicked on the link, and his computer downloaded a PDF file.

Congratulations on becoming an Affiliate member of Sky Cloud Dreams! Your decision to join our group is one of the most important choices you'll make in your life. A whole new world is about to open up to you, not in the realms of science fiction or fantasy, but right here on earth—in your *mind.*

Jake glanced at the wall clock—2:55 p.m. He didn't have much time; he had work to do on the Madigan case. Skimming through the PDF handbook, he searched for telltale signs of what Sky Cloud Dreams was really about. The setup was too elaborate to be a simple marketing tool. He found biographies of Campbell Bradley and Benjamin Bradley, descriptions of Campbell's novels and the movies based on them, "A Guideline to Space Cloud Dreams Etiquette" (*Smile! Always be upbeat! Show respect to your fellow Dreamers!*), and invitations to free lectures held in the Dream Castle.

Finally, he came upon a short essay written by Benjamin Bradley and searched the double-talk before discovering a nugget of information:

COSMIC FORCES

Do you believe in a higher power but reject the dogma to which you've been exposed? Sky Cloud Dreams was founded on the belief system that our world was colonized by extraterrestrial beings who will one day return to earth to take believers to a better world. We call these beings the Imago. For more information, please arrange to attend one of our special seminars at Sky Cloud Dreams, exclusive and free to our members. Discover why governments and traditional religious organizations do not wish you to open your mind to the life-changing possibilities offered by the Imago.

Jake entered *Imago* into his browser, and two definitions appeared:

1 : an insect in its final, adult, sexually mature, and typically winged state

2 : an idealized mental image of another person or the self

Idealized insects, he thought as he pressed autodial on his cell.

A few rings later, Joyce answered.

"How's Martin?"

"Sullen," Joyce said. "He's in his room as usual."

"Did you search his websites like I suggested?"

"Of course. He spent all of his time on HyperSpaceBook and that site for the Dreamers. I blocked them like you told me to."

"Good. You also need to confiscate any books written by Campbell Bradley and any of those *Celestial* movies on DVD. The problem is, he can download them, too. Look for any brochures or literature from Sky Cloud Dreams, and check his computer for downloaded files. You really need to monitor his computer activity. Move his computer downstairs where you can keep an eye on him."

"He's going to hate me."

"He'll *resent* you but he'll get over it."

"When?"

"One step at a time. Another thing: Martin had to pay a membership fee with a credit card to join the Dreamers. I think the fee is just a rouse to collect data on members. They know your address, and they know your phone number. If you didn't buy that membership for him, you'd better keep a closer watch on your credit cards. Don't let him have any visitors for the time being."

"Thank you, Jake."

After saying good-bye, Jake checked the time again: 3:10 p.m. *Time to go to work.*

CHAPTER
4

Dressed in black beneath a gray duster, Jake stood in the crowd of uniformed police officers, media personnel, and interested citizens facing the new annex to the Central Park Police Station on Tranverse Road and West Eighty-sixth Street.

Mayor Myron Madigan stood on a platform erected for the occasion, flanked by police officials in their dress blues and his security detail, comprised of plainclothes, off duty cops. Red, white, and blue ribbons adorned the platform, and a large American flag provided a backdrop. Madigan waved to the crowd like a true politician and traded smiling remarks with the men around him. His red hair swept back from his receding hairline, his bushy eyebrows underscoring his stubby forehead.

A uniformed captain with craggy features stepped up to the microphone. "Good afternoon. I'm Captain John Collier, and I'd like to welcome you to today's ceremony. The Central Park Police Station, headquarters of the 22nd precinct command, is the oldest police station in New York City. It was designed by Calvert Vaux and built in 1871. That's almost a hundred and fifty years of NYPD history."

The crowd applauded, the police showing the most enthusiasm.

In one of the quietest neighborhoods, Jake thought.

"Our new annex will provide much-needed modernization and additional space to the command that protects twenty million visitors annually, and the original building will continue to serve as a base for New York's finest. It is my honor to introduce to you the man who made this upgrade possible, Mayor Myron Madigan."

The crowd whooped and cheered, and Madigan came forward. Collier lowered the microphone so the mayor did not need to, sparing him embarrassment. Madigan continued to wave to the crowd, beaming.

Jake disliked the man, but his feelings went no farther than that. Madigan was a political animal with grand ambitions, but Jake had known much worse men and women. If Marla told the truth about her husband confining her to a psychiatric facility, the man in the tailored suit and camel-hair coat warranted at least a spot in Jake's rogues gallery. But Jake still didn't know how much of Marla's tale to believe.

"Thank you and good afternoon," Madigan said. "I see a lot of familiar faces here."

Oil those wheels.

"The 22nd precinct may not have the highest crime statistics in the city, but I attribute that to the excellent performance of our uniformed men and women who serve it."

The cheers grew louder, and Jake found his distrust of the mayor intensifying for no particular reason. Marla certainly struck him as being more sincere, but he tried not to allow his personal feelings to cloud his judgment. He had a job to do, and emotions didn't figure into that job. He needed to be a detached observer, hoping to obtain the evidence his client desired.

"The Central Park Police Station is an important symbol in this department. It represents over a century's worth of dedication, service, and tradition. One year ago, this city stood poised on the brink of disaster. Our economy faced total collapse, we were forced to lay off two thousand uniformed officers, homeless people crowded our sidewalks, and Black Magic ravaged our streets."

A tide of boos rose like a chorus, and Madigan raised both hands as if a robber had instructed him to do so at gunpoint. The placating gesture quieted the restless crowd.

"I worked tirelessly with Governor Santucci to roll back the layoffs at a critical moment in this city's history and authorize the rehiring of those two thousand officers and an additional five hundred."

Applause thundered.

"Under the direction of Commissioner Bryant"—Madigan gestured at a jowly man with thick white hair who nodded to the crowd—"we dismantled the ruthless gang responsible both for polluting our streets with Black Magic and for committing the notorious Machete Massacres."

The crowd roared its approval, and Jake suppressed a smirk. He alone had stopped the drug operation run by Prince Malachai and Katrina. Both drug lords were found dead at the bottom of a construction site after tangling with him.

"We took back our streets and our neighborhoods. New York

GREGORY LAMBERSON

City has never been safer than it is today, thanks to the efforts of our entire police department." Madigan waited for the cheers to reach a deafening crescendo. "Not only that, but employment is up and homelessness is down. With our economy on the rebound, we can all tell our children that we truly live in the greatest city in the world!"

The crowd roared.

I think I won this little thug a second term.

Grinning, Madigan gestured to Collier, who produced a pair of oversized scissors, and the two men walked over to a yellow ribbon strung across the entrance to the new annex. Madigan posed with the giant scissors, allowing camera flashes to create a halo around him, then cut the ribbon in two with one decisive snip. The ribbon billowed in the breeze and landed on the concrete as the crowd chanted Madigan's first name.

Sliding his hands into the pockets of his duster, Jake made his way through the crowd and crossed the soft grass to the parking area. He spied a pair of black SUVs in a separate, reserved parking area: the mayor's security detail. A single plainclothes cop stood outside the vehicles. Mayoral security was a sweet assignment, one that could lead to discretionary promotion.

Jake programmed Karlin Reichard's address into his GPS and started out for the Henry Hudson Parkway. Forty minutes later, at the outskirts of Scarsdale in Westchester County, he followed a road that cut a swath through dense woods. Occasionally he'd spot a mansion arching up into the sky. A quarter of a mile before Reichard's estate, he turned into a service road and parked twenty feet from the main road, the Maxima cloaked by trees.

As the sun descended, Jake changed his clothes in the backseat without much grace. Multiple shades of green camouflaged his cargo pants and army jacket, and he had painted a pair of running shoes to match. He put on a rolled-up olive-green ski mask, then circled the car to its trunk, which he popped open. Removing a compartmentalized backpack, he slid his arms through its straps. Then he pulled the ski mask over his face, closed the trunk, and locked the car with his remote.

Jake Helman, Ninja Detective.

Checking his watch, he walked between the trees, parallel to the main road. Across the street he saw a stone fence that ran the entire length of the property. He knew from the satellite photos he had studied of Reichard's estate that he had been following the grounds even before he had pulled over. He slowed down when he spotted a parked SUV outside a gated driveway. Moving into position, he observed a manned security booth on the other side of the gate. The winding driveway led to a mansion on top of a hill surrounded by woods. The black SUV was identical to those he had seen at Central Park, the lead vehicle in the mayor's security caravan. The man inside, either a lieutenant or a captain, had traveled to Madigan's destination ahead of the other vehicles to ensure the location was secure, following proper protocol.

Crouching on a log and safely hidden by bushes, Jake waited for the other vehicles to arrive. The woods grew dark, then the street. Marla had told him that Madigan was visiting Reichard's for the weekend following the ribbon-cutting ceremony at the Central Park Police Station annex.

"Myron spends one weekend a month at Reichard's," Marla had said. "And I'm never invited. He claims they're strategizing his future, but I'm convinced this is where he's cheating on me. Maybe he's got his own love nest inside that goddamned mansion, or maybe they stage Roman orgies there. I wouldn't put it past Myron to sodomize little boys. Anything that suggests the rarefied behavior of men who can get away with anything draws him to its flame."

Jake didn't realize how dark it had gotten until he saw approaching headlights illuminate the parked SUV. The other two department issue SUVs slowed to a stop behind the first. A moment later, the security gate ground open, and the SUVs filed through it and up the driveway, their movement triggering motion detectors that activated floodlights. Because of the steep incline and the twists and turns, it took them almost a full minute to reach the mansion's entrance.

Raising high-powered night vision binoculars to his eyes, Jake saw Madigan disembark the middle SUV alone and walk between massive columns to the enormous front door.

Definitely not protocol.

A man silhouetted by a bright overhead light opened the door and admitted Madigan to the mansion. All three SUVs descended the driveway and exited the property. The two lead vehicles drove away, while the third parked outside the property, and the security gate closed.

Jake frowned. *They're working three shifts outside the security perimeter.* No NYPD security detail would guard their assigned figure in such a haphazard manner, especially the mayor's detail. Half of those men belonged inside the mansion with Madigan. *Unless he's really throwing his weight around.* But for what purpose? *To keep his sexual antics a secret?* Marla no longer seemed paranoid.

Rising, he backtracked one hundred yards and moved closer to the road, where he waited. Floodlights illuminated the grounds in a continuing pattern that suggested a roaming security patrol.

Twenty minutes later, headlights appeared on the road in the distance, moving closer. A silver SUV roared past him, and when its headlights shone directly on the department's SUV, blinding the plainclothes detective inside if he happened to glance in his rearview mirror, Jake sprinted across the road and scaled the six-foot wall and crouched atop it like a gargoyle. Darkness enveloped him. Standing straight, he slid the pack from his back, unzipped one compartment, and walked along the wide fence in the direction of his car, invisible to the world. He deliberately scuffed the soles of his running shoes on the stone surface. It didn't take long for floodlights to light up the grass below him.

When he made it to the corner wall, he heard dogs racing in his direction, their sharp barking causing him to jump. As he reached inside his pack, three Doberman pinschers leapt snarling for his feet. Instead of jumping back to safety behind the wall, he squatted low to the stone and tossed three handfuls of ground beef onto the ground, then watched the dogs gobble the meat.

Underfed so they'll tear any trespassers to pieces, Jake thought.

With the meat devoured, the animals circled each other, panting. One of them whimpered. Within seconds, they rolled over and stopped moving, drugged by the over-the-counter drugs Jake had purchased earlier, designed to relax pets during travel. Jake had laced the meat with four times the prescribed dosage.

Dropping to the ground beside the unconscious canines, he jogged uphill with the new section of wall to his left side so he could escape in a hurry if necessary. No longer able to see the security booth, he slowed to a walk when he reached a stream that circled the hill like a moat. Sliding down the embankment upright, with his arms outstretched like those of a surfer, he leapt to a flat stone in the middle of the little stream and hopped onto the opposite embankment, which he climbed without difficulty.

When he passed a tennis court carved into the hill, security lights illuminated him. Making certain he was surrounded by grass, so that his camouflage garb rendered him invisible, he broke into a run but didn't sweat the lights because he knew the guard dogs must regularly trip them. As long as the dogs were loose, no one would activate more sophisticated security devices. Sixty yards higher, he circled a self-illuminated, glass-enclosed swimming pool. At last he stood facing one side of the mansion. A row of tall windows spilled yellow light onto the landscaping along the mansion's exterior.

Raising his binoculars, Jake saw men dressed in suits and tuxedos enter the room and sit at a table.

Dinnertime. How many men?

He walked to his left so he faced the next window and saw more men dressed in formal wear sit at the table. Two Mexican women in blue frocks served their food.

At least six, possibly eight.

Returning the binoculars to their designated pocket, he took out his small high-definition video camera and moved fifty yards to his right. Once the dining room windows were out of sight and he knew he could not be seen by the men, he ran straight to the mansion's corner, triggering security lights. He felt fully exposed but knew he blended into the lawn and bushes. Reaching the mansion, he crept through the shrubs to the first dining room window and peeked through the glass with his camera recording.

Eight men, all right, Madigan among them. All Caucasian, and all but Madigan had white or silver hair. Gleaming silverware and fine china covered the silken tablecloth. Ignoring their servers, the men laughed and traded cocky looks with each other. They all reminded Jake of Old Nick. A roasted pig occupied the table's center, surrounded by side dishes so exotic that Jake couldn't identify them. The men ate the food with the refined manners of

50

those accustomed to high society, yet their ravenous appetites repulsed Jake.

Captains of industry, he guessed. Reichard dominated the conversation, the others hanging on his every word. *Powerful men.* But no women. Marla may have been correct that her husband was up to no good, but based on what Jake witnessed, she was wrong about him having an affair, at least at these weekend retreats. *An all boys' club, and none of them seem effeminate.* The old men seemed to take extra care to include Madigan in their exchanges. *He's new to the choir.*

The servers filled their glasses with alcohol, and one circled the room toward Jake, who ducked with his back pressed against the cold brick wall. Staring at the window light on the ground, he saw the rectangle narrow to a sliver as the woman closed the drapes. The drapes in the next two windows closed as well. Standing, Jake still observed enough through the slit between the drapes to know the men remained engaged in conversation.

With a glance at his watch, he estimated he had maybe another hour before the guard dogs regained consciousness. Tiptoeing along the shrubs, he made his way around the mansion. His shoulder brushed ivy clinging to white latticework, and he gazed across the property. Two guest homes, a maintenance building, an enormous parking garage, and a horse stable divided the rear half of the hill.

A footstep to Jake's right made him flatten his back against the wall again: a man in a classic chauffeur's uniform exited the mansion through a side door and activated one of the garage doors. Lights flickered on, illuminating a white stretch limo. The chauffeur got into the car, started its purring engine, and backed the limo out of the garage.

When Jake lost sight of the limo, he circled around the way he had come. Although he didn't see any cameras, he knew they were mounted in the nearby trees and trained on the entrance. Camouflage or no, the guard in the security booth below would see him crossing the front of the mansion if he was paying attention. Jake walked in a straight line from the mansion's front corner, passing the trees. Then he walked along woods facing the opposite side of the mansion. Once he had passed a gazebo, he saw the limo idling beside the mansion with the chauffeur standing beside it.

He expects to be needed soon.

Jake made himself comfortable. Somewhere behind him a twig snapped, and he jerked around. Peering through his night vision binoculars, he scanned the woods but saw nothing but trees. He did his best to relax, but the hair on the back of his neck stood on end.

Not much later, the side door opened, and the dinner party members exited. The chauffeur opened the passenger door, and the men climbed into their luxury ride. Then he closed the doors, got in, and drove forward, not toward the entrance but to the rear of the property.

Jake's heart beat faster. What the hell were they up to? Staying close to the woods, he jogged after the limo. The driveway dipped down the opposite side of the hill, and the limo drove a quarter of a mile away and stopped. Clearing the trees, Jake saw a stone building with Gothic architecture that resembled a giant crypt the size of a two-story home: a domed roof capped angular abutments and narrow windows. Floodlights rendered the scene visible.

The old men exited the limo, and Reichard led them up stone steps to the front door. He keyed in an alarm code that also activated lights inside the building, and the men followed him inside. Once the door had closed, the chauffeur got into the limo and headed back to the mansion.

Jake narrowed his eye. The big shots liked to surround themselves with underlings but kept them far away from the main action. As the limo climbed the hill, he estimated he had ten seconds before the floodlights went off and he would have to worry about triggering them again. He ran to the stone building and inspected it. Glass block windows: even if they weren't covered with dark drapes, he would be unable to see inside. Avoiding the front door and its alarm, he circled the building, and the floodlights darkened behind him. He stood in the back, gazing up at the stone ledge around the dome, framed against the night stars.

Watch the stars . . .

He had reached a crossroads: if he continued circling the building, he would trigger the lights again. Reaching up, he grabbed a handhold of cement. The structure had all kinds of angles, and with relative ease, he climbed to the top and stared at a skylight centered in the domed roof.

Bingo.

Crossing the roof, he hunched down beside the skylight and focused on the room below. A fire blazed in a wide fireplace. Leather-bound books filled recessed bookcases. Eight black leather reading chairs, each with its own mahogany stand, circled an elaborate Oriental rug. Leaning closer to the skylight, Jake saw a sofa and at least three doorways leading into dark rooms. The dinner guests took their seats and lit cigars, and Reichard, speaking, poured drinks. Then he disappeared into one of the darkened rooms. The other men spoke to Madigan, who sat on the edge of his seat, his belly spreading like batter.

Jake took out his camera and recorded the scene, zooming in

on each man. He recognized none of them but believed they were important enough that they would be easy to identify.

Reichard emerged from the room, and to Jake's surprise, not alone. The kingmaker escorted a woman in her twenties into the center of the rug. Her long dark hair spilled over her silken robe, which clung to the curves of her body. She walked with deliberate sexuality designed to trigger a response from the men around her.

Hooker? Jake wondered. *No, too classy. A call girl, maybe.*

Reichard presented the brunette to his guests, who rose and bowed to her.

The woman smiled, her eyes shiny.

Drugged, Jake surmised. *If she's about to do all of them, I don't blame her.*

The men returned to their seats, but Reichard gestured to Madigan and said something, and the mayor stood again. Reichard escorted the woman over to Madigan, whose tie she loosened. Looking uncomfortable, Madigan spoke to her and she responded. Then she kissed him on the mouth, and the men leaned forward in their chairs. Jake captured the kiss with his camera.

Well, Marla, you're not crazy after all.

Still kissing the woman, Madigan extended his open right hand behind her back. Before Jake had time to react, Reichard set a gleaming dagger into Madigan's waiting hand, and the mayor drove it between the woman's shoulder blades, piercing her heart. She arched her back and stared straight up with her mouth open, making eye contact with Jake, who snapped his head in disbelief.

You son of a bitch!

Madigan allowed the woman to slip to the floor and crouched over her. Jerking her to one side, he wrenched the dagger free, then rolled her onto her back, her arms flailing. He made a motion with his arm that sent arterial spray splashing across the rug. Madigan stood, his chest heaving, and Jake saw that he had sliced her throat. Crimson gushed onto the floor as she bled out. Reichard gave a handkerchief to Madigan, who wiped his face. The other men brought their hands together in applause.

Jake felt his brain pulsing. *What the hell is with these guys?*

Reichard reached into his jacket pocket and removed something too small for Jake to discern at first. Then Madigan extended his right hand with his fingers spread apart, and Reichard slipped a ring onto one finger.

Some sort of initiation ceremony . . .

Jake rose on weak legs, uncertain what to do next. The woman lay dead below, blood pooling around her, her murder preserved on his camera's memory card. Her glazed eyes continued to stare up at him, and his mind catalogued the victims whose murders he had investigated in Special Homicide. As he took a step back from the skylight, an inhuman shriek pierced his ears from behind him, causing his body to jump and constrict at the same time.

Spinning around, Jake saw a figure standing eight feet away. He could not tell if it was male or female, only that it wore a brown robe with a cowl that masked its features. It stood maybe five and a half feet tall, with stooped shoulders.

Jake's mind raced. No human being had made the shrill sound he had just heard.

The thing shuffled forward, its feet hidden by the robe. The canvas fabric undulated from the waist down, as though the thing moved on legs that lacked a skeletal structure.

Shoving his camera into his pocket, Jake reached for his Glock, holstered beneath his left arm. Before his hand closed around the gun's grip, the thing emitted a loud gurgling sound that chilled his blood, and something shot out at him from beneath the cowl. He ducked to his left, and the protrusion darted onto the space where he had just stood, then retracted into the darkness within the cowl like a tape measure. It must have been four feet long.

That's a tongue!

With his heart hammering, Jake pulled the Glock free, thumbed the safety off, and aimed at the approaching thing. The tongue, as thick as a snake, lanced out again, and he cocked his arm, aiming the Glock at the sky. The tongue wrapped around his forearm several times, its tip shaking in the air inches from his face. A vertical slit opened in the grayish-pink flesh, and Jake jerked his arm away as a stream of yellowish-green fluid sprayed out of the orifice.

Venom!

With the fluid discharged, the figure retracted its tongue, but Jake gripped it with his free hand and jerked it back, dragging the thing straight for him. The creature lunged at him with open arms, and Jake glimpsed thick claws protruding from the digits on each scaly hand. He batted the hands away from his throat, and the thing crashed into him. The impact jarred Jake, who pivoted on one heel as he fell backwards with the thing on top of him, reversing their positions in midair before they landed on top of the skylight. Below them, the men looked up at the sound.

With the stench of fish overpowering him, Jake heard a splintering sound, and a moment later the glass gave way. He and the creature plummeted to the floor twenty feet below, and as Jake felt his stomach crawling up his throat, he saw the men scattering in all directions. The floor rose to meet him, and the thing beneath him broke his fall, the impact forcing Jake to drop his gun. He felt the creature's ribs snapping and ruptured flesh spreading beneath the robe like buckets of jelly. The thing emitted a wet-sounding wail and vomited black blood in a stream over the top of its head.

Jake leapt to his feet, untangling the limp, sandpapery tongue from his wrist. Surrounded by shards of glass, the creature writhed on the floor beside the dead woman. Its cowl had fallen back, and Jake gasped at its features. He saw no eyes, nose, or mouth, just a dozen feelers, perhaps ten inches long and an inch thick, with tapered ends that twitched in the air like tentacles. Its hands and feet were webbed and scaly, with black claws. All of the visible flesh was as pallid as the belly of a fish. Three suckers, like those found on the tentacle of an octopus, glistened on the inside of each finger. A rattling sound issued from deep within the creature, and the feelers stopped moving. Then the air turned even more foul.

Jake scanned the stricken faces staring at him. Somewhere in the room a glass shattered on the floor. Reichard appeared puzzled more than anything, but Madigan stood paralyzed with his eyebrows raised and mouth open. Was he horrified that his crime had been witnessed or that a monster lay dead at his feet? One man with a widow's peak and a square jaw glared at Jake, and Jake sensed the man coiling to make a move. Jake dove for his Glock, rolled across the floor, and came up in a crouch. He swept the gun past the face of each man, causing them to stiffen. At least they couldn't see his face beneath the ski mask. He bolted for the front door.

"Don't shoot!" he heard one man croak to the rest. "You'll bring everyone on the grounds running. He'll never leave the property alive."

Jake threw the door open, darted outside, and slammed the door shut. He charged into the night, triggering floodlights as he ran at a forty-five degree angle across the estate. He sprinted before the mansion, his shoes slapping the brick driveway, and cut a path toward the far corner of the stone wall. As he passed the glass-enclosed swimming pool, he thought he saw silhouettes keeping pace with him right outside the light, and then he heard the same shrieks that had been made by the creature he had just killed.

There are more of those things!

His body turned numb with fright. He ran faster, which was hard to do going downhill. When his movement triggered the floodlights around the tennis court, he counted at least three of the robed figures in his peripheral vision. He had to turn his head all the way left to check the terrain in that direction with his sole eye, and this caused him to stumble and roll down the hill. He clutched his Glock tight in his right hand, refusing to drop it again. Rising without coming to a stop, he stutter-stepped toward the stream that circled the hill's base. Rather than descend one embankment and hop across the stream to the other one, he leapt from the edge of the grass over the stream and landed on the opposite embankment, his lead foot sinking deep into mud. The mud made a sucking sound when he pulled his foot free, and he scrambled up the earth.

When Jake reached the top, he found himself looking straight into dark brown fabric. Craning his neck to look up, he saw one of the creatures as it dove straight at him. Before he could dodge the thing, it slammed into him and drove him onto his back in the cold stream. Ignoring the pain inflicted on his lower back by sharp rocks on the streambed, he struggled in water almost a foot deep, the thing straddling his stomach. He had to sit up to prevent his head from going underwater, which brought him closer to the thing. The monster seized Jake's throat in both hands, its slimy flesh causing him to shudder, and he felt a sucking sensation on his skin.

He did not want to reveal his location to the other creatures by firing his gun, but he knew the thing intended to shoot him full of venom. He swung his Glock at the creature's head, throwing it off balance, then shifted the gun into his left hand and grabbed a rock, which he slammed into one side of the monster's head with a soggy impact. The thing shrieked and leaned forward, as if preparing to lash out with its tongue. Jake traded the rock for a piece of driftwood, which he drove into the thing's face with all of his strength. The creature fell back, groping for the wood protruding from beneath its cowl with both hands.

With his wet clothing clinging to him, Jake managed to get up on his knees. When the creature pulled the wood free of its head with a wet sound, he leapt onto its torso and forced its head beneath the water, careful to turn it sideways so it could not sting him with its tongue. The feelers writhed beneath the surface like water moccasins, and the creature kicked its feet, bubbles rising as Jake attempted to drown it. After a good thirty seconds' worth of effort, he realized he *couldn't* drown the damn thing because it was amphibious. Clutching the driftwood again, he raised it high over his head like a stake and plunged it straight down through the water into the thing's head, causing his attacker's body to spasm. Then he placed both hands on the end of the wood and leaned on it with all of his weight until he felt it crush the creature's skull. All at once, the thing stopped struggling.

Gasping for breath, with his heart thudding in his chest, Jake staggered out of the stream and scrambled back up the embankment and onto the lawn. Swallowing the night air, he rolled to one side and stood, his clothes dripping, and ran for the stone wall. The dogs no longer lay on the ground.

Great. Just what he needed. He heard shrieks all around him as the things communicated with each other. His feet pounded the ground, and when he reached the wall, he scaled it as fast as he could. He had one foot planted atop the wall when he felt claws seizing his other leg. Before he knew it, two of the things had yanked him to the ground. The robed figures hunched over him, their shrieks projecting distinct anger, and he inhaled breath that reeked like sewage. Lying on his back, he wondered which of the monsters would shoot its tongue at him first or if they would launch a simultaneous attack.

Screw this!

Gripping the Glock in both hands, he fired at one creature, then the other, then returned to the first figure. The gunfire echoed in the night, the muzzle flashes leaving spots flickering in his eye. He fired a total of four times before the monsters sprawled out on the grass. As he climbed the wall, he heard more of the things heading in his direction.

No wonder the dogs beat it.

Dropping to the ground on the other side of the wall, Jake heard shrieks behind him. The police SUV pulled right up to the security gate, and the driver honked the horn. Jake sprinted across the street and into the woods, where he took out his binoculars and used the night vision function to search for his car. Spotting it, he scampered between trees. He slammed his left shoulder against one trunk, twisted his right ankle, and just missed smashing his face into bark. Why the hell couldn't there be a full moon tonight?

He used his remote control to unlock the Maxima's doors and prayed none of the things prowled the woods opposite Reichard's estate. Jerking the car door open, he jumped inside, hit the locks, and started the ignition. With only his fog lights providing illumination, he turned around and drove into the main road. A glance at the rearview mirror revealed the SUV still waiting at the security gate. He increased his speed, leaving the Reichard estate in his dust, then switched on his headlights and pulled the ski mask from his head.

"Shit!" He pounded the dashboard. *How the hell is this happening to me* again?

CHAPTER
5

As he sped back to Manhattan, Jake kept checking his rearview mirror for signs of a tail. He assumed the other members of Madigan's security detail had checked into a hotel in Scarsdale, but for all he knew they were staked out waiting for anyone fleeing Reichard's mansion.

I'm just being paranoid.

He swallowed.

Like Marla was paranoid?

Karlin Reichard and his gang inspired such paranoia.

Monsters in Scarsdale!

Picturing the creatures, he thought he had seen them before. He would know the answer soon enough.

Parking in the Twenty-third Street garage one block away from his office, Jake felt great relief and comfort when he breathed the Manhattan air. Nothing put his mind at ease like the city's stench of garbage and pollution.

Too hurried to change his clothes again, he had merely pulled his soaked outfit and carried his backpack in one hand. Passing Laurel Doniger's storefront, its neon Spiritual Advisor sign dark, he gave the Tower his customary glance and entered the foyer of his building and keyed in his alarm code. Unwilling to wait for the lone elevator, he ran up four flights of stairs, passing darkened corridors and closed offices, and hurried to his suite. He inserted separate keys into the three locks, entered his waiting room, flicked on the lights, and keyed in another alarm code. After relocking the front door, he hung his duster on a coat rack and peeled off his jacket.

In his main office, Edgar cawed when Jake switched on the lights.

Shedding the rest of his wet clothes, Jake said, "Edgar, don't ask me how I did it, but I'm waist deep in craziness again."

Edgar croaked and Jake sniffed his arm. "I know. I stink like rotten fish."

In the narrow bathroom off the kitchen, he stood at the sink and gazed at the mirror. "What the hell?"

Red circles the diameter of a nickel covered his throat, so many that they almost resembled one large bruise. He counted thirty of the burns. Remembering that each finger of the creature he had killed in front of Reichard's crew had three suckers, he did the math. When the second creature had seized his throat in the stream, it had either burned or sucked away a layer of his flesh. Grabbing a tube of disinfectant from the medicine cabinet, he rubbed the ointment into the wounds and let out a pained hiss. Now his skin really burned.

"Son of a bitch." Jake walked naked into the shower stall in his bedroom. He ran hot water, stepped into the spray, and scrubbed his body with soap and more disinfectant. His throat itched like mad.

Once dressed, he returned to his office and opened the iron safe in the far corner. Each of the three combination locks on the safe door had its own combination, and he threw the lever and opened the heavy door. Reaching inside the safe with both hands, he took out the laptop he kept there, next to two case folders: one for Old Nick and the other for Katrina. A third file might join them soon, if he lived long enough to document his current predicament.

Powering up the laptop at his desk, he booted the program contained on the DVD in its tray. The laptop was dedicated to this sole function, and Jake kept it disconnected from the Internet to prevent anyone from hacking into the invaluable program. Old Nick had spent millions of dollars funding the research that resulted in Afterlife, and Ramera Evans—Katrina—had almost destroyed the city in her quest to get her hands on it.

Edgar hopped onto the desk as Jake accessed the program. He located the word *biogenetics* in the menu and jumped to that section. He had first viewed the images of Tower's genetically engineered monsters when he had broken into the apartment unit of Kira Thorn, Tower's second in command, and sneaked onto her computer.

Since then, he had reviewed the footage and had secretly even provided copies of it to the ACCL: Anti-Cloning Creationist League. The videos, stills, and schematics had appeared on YouTube and other websites, but the government had taken no direct action against Tower International. The phrases "Tower makes monsters" and "Tower brings bad things to life" had become Old Nick's legacy, even if the world at large considered the footage leaked by Jake a hoax. The new urban legend had become as associated with Nicholas Tower as the catchphrase, "Where's Old Nick?"

Monstrous images filled the screen: drawings, photographs, X-rays, and videos of genetically engineered monsters—bipeds, quadrupeds, slimy things with tentacles; hateful eyes, protruding fangs, spiked skulls; variations of snakes, lizards, and spiders. Creatures that should not exist, which had not existed until Old Nick directed his scientists to create them. Flesh-and-blood weapons of war—the new frontier.

Jake clicked on one dossier after another, searching for a match for the things he had encountered on Reichard's estate. He found none.

Closing the program, he stood at the window and gazed at the Tower across the street.

There's a connection. I feel it in my bones.

Jake lay awake in bed, replaying the night's events in his mind. He had viewed the digital footage of Madigan murdering the drugged woman. He had not captured footage of the scaly creatures that had come after him, but he did not need to see them again to picture their ghastly feelers and venom-spewing tongues or to imagine their scaly fingers and suckers upon his skin. He would never forget them.

What did Reichard need them for? As far as Jake had seen, they served no purpose that could not have been filled just as well by a human security force or the dogs. There had to be more to their presence than met his eye.

Early the next morning, Jake rapped on the front door to Laurel Doniger's parlor. With the curtains drawn, he could not see inside the storefront. When Laurel didn't answer, he knocked again louder.

A minute later, she opened the door. She appeared wide awake but had not put on her makeup yet, though Jake found her attractive in the morning light. She wore a lilac-colored dress belted at the waist, and her gaze dropped to Edgar, who occupied the birdcage Jake held. Without saying anything, she stepped away from the door, allowing Jake to enter.

As he closed the door behind him and locked it, he watched her sit at the round table in the middle of the sunken floor, folding one creamy leg over the other. Laurel didn't see much sunlight, and Jake averted his eye from her flesh.

"I take it you're in trouble, or you wouldn't have brought Edgar," she said.

Jake set the cage on the table, and Edgar cawed at Laurel. "You could say that."

She stared at him as he sat opposite her. "Do you want to tell me about it?"

Leaning forward, Jake clasped his hands on the table. "Marla Madigan."

"The mayor's wife?"

Jake nodded. "Did you send her to me?"

"No. Why?" She seemed concerned, a trait Jake appreciated.

"Because she hired me to spy on her husband, and that's what jammed me up."

"What makes you think I sent her to you?"

"Because that's what happened the last time I got mixed up in crazy shit like this." Laurel had sent Carmen Rodriguez to Jake, and Carmen and her grandson Victor had been dismembered by her other grandson, Louis, who had become one of Katrina's undead soldiers.

Laurel offered him a cautious smile. "You need to realize something. You've been exposed to powerful forces during the last year and a half, spiritual and supernatural alike. You know they exist—and now they know *you* exist. You're marked. I sense it in you very clearly. Others may sense it intuitively, without knowing why. I've never known anyone with your experiences, but you give off a certain vibration that draws people in need of a certain kind of help to you, almost like a beacon. You're drawn to similar vibrations."

"I'm beginning to think it's a curse."

Sliding her hand forward, Laurel turned it palm up. "Care to share?"

Jake looked at her hand, then back into her eyes. "The last time you got information from me you used a different method." In fact, Laurel measured the energy of her clients through sense of touch. She had given Jake a healing massage that had climaxed with him climaxing.

Now she studied Jake like a poker player trying to read an opponent. "Is that what you want me to do now?"

"No, let's keep this strictly professional."

"I'll send you a bill for services rendered."

Jake reached out and grasped her hand.

Laurel glanced down at his hand. She raised her eyebrows and shaped her face into an expression of fear, then recoiled as if she'd been struck. Jake saw terror in her eyes, and he knew what her mind detected.

"The bastard killed her in cold blood, and all of those twisted fucks just watched and clapped," he said.

Laurel flinched again, this time trying to jerk her hand away from Jake's in a defensive motion.

"Easy . . ."

Laurel's breath came in sharp gasps. Her lips quivered, as if ready to scream. At last she snatched her hand back and covered her eyes, shielding them. When she removed her hand, water filled her eyes.

"Hey, I'm the one who lived through that."

Laurel fanned herself with one hand. Her chest rose and fell, fighting for breath. "You don't know . . . When someone's memories are recent, I really experience them. I'm there, watching, and I can't get away. What the hell were those things?"

"I was hoping you could tell me."

She gave him an uncertain look. "I'm not some expert on monsters, whatever you think."

"You sure knew a lot about those zonbies I went up against last year."

"That was different. There's research on vodou. Documented cases. I've never seen anything like *these* things. And neither has your Afterlife file."

"I really wish you'd stop doing that."

"Let me see those wounds on your neck."

Jake frowned. "I told you to stop." Tugging on his turtleneck, he revealed the suction wounds to Laurel, who rose and stepped before him. She slid her hands over the wounds, grimacing as she massaged his flesh. The soreness evaporated from Jake's body, and he knew she was working her magic on him. When she stopped touching him, she ran from the room with one hand over her mouth.

A moment later, Jake heard her vomiting in the bathroom, and he experienced a twinge of guilt. He had not asked her to go through that for him.

"What will you do about the mayor?" Laurel said when she returned.

Jake blew air out of his cheeks. "Good question. As a PI, I'm required to report any crimes I uncover . . ."

"But?"

"Karlin Reichard is a heavyweight, and I have to assume his peers are, too. Hell, Madigan is no cream puff."

"But you recorded that woman's murder."

"Yeah, there's that. And Marla hired me to get her footage she can use against Madigan. But these guys can pull massive strings to make sure that footage never sees the light of day."

"They don't know who you are. You can give Marla the footage and tell her to say it's from an anonymous source."

"If Marla takes possession of that footage, it will put her life at risk."

"Then send the footage to the authorities anonymously."

Jake considered this. "I tried something similar with the footage of Tower's Biogens, and it got me nowhere. And he was *dead*, for Christ's sake. I'm telling you, these rich bastards have long arms. Madigan alone has a lot of contacts in the police department and DA's office. Reichard's reach goes even higher. I have to tread very carefully."

Laurel cocked one eyebrow. "Fear doesn't suit you, Jake."

"Are you kidding me? It's one of my finer qualities. I seem to handle myself okay against ghosts and goblins, but throw a white-haired, rich old fart my way, and I know to duck and cover."

"You have the advantage. You have the evidence, and you know who they are."

"I know who two of them are."

"And none of them knows who you are."

Jake looked around the parlor for something to focus on besides Laurel's probing gaze. "I knew the second I took this case it was going to be trouble. I just didn't know it would involve creatures from the black lagoon. I was so sure those things were some of Old Nick's Biogens. Whatever they are, they're the key to this."

"Our mayor committed murder. Reichard and his partners are accomplices."

"Madigan committed a human sacrifice. It was the price of admission to their great explorers' club. I bet each one of them did the same thing."

Laurel's features remained firm. "They have to pay for what they've done, and they have to be stopped from whatever else it is they're doing."

Jake snorted. "You make a pretty convincing argument for me to risk my life considering you never leave this place."

"I do what I can from here. Do you do everything you can to help people?"

He weighed her words. "I try."

"I think you need to take a trip."

Jake tried not to wear his suspicion on his face. "Where to?"

"Lily Dale. It's a spiritualist community in Western New York, an hour south of Buffalo. Find a woman named Abby Fay. She's the most powerful psychic I know. She'll tell you what those creatures are."

"Why do I need a psychic more powerful than you?"

"Because I can't help you. She can. She's also helped a lot of police with unsolved murders and kidnappings. Leave Edgar here. That's why you brought him, isn't it?"

Jake nodded.

"Have a safe trip."

✳

Jake bought coffee and a bagel at the coffee shop down the block, then entered his building and rode the elevator to the fourth floor. When he opened the door to his suite, he was not surprised to see Carrie sitting at her desk, but he turned rigid at the sight of two men in suits sitting in the chairs against the wall. One had blond hair, the other none. Carrie looked even paler than usual. The men rose as Jake closed the door.

That didn't take long.

"Detective Storm," the blond-haired man said, showing Jake his gold shield.

"I had a toy named Sergeant Storm when I was a kid," Jake said.

"I'm not a sergeant. I'm a detective."

"That's okay. He was an astronaut."

Storm gestured to his partner. "This is Verila."

Jake nodded to them. "What can I do for you?"

"You can come downtown with us," Verila said.

"Farther downtown than this?"

"One PP," Storm said.

One Police Plaza: *the Puzzle Palace.* "What's this all about?"

"Lieutenant Geoghegan wants to see you," Verila said.

"Oh, does he?" Jake knew Theodore Geoghegan. The gruff lieutenant had questioned him after he had crashed his Chevy Malibu into the barricade outside One PP after being chased by Katrina's zonbie hit men. Geoghegan was Major Crimes. Something told Jake that Madigan was already reaching deep. *But how did they know to come to me?* And why would Madigan want to involve the police? "Then why didn't he come here?"

"Because he's Lieutenant Geoghegan," Storm said as if that explained everything.

Jake held up the paper bag in his hand. "I was just about to enjoy my breakfast."

"Enjoy it in our car," Verila said. "We'll try to avoid the potholes."

"You know, fellas, I run a business. I don't really feel like leaving that business just on Teddy's say-so. Why don't you give me a little something to go on here so I know this little jaunt is worth my while?"

Storm gave him a patronizing smile. "The lieutenant will fill you in."

Jake turned to Carrie. "Hold down the fort."

The day had gotten off to a great start.

CHAPTER
6

Jake did not remember the last time he had seen One Police Plaza in daylight, but it sure looked different than it did when he had seen it last at night, with his car flipped upside down against a cement barricade and its windows shot out. Geoghegan and a uniformed PO had pulled him out of the wreckage, and Geoghegan had been one of three men to interview him about the incident that night. Gary Brown, Jake's old partner in the Street Narcotics Apprehension Program, and a suit from Homeland Security had been the other two.

Gary had died the very next day, his body riddled with cancer. It had been a peculiar death, having occurred on the street next to a department issue SUV outside the apartment building of his partner, Frank Beck, who had died of a cocaine overdose at almost the same time. Jake learned the two crooked cops had been murdered by the vodou bokor Katrina. He felt sorry for Gary, who had invited a world of trouble into his life.

Walking through the halls of police power, escorted by Storm and Verila, Jake now felt isolated. He had once belonged to this brotherhood and had partners and friends and backup. Now what did he have? A dwarf assistant, a pet raven, and a psychic lady friend. Maybe Martin had been right when he had accused him of belonging nowhere.

Entering the Major Crimes Unit bull pen, he scanned the faces of the half dozen detectives working the phones. The gold shields who worked MCU dressed a little better, carried themselves a little straighter than precinct detectives. They had to, working in the Puzzle Palace, with bosses around every corner. Some of these well-dressed detectives glanced at him now. Jake didn't know any of them, but he sensed their disapproval. What the hell was going on?

Verila knocked on Geoghegan's door, and a gruff voice answered, "Come in." The detective opened the door, and Geoghegan looked up from his desk. Seeing Jake, he took off his reading glasses and rose. The burly lieutenant had put on weight since Jake's encounter with him six months earlier. "Thanks for coming, Helman."

"It's not like I had a choice." Jake glanced at Storm and Verila. "You boys run along now and let the grown-ups talk. You've done your errand for the morning."

Storm's face scrunched up and Verila tugged him away.

"What can I do for you now that I'm here, Lieutenant?"

Geoghegan avoided his eye. "Let's do this in an interview room."

Wonderful. "Whatever you say."

Jake followed Geoghegan through the bull pen into an interview room. "Just like old times."

Geoghegan eased into a metal chair at the table, and Jake sat opposite him. The hefty lieutenant took out a yellow notepad and a pen, each bearing the NYPD logo.

Jake looked around the room. "No camera?"

"Not at this stage," Geoghegan said with a thin smile.

Jake folded his arms. "Okay, the suspense is killing me. What's on your mind?"

"A few things have happened since our last conversation. For one, your partner disappeared."

He's playing games. "Edgar was my ex-partner."

"Still, that's some coincidence. You get chased over the Brooklyn Bridge by machine gun–toting drug dealers when Hopkins is serving on the Black Magic Task Force, and two days later he goes MIA, never to be heard from again."

"I don't know anything about his disappearance. I gave a full statement to Missing Persons."

"I know. I read the file. I just thought maybe you remembered something you forgot back then. Some little detail gnawing at your insides."

"I'm afraid not. Can I go now?"

"Now it's my turn to 'fear not.'"

"You mean you're going to get down to the real reason you hauled me down here now that you think you've got me off balance?"

"I keep forgetting you're an old hand at this. Except that you used to sit on this end of the table."

"From where I'm sitting now, it really doesn't matter. Stop wasting my time, or I'm walking out of here."

"Still a wiseass. Still a tough guy."

"And I still don't suffer fools gladly. Your meter's running."

"Working on any big cases at the moment, Sam Spade?"

"They're all big to a little guy like me."

"Yeah, sure. Show some humility now. Switch up your dance moves. It won't do you any good. I'm an old hand at this, too."

"Are we going to cross swords in a pissing contest, or are you all warmed up now?"

Geoghegan sat back. "Mayor Madigan's wife hired you to do some lifting for her."

Damn. He had hoped there was no connection between Marla and this dog and pony show. "Confidential."

"I'm not asking you if she hired you. I'm telling you she did. And now the lady is missing."

Jake's heart skipped a beat. Had Marla fled Madigan, or had something happened to her? "I'm listening."

"How about you start talking instead? We can trade information."

"What happened to Marla?"

"Oh, you're on a first name basis?"

"What makes you think she hired me?"

"Because when she disappeared she left her cell phone behind. Your number's in there, and you left two messages on her voice mail."

Jake tried to maintain a passive expression. "She wanted me to dig up some dirt for her. When did she go missing?"

"Last night. She snuck out of Gracie Mansion and never came home."

"Then it hasn't been twenty-four hours . . ."

"When a high-ticket politico's wife disappears, we like to get a jump on the case."

"Especially when your boys were responsible for keeping an eye on her. You don't want to piss off the mayor or anything."

"Do you want to piss off the mayor?"

No, I want to kill him. "I never met the man."

"He's rushing back to the city now from some retreat. What did Mrs. Madigan want you to find on him?"

"She wants me to prove he's cheating on her so she can get out of their marriage without him making her life miserable." *The truth will set you free.*

"There, that wasn't so hard, was it? A straight answer. Why would Madigan penalize his wife just because she'd lost that loving feeling?"

"You'll have to ask her. Or him. All I know is he had her locked up for psychiatric evaluation when she tried to leave him once before, and he's threatened to do it again."

"You buy that?"

And a lot more. "Lock, stock, and smoking barrel."

"Proof?"

"Just her word. But I bet some official legwork will find more than enough evidence to back up her story."

"She's known to be a little high-strung."

"Her husband is an ogre." *And a murderer.*

"Did you get what she wanted?"

Decision time. But the decision was easy to make: if Jake planned to take down Reichard and Madigan as Laurel had suggested, he needed to do it from behind the scenes, which meant keeping what he'd witnessed to himself. "Not yet."

"Why doesn't that surprise me? I guess your meter's running, too."

Jake ignored the shot. "What's her security detail say?"

"She got out of Gracie Mansion without them knowing it."

"Some security."

"Look who's talking. Carmen Rodriguez hired you to find her grandson last year and got dead instead. Come to think of it, Kira

77

Thorn disappeared while you were head of security for the Tower, didn't she? Your clients have a way of disappearing. Maybe you're some kind of whacked-out serial killer, like the Cipher."

A low blow. Geoghegan knew that the Cipher had murdered Sheryl. He also knew the Cipher had been murdered by an unknown vigilante. "Actually, Kira disappeared after I resigned from the company, and given the way the feds moved in on Tower International, I'd say it's a safe bet she's living overseas under an alias. You have been checking up on me, haven't you, Theodore?"

Geoghegan spread his hands apart. "Guilty as charged. You fascinate me, Helman. And every good detective loves a good mystery."

Who says you're good? Geoghegan struck Jake as nothing more than an ambitious paper pusher. "It doesn't make sense that she ran away from home and left her children behind."

"Those kids are in boarding school."

"See? You know more about her than I do. It also doesn't make sense that she didn't take her cell phone with her."

"What are you suggesting, that she was kidnapped out of Gracie Mansion?"

Jake let the question hang in the air between them.

Geoghegan picked up the slack. "How about this: she's the one cheating on Myron, and she's in a love nest right now."

Jake shrugged. "Who am I to disagree with a good detective like you? Let me know how it all turns out."

"I gather this interview is over?"

"Unless you have anything else to ask me."

Geoghegan's chair squeaked beneath him. "Okay, let's give it a shot. Where were you last night?"

Jake felt his body turning numb. Why the hell hadn't he seen *that* coming? "Working."

Geoghegan tapped his pen on his notepad. "Do tell."

"My work is confidential between me and my clients."

"Oh, you have more than one damsel in distress at a time?"

"I keep busy."

"Where were you last night?"

"I don't think I'll tell you at this stage. It isn't germane to what we're discussing."

"I'll be the judge of that." Geoghegan sat forward. "And *confidentiality* doesn't apply to private eyes the way it does to doctors and lawyers."

Jake rose. "Don't forget priests."

"Sit down." The words came out with the edge Jake suspected Geoghegan reserved for street punks.

Setting his hands on the table, Jake leaned forward. "This is your house. You invited me here. That makes me your guest. Right now, I say that it's none of your business where I was last night. You want to pull that information out of me to satisfy your own curiosity about what it's like to be a PI and not have to appease bosses, then arrest me. Otherwise, I'm leaving."

Geoghegan got to his feet with a grim expression. "You really don't want to make an enemy out of me."

Jake stood back from the table. "No, I don't. But I've answered all the questions I intend to. You want more, charge me. We both know you don't even have enough to hold me for questioning. I've told you everything I know about Marla Madigan."

Geoghegan seethed without speaking, then jerked his head toward the door. "Get out of here."

As Jake reached for the knob to the steel door, Geoghegan called his name and he turned around.

"Don't leave town, okay?"

"Yeah, sure."

"I've always wanted to say that."

Jake exited the interview room.

*

As soon as his feet struck the sidewalk outside One PP, Jake whipped out his cell phone and hit autodial.

"Helman Investigations and Security," Carrie said in her most professional voice. No one who heard her would suspect that tattoos covered most of her body and metal piercings filled in the blanks.

"Carrie, book me a flight to Buffalo. I'll need a car, too, and five hours on the ground. I'd like to fly back tonight, but if you don't think I have time, get me a hotel."

"Any preferences?"

"Nothing in the city. Do a little detective work and get me something in between the airport and someplace called Lily Dale."

"Right, chief."

"Leave my itinerary on your desk and take the rest of the day off."

"I hear that and I like it."

"You're on call, though. Keep your cell handy in case I need you."

"Whatever you say."

Jake closed his phone and hailed a taxi. His thoughts returned to Marla. If Madigan had confined her to psychiatric observation again, she was already a big concern to him. Most likely, he had confided her distress to Reichard and his alliance, in which case she had become a concern to *them*. Had they been monitoring her cell phone all along, or had they simply concluded she was somehow responsible for the camouflaged intruder who had literally dropped in on their ritual uninvited?

She was depending on me to help her. She would have called me if she could have. And she wouldn't have left her cell phone behind.

His gut told him the best thing he could do at the moment was follow Laurel's lead and see if it yielded any useful information.

Exiting his building's elevator, Jake crossed the fourth-floor corridor to the front door of his suite and unlocked it. Carrie had turned off the lights on her way out, but sunlight flooded the reception area. Jake entered his code into the alarm pad, then locked the door. His itinerary covered Carrie's desk: a flight out of JFK in three hours, one night at the Fulbright Inn somewhere called Chadwick Bay, and a return flight first thing in the morning. Carrie had made the correct call: better to be safe and spend the night in Western New York and make sure he obtained whatever information he could.

Switching on the kitchen light, he opened his office door and froze. A woman sat with her back to him in the chair facing his desk. How the hell had anyone gotten inside his suite with the security system activated? He had even wired the windows with sensors after AK had climbed in from the fire escape six months ago and stabbed him in the eye.

Unless Carrie let her in . . .

"Marla?"

The woman did not react to the sound of his voice, so Jake flipped the switch beside him, and the overhead light came on. The woman had long, sleek black hair and sat as still as a shadow.

Even from behind, Jake recognized her, his heart beating faster as his blood chilled.

Not Marla.

The woman rose with elegant poise and turned to face him, her every movement familiar to him. "Hello, Jake."

He swallowed as his blood rushed to his feet. "Sheryl . . ."

CHAPTER
7

Jake swallowed air, speechless as his dead wife circled the chair. She wore a sleeveless turquoise-colored dress that he had always liked, with knee-high leather boots. Her dark brown eyes captured the morning light and reflected it back at him, her oval face almost gleaming.

Sheryl. His heart ached for her, an open wound he feared would never heal.

She looked him up and down. "You look good. I'm glad to see you've been taking care of yourself."

"You look good, too. Amazing, in fact. Especially for someone who's been dead a year and a half."

Sheryl moved closer to him, the heels of her boots making soft clacks on the hardwood floor. "Dead in your world, not mine. And mine is much larger than yours." She took in the room. "I like your office. Don't you think it's time you got a real apartment, too?"

"I can't afford one on top of the rent I pay for this place."

"You can manage."

"Maybe. But I'm comfortable here. It makes things easier."

"You can't watch the Tower full-time, just like you can't guard Afterlife around the clock." She cast a sideways glance at the open door to Edgar's caged quarters. "And you can't babysit Edgar full-time, either."

He thought he heard sadness in her voice.

"Where is he, anyway?"

Suspicion surged through Jake's veins. Why didn't Sheryl know about Laurel? As soon as the thought formed, he constructed a mental image of a brick wall, a trick he had seen in an old science fiction movie dealing with telepaths.

Standing before him, Sheryl looked into his eyes. "Relax. I won't invade your privacy. I watched you deal with Prince Malachai and Katrina. I couldn't help myself; I care about you too much. They're both in the Dark Realm now, suffering along with Old Nick and the Cipher."

He took a deep breath. "If I remember correctly, you 'agents of Light' aren't supposed to divulge classified information like that."

"We're not even supposed to communicate with humans or make our presence known to them. But you're a special case. You prevented the Dark from swallowing the Light. And you saved my soul." She caressed one side of his face. "Thank you."

Jake felt emotion flooding through him. Sheryl felt real: warm and vibrant, just as she always had. Setting one hand over hers, he threw his other arm around her and felt her hands on his back. He buried his face in her hair and recognized the familiar coconut scent of her shampoo. He fought tears. "God, I've missed you."

Sheryl rested her head against his chest. "I know you have. But it's different for me. I can observe you whenever I want, and the Light offers me so much more than I ever had here. It's the same for everyone who ascends."

He felt her heart beating against his chest. Gazing down at her, he set one hand under her chin and raised her head. Her lips were full and inviting.

She looked him in one eye, then the other. "Your poor eye . . ."

Unable to control himself any longer, he kissed her on the mouth and tasted her tongue. She did not resist, but he felt an odd sense of detachment on her part.

Then she drew away from him. "This isn't possible. I'm here to talk. We can share this moment, but that's all. No physical contact, sexual or otherwise. It wouldn't be real, anyway."

He did not want to accept that. "I love you."

"And I love you. I always will. But I'm not human anymore. I'm just particles in a vast field of energy. You and I can never be what we once were, because I can never be what I was." Sheryl gestured at her body. "This is an illusion for your benefit."

"I figured, when I saw your hair was long again, the way I always liked it. Abel said I'd never see you again unless I ascended to the Realm of Light."

She cocked her head, the way she always did when explaining something to him with the patience of a grade school teacher. "He told the truth. I was never meant to materialize before you."

"Against company policy, huh?"

She smiled. "Something like that."

"You sound like Abel."

"In a sense, we're all of one mind in the Realm of Light."

"Sounds like a commune."

Sheryl continued to smile. "We don't choose what we become when we ascend; we just become. The choices are made here on earth. Those decisions determine which plane we reach."

"I'm glad you achieved heaven."

She raised one eyebrow, as if puzzled by the term. "You can ascend to the Light too, Jake. I know you can. You're a good man."

"I'm trying. I want to get there, to be with you."

Her face and voice turned serious. "You need to want to ascend for yourself, not to be with me. It's all about your personal being. You can't have selfish motivations."

"I can't help it. I love you, and knowing that you're still alive in some higher dimension makes me want to do anything I can to be there with you. It's hard, though. I keep getting monkey wrenches thrown at me. Like Katrina."

"Edgar killed Katrina, not you. You tried to save her. Killing in self-defense, or to save someone else, will not prevent your ascension. But you have to live your life to its fullest."

He felt his eyebrows knitting together. "My life is hollow without you."

Sheryl shook her head. "That isn't true. Like I said, you're a good man. You always were. You just allowed yourself to get side-tracked from who you are. You're on the right path now, trying to help those you can."

You're the only woman I've ever loved, Jake thought. *The only one I ever can love.*

Her face took on a shade of sympathy. "That isn't true. You'll find love again. I appreciate your devotion to your memory of me, but please understand that it stems just as much from loss and misplaced guilt as anything else. You want me because deep inside, you know you can no longer have me, and you blame yourself for the Cipher killing me."

"It was my fault. I should never have gone home that day . . ."

"Marc Gorman would have killed me anyway. Kira Thorn ordered him to steal my soul, and that's what he would have done." She shuddered, a distinctly human reaction, as if remembering her murder.

"If I hadn't screwed everything up . . ."

Sheryl moved close to him again, a smile on her lips despite the glistening in her eyes. "No one is perfect. Everyone makes mistakes. That's what human life is: making a series of decisions that impact your life and the lives of those around you. But you can't blame yourself for my murder. Do you understand?"

"If I hadn't messed up with the coke, I never would have been forced to resign from the department, and then I never would have hooked up with Tower and Kira."

"You don't know that. You still might have walked into that bar and killed those two robbers."

Dread and Baldy: Kevin Creed and Oscar Soot. The lowlifes had returned as minions of the demon Cain, who had tortured Jake. "I doubt it."

"It doesn't matter. You made a mess of your life, but you atoned for it. You freed me and the other captured souls and saved the Realm of Light from being destroyed by our enemies. That couldn't have happened if you hadn't wound up working in the Tower. My energy still exists, just like it always did. But if things had been different, we'd *all* exist in a very different reality right now, one impossible for you to imagine. You saved me, Jake. You saved the world. You saved everything. My death was inconsequential in the long run. You have to stop blaming yourself and get on with your life."

"I don't want to get on with it. I want to be with you."

"You're as stubborn as ever. Hopefully, one day you'll ascend and we'll be reunited, but in a different manner than you expect."

"Different how?"

"I can't tell you that."

"Will the home office dock your bonus?"

"Don't be angry. It accomplishes nothing."

"That isn't true; it makes me feel better."

"No, it doesn't. You only fool yourself into believing it does."

"Did you come back just to lecture me?"

Closing her eyes, Sheryl shook her head again.

"Then why are you here?"

She opened her eyes and locked them on his. "I need your help."

Jake did a double take. "You need *my* help?"

"I'm afraid so."

"You're an angel. How the hell can I help you?"

"You know that 'angel' is a primitive term for what I've become. That's like me calling you a monkey or a fish."

"Forgive my inadequate linguistic skills. Compared to you, I am a primate. So I'm having a difficult time grasping how I could possibly help you. I don't play a harp, and I don't walk on clouds."

"No, you don't. And that's exactly why we need you."

"We?" he said, knowing exactly what she meant.

"The Realm of Light."

"I think my brain just flinched. Can we sit down?"

"Please."

Jake sat on the sofa and Sheryl joined him. The furniture had come from their old apartment in the Upper East Side. He never thought they would share it again.

Sheryl turned her body so it faced him as much as possible, her exposed knees close to him.

"All right," he said. "Let's have it."

"There are powerful forces in the universe beyond your ability to comprehend."

"You said that before, and you can say it again."

"Most of them we know about. But there are mysteries even for us. Only God knows everything."

Jake grunted. "Abel never actually told me that God exists."

"I believed in God when I walked this earth. Why wouldn't I believe in Him now that I live in the Light? Surely you're not still an atheist after everything you've experienced?"

"No. Not an atheist. How could I be? I've seen Abel. Cain. *You.* I accept this world is just a stepping stone to more evolved dimensions. But I still don't buy the dogma. No man knows what God expects from us, if God expects *anything* from us, *if* God exists."

"You'll understand everything better when you evolve to your next form, whichever Realm that's in."

Jake blew air from his cheeks. "I know so much already that sometimes I feel like my head will explode. Knowledge may be good, but it can also be frustrating."

"You carry a burden you can't share; it's true. But you also have reassurance that no one else on this planet truly has: that in the grand scheme of things, there's more than this." Sheryl gestured at the office. "Your brain will be fine."

He tried to read her eyes. Once easy, he now found it impossible. "What can I do for you? I have a plane to catch, and I haven't even packed."

"I know how you pack. That will only take you two minutes."

She knew him so well. He didn't smile.

"You understand that life begins here and evolves to the higher planes. If life on earth ceases, then no new energy ascends to the realms. The Dark Realm and the Realm of Light will reach their final densities and will be locked in an eternal status quo."

"So what? I mean, bad for the planet, but if everyone gets where they're going anyway, no harm, no foul, right? It's just a roll of the dice whether the demons or angels hold the majority."

"If the Dark Realm obtains more energy than the Realm of Light, the amount of suffering that will result will be immeasurable. Since the dawn of time, the agents of Light have kept this from happening, sometimes with ease, sometimes with great difficulty. When the Cipher captured my soul for Tower, the balance was perilously close."

"I know: thirteen souls made all the difference."

"*You* made the difference. That's why we need you now. There's a reason why that soul count was so critical."

"Those powerful forces you mentioned."

"Both the Light and the Dark have a vested interest in what happens to humanity, and we're natural observers. But there are places on this world even we cannot see. Blind spots: areas that have developed with increasing frequency, which we can't even enter to investigate."

"Like the Tower, shielded by the security spell that Kira cast."

"Exactly. Some of these blind spots have been created by human beings who have tapped into greater cosmic resources. We saw these situations developing but were powerless to intervene. Others are completely beyond our comprehension."

"Is it possible the Dark Realm is establishing beachheads here?"

"We would sense if that was the case. Positive and negative energy detect each other. These blind spots are simply blank to us."

"So there's a new player in town?"

"We think so. It's powerful and hungry. For almost three centuries, it's been devouring souls in their human form. Those souls have not ascended. They've simply ceased to exist."

"How many souls?"

Sheryl's expression turned grave. "Over half a million."

Jake blinked. "Holy shit."

"Some of them should have reached the Dark Realm, but most were bound for the Realm of Light. That's why my soul and the others you freed from Tower's Soul Chamber were so crucial in holding the Dark forces at bay. Mathematically, souls are now vanishing at a rate of at least six per day."

"Can't you protect them?"

"No. We can't directly intervene, even to save ourselves. And it's impossible for us to know which souls are at risk. They simply vanish from our radar."

"There must be patterns—"

"The souls that disappear do so in pairs."

Jake divided six by two. "Breakfast, lunch, and dinner."

"So it would seem."

"And you believe they're disappearing into these blind spots?"

"It's the only explanation for why we're powerless to detect what's happening. We call this new enemy the Destroyer of Souls."

"How many blind spots are there?"

"I can't tell you that."

"Then how do you expect me to help you?"

"Ask me the right questions."

Jake rose. "Look, I'm no idiot. Abel sent you here because he knew he could play on my emotions that way and I could never say no to you. But I really don't have time to play games. If you want me to go find this Destroyer of Souls, then you'd damn well better point me in the right direction. I won't jump through hoops blindfolded, you understand? I won't be a pawn for heaven, hell, or even you."

Sheryl rose as well. "Abel didn't send me. It was my decision to come here. Abel is partly the reason why I'm here."

"Oh?"

"He's missing."

Jake narrowed his eye. "How is that possible? He's one of you."

"He made it his mission to find the Destroyer and stop it. It's been a goal of his since the first soul disappeared. During the last year and a half, since we almost lost the war with the Dark Realm, it's become an obsession with him. He finally got close to the answers he sought when he disappeared. We can't detect him any more than we can the souls the Destroyer's already consumed."

Jake searched her eyes for sincerity. He thought he saw it, but as Sheryl had already pointed out, she had created her present form for his behalf. "Are you telling me Abel is dead?"

"Abel hasn't been alive for centuries. He's energy, just like me. And that energy has vanished. Abel was the first being to ascend to the Realm of Light. We don't have leaders, but Abel was the oldest and wisest of us. His absence has left a huge void in our dimension. If his energy has somehow been destroyed, that poses a far greater threat than we ever imagined. I'm not talking about souls that will never ascend. I'm talking about something destroying the earth, the Realm of Light, *and* the Dark Realm—everything that we know exists."

Jake sank back into the sofa. "You want me to find Abel and

slay this soul-eating dragon, is that it?"

"Find Abel. We'll do the rest."

He looked at her. "And if my soul disappears?"

"You carry some of my energy inside you, remember? I gave you a part of myself. I'll know where you are and when you need me."

He felt resignation settling over his body. "That won't really help me if I disappear into one of these blind spots, will it?"

Sheryl offered a weak smile. "Maybe not."

"I don't suppose Abel kept any sort of files I can see?"

She shook her head. "I can't share specific information with you, anyway."

Jake pounded the arm of the sofa. "Damn it! You've got to give me something to go on."

Sheryl slid her hand over Jake's left wrist. "You have to understand. There are laws of physics that govern the higher realms. It's against my nature to break those laws. If I do, my energy will change. I could wind up in the Dark Realm, never to return. I'm willing to make that sacrifice to stop this Destroyer. I really am. But I don't think it's necessary. I have faith in you, Jake. Have faith in yourself."

"I don't even know where to start looking—"

In the blink of his eye, Sheryl disappeared.

Jake leapt off the sofa and spun around the office. "Sheryl?"

Gone.

Again.

First the tears came, and then he closed his hands into fists.

CHAPTER
8

Jake tossed a light load of clothing into a duffel bag, just enough for one change, and packed a laptop. He had planned to drive to JFK since he only intended to park the car overnight at most, but Sheryl's visit had left him too shaken to drive, so he took a cab.

During the car ride, the wait in the airport, and the flight, he grappled with the extreme emotions that had surfaced within him. He had seen Sheryl, touched her, kissed her even. She had reentered his life, something he had considered impossible seventeen months earlier, and his refusal to enter into a new relationship felt justified. But she had made it clear to him that reviving their relationship was impossible, at least according to the angels' handbook.

Crushed against the airplane window, a heavyset couple beside him, Jake switched on the mini-TV recessed into the seat before him and inserted his earphones. At the same time, he opened the stapled research he had printed out on Lily Dale. He jumped from a game show to a talk show to a nature documentary before locating a cable news channel. He disliked the station, but it was the only news he could find, a situation he had experienced before, everywhere from doctors' offices to pizzerias. Mindless partisan propaganda, but at least they dished up what little actual news they delivered in bite-sized bits that didn't require much concentration. As a newswoman with hair as plastic as her smile did everything in her power to make a political candidate favored by the network appear charismatic, Jake drummed his fingers on the arm of his seat.

How the hell did Sheryl expect him to find Abel with zero concrete leads to follow? It was impossible. The heavenly confidentiality clause frustrated the hell out of him. Six people would die every day that this Destroyer Sheryl mentioned continued devouring souls unchecked. By his calculation, 42 people disappeared a week, which amounted to 168 a month, 2,016 a year, 20,160 a decade, and 201,600 a century.

That's just a drop in the bucket with a current global population of more than six billion people.

Despite her professed concern for those souls, Sheryl seemed much more worried about the implications behind Abel's disappearance.

There's nothing like losing a member of your own team to awaken you to the presence of an encroaching enemy.

He imagined she and the other agents of Light were more than a little alarmed to realize their existence had a possible expiration date after all.

Eternal bliss: one more bill of goods sold by the power brokers.

The story Jake had been dreading came on the air: another

blonde newswoman stood before Gracie Mansion, surrounded by other media people and police personnel.

"Carol," she said to her anchor, "we're being told very little by authorities at this moment, but our own sources tell us the calamity you see behind me centers around the possible disappearance of New York City's first lady, Marla Madigan. Mayor Madigan was out of the city last night but returned this morning when the Gracie Mansion security detail alerted city hall to Mrs. Madigan's unexplained absence. The mayor's spokesperson has not issued a statement yet, but we'll keep you posted when he does."

So it's out there. No mention of Reichard or where Myron Madigan was when Marla disappeared. *Not surprising since Reichard owns the network.* Jake sighed. He could not believe Marla's disappearance was a coincidence or that Madigan had nothing to do with it. And the mayor wouldn't have just sentenced her to another stay in an institution if he was making her disappearance public. *She's dead.* He knew it.

The clouds parted and the aircraft descended, circling Buffalo Niagara International Airport. He had visited Buffalo with Sheryl once because she had wanted to see the Albright-Knox Art Gallery, and they had timed their trip to coincide with an arts festival downtown. Jake had been impressed by the city's architecture, particularly its grand mansions and churches.

Sheryl.

His thoughts always returned to her. Was she watching him now? He had to assume so.

Among the last to depart the plane, Jake followed the other passengers through the small airport to an escalator that led to the baggage claim. From there he stepped outside and crossed the asphalt to the car rental facility.

COSMIC FORCES

Fifteen minutes later, in a black Ford Escape, he looped the Cheektowaga airport and accessed a highway. Fifteen minutes after that, he was surrounded by trees and caught himself scanning the open sky for high-rises, only to find clouds. He enjoyed the drive, speeding up only to pass numerous semitrucks, and ticked off the signs he passed bearing Indian names: Lackawanna, Fredonia, Cassadaga.

He turned off at the Dunkirk-Fredonia exit and checked into the Fulbright Inn, where Carrie had booked him, which faced Chadwick Bay. Inside his room on the second floor, he tossed his bag on the second bed, used the bathroom, and then hit the road again. It took just fifteen minutes to reach Cassadaga Lake, and then the sign for Lily Dale loomed before him.

According to his research, Lily Dale was founded in 1879 as a retreat for Spiritualists. The 167-acre community was owned by "the assembly," a religious order comprised of freethinkers who believed death merely served as transition for living creatures into nonliving entities. Jake gave the Spiritualists credit for getting that right, even if their belief in spirits veered toward the creaky spectrum of what he knew to be true.

A single road led into Lily Dale, and that same road provided the only exit. As he neared the empty tollgate, he reminded himself that only 250 people lived in Lily Dale year round, 35 of them as registered mediums. The population swelled during the summer season when as many as 22,000 tourists flooded the assembly.

With the season still two months away, Jake coasted past the gate and into the hilly village's empty streets. New Age crystals and signs for psychics, healers, and tarot card readers filled the windows of the cottages that crowded the hills. Jake drove along the main street, turning his head from side to side as he searched for Deer Lane. Finally, he parked in the gravel parking lot of a gray Victorian house that appeared to be an inn and set off on foot. He passed a library, a museum, a post office, and a volunteer fire department, but he saw no police station, which led him to wonder if crime existed in a town full of psychics.

His trek became a walking tour, which he didn't mind, even though the temperature felt a good ten degrees lower than in Manhattan. At last he saw someone, an older man who stood on a stepladder, dislodging clumps of rotten leaves from the gutters of his house with a garden rake. The man wore a blue baseball cap that shaded his eyes as he turned in Jake's direction. Jake smiled and waved, but the man just gave him a sullen nod and returned to his chore.

Jake passed a dirty white building on top of cinder blocks. At first he thought it was a church, but on closer inspection he saw it housed public bathrooms. The trees around the road grew denser, and he found himself standing in the middle of an outdoor meeting place with wooden benches facing a pulpit carved into an enormous tree trunk. A chill ran down his spine, and he looked around for signs of life. He knew it was silly to be frightened of the gathering place, but he couldn't help himself. Inspecting the pulpit, he imagined druids and pagans dancing naked at night rather than tourists attending a lecture by Deepak Chopra.

Wind blew his hair, and he followed a path that took him through what appeared to be a makeshift graveyard. Inspecting the names and inscriptions on the markers—some stone, some wood—he realized that he had stumbled onto a pet cemetery. He detected movement near the ground not far from him and jerked his head in that direction, his arms recoiling.

A black cat wandered between two graves.

"Visiting deceased relatives?" The sound of his voice caused the cat to bolt. "I don't blame you."

Emerging from the woods, Jake crossed a road and saw the street he wanted ahead. His thighs tightened as he climbed the hill, and as he located the house number he sought, the front door opened and a thick woman wearing work boots, jeans, and a curly blonde wig stepped onto the wooden porch.

Jake stood on the concrete walkway, uncertain how to introduce himself.

The woman's mouth opened but no sound came out.

Jake raised his eyebrows, wondering why he had startled her so much.

"Come on," the woman said at last, composing her wits. "You'll catch cold standing in the damp air like that. I know you're here to see me."

Jake climbed the wooden steps, which squeaked beneath him. "I'm Jake Helman."

The woman smiled as if she already knew or just didn't care. "And I'm Abby Fay."

Entering the house, Jake faced a wooden stairway with a living room to his left and a dining room to his right. The interior seemed dark even with the blinds open and lights on, and a damp, musty smell assailed his nostrils. Abby Fay had lived here a long time. The door closed behind him, and he heard the woman moan.

"Oh, my . . ." Abby brushed against him on her way to the floor, where she sprawled out.

Jake kneeled beside the woman and rolled her onto her back. Her mouth opened and closed and her eyelids fluttered, and her wig sat lopsided on her head. Jake set his hands on the back of her head, attempting to raise it.

Her eyes snapped open and she recoiled. "Don't touch me!"

Jake held his hands up for her to see. "Okay, okay . . . What can I do to help you?"

Abby drew in her breath and swallowed, searching the confines of her own home. "Nothing. I'm sorry. I've never felt anything like this in my life." She focused on him. "I'll be all right. I just need to get up—please don't help me."

Rising, Jake spied a walker in the corner by the door. He moved it within her reach.

"Thank you." Abby grabbed the walker with flabby fingers and pulled herself upright, then struggled to her feet. "Hoo, boy." Adusting her wig, she regarded Jake with what appeared to be wonder. "You've got some powerful mojo." She gestured in the direction of the dining room. "Let's go in the kitchen."

Using the walker, Abby led him through the dining room, which overflowed with stacks of newspapers, magazines, and books, and into the kitchen, where she removed some dishes from a table and set them into a deep sink. She filled a glass with tap water and gulped it down. Water marks stained the ceiling, and the linoleum on the floor peeled in several places. The chairs at the table did not match. Liquor bottles covered the counter.

"I hope you don't mind conversing in here," Abby said. "My parlor's a mess. I haven't even started cleaning up for the summer season."

Jake saw a row of prescription drug vials arranged on the counter.

"Not that I expect to live that long." She pointed at her wig. "Cancer. The doctors give me three months, tops."

"I'm sorry." Jake wondered what malady had caused the woman's collapse.

"Don't be. Only half of these drugs are for my physical illness. The others are for migraines and psychosis." She offered him a weak smile. "The voices in my head sometimes make me a little batty."

He did not know how to respond.

"Don't say anything. Just have a seat."

Just like Laurel.

They sat opposite each other, and Abby drew a cigarette from a half-empty pack. "You don't mind if I smoke, do you? There's no point in quitting now."

"Go ahead." He paused. "Outside, you seemed as if you were expecting me."

Hand trembling, Abby lit her cigarette with a match, which she shook out and deposited in the ashtray. "I sensed you. There's a difference."

Laurel probably called or sent psychic smoke signals.

"Nobody told me you were coming. I sensed you, like I said. That's what I do." She narrowed one eye at him. "She calls herself Laurel now, eh? Laurel Doniger?"

Jake nodded. He had always suspected that Laurel used an alias. "How do you know each other?"

"We didn't meet on the psychic hotline. If she didn't tell you, I'm not going to, either. She's got her secrets. I've got mine. Actually, that isn't true. I'm a pretty open book. I've lived here for thirty-five years, ever since I left my husband. Couldn't stand sensing his thoughts: how I scared him, how he cheated on me and wished I'd die. So I made it easy on him and came here." She tapped her cigarette in the ashtray. "I normally charge seventy-five dollars a session, but this one's on me."

"I can afford the fee."

Abby took a long drag on her cigarette. "Good for you, but I don't want your money. Don't need it where I'm going. The doctors want me to prepare myself for hospice, but I'm not going anywhere. I figure I can wipe my own ass, and when I can't, I've got plenty of friends here who can. Besides, they'll just try to keep me alive, and I'm ready to be on my way."

"I guess you're a staple of this town."

"We're not a town; we're an assembly. Every person who owns a house here belongs to the assembly, and every practitioner is licensed by the assembly."

"I suppose that's one way of making sure the neighborhood never changes."

Whenever he spoke, Abby's eyes widened.

"You got me figured out. I don't need to touch people, like Laurel does. My receivers are more finely tuned than that. I read vibrations, never more clearly than when someone speaks to me. And, boy, I'm reading a whole lot in your voice—more than I've ever read in anyone else's. It's not every day I meet someone who completely alters what I've believed for fifty years."

She had a habit of putting him on the spot. "How did I do that?"

"Do you know who Margaret and Kate Fox were?"

Jake nodded. He had read about the Fox sisters during his flight, though he had been unable to concentrate on the information.

"Don't keep your thoughts bottled up. I can read your mind well enough to get the answers to my questions, but I need to hear your voice to get a more complete picture of your problem."

"They were two teenage girls who supposedly communicated with spirits. It's because of their fame that mediums and psychics settled here."

Abby showed her approval by giving Jake a slight bow. "The Fox family lived in Hydesville, New York, outside Rochester, in the nineteenth century. That's just over an hour from here, but don't go looking for the town. It doesn't exist anymore. The house was supposedly haunted even before the Fox family moved in, and it wasn't long before they started hearing sounds inside the walls, like someone tap-tap-tapping in code. Margaret and Kate, the two youngest daughters, began communicating with the spirits in the house, tapping and rapping on the walls in response to the sounds they heard. Alarmed, their parents sent them to live separately with different relatives. But the sounds followed each girl wherever they went. Mediums confirmed their story and abilities, and word spread like wildfire. All across the state and then across the country, people wanted to see the girls who communicated with the spirit world. Their older sister, Leah, became their manager, and they conducted séances for celebrities and became darlings of high society, attracting thousands of fans and followers."

"The birth of Spiritualism," Jake said.

"Spiritualism became linked to radical political movements of the time, like abolition and equal rights for women, and Lily Dale became a Mecca for those movements. This was the place for freethinkers and mentalists who operated outside the mainstream. Susan B. Anthony spoke here when no one else would have her. We're still proud of that legacy."

"But it was all a hoax, wasn't it?"

"Margaret and Kate became heavy drinkers. This is sadly common among mediums, as you might guess from all the bottles in here. Sometimes we have to dull our senses so we can hear ourselves think. Margaret and Kate had a disagreement with Leah and other leaders in the Spiritualist community, who basically served as their handlers. In a blow to the movement, Margaret appeared before a crowd of two thousand people and announced that the entire affair had been a sham. The Foxes' finances dried up, and all three sisters died inside of five years."

"So Lily Dale was built around lies."

Abby smiled. "It didn't matter. The Fox girls brought believers together, and here we remain. People think New England is the most haunted place in the country, but New York has always been the focal point for psychics and mediums. There's something in the earth here, in the air and in the water. The Fox sisters never lived in Lily Dale, but after their deaths, their cottage was relocated here to serve as a museum piece and a symbol. It burned down back in 1955."

"Let me guess: the ruins are haunted."

"No. But with so many psychics and mediums gathered in one location, a lot of spirits have passed through Lily Dale."

"I'm sure plenty of frauds have passed through, too."

"Oh, there are con artists, all right. Predators and charlatans exist in every field. I've seen them come and I've seen them go. But I've never seen anyone like you, Jake Helman—never *felt* anyone like you. You've touched the spirit world and been touched *by* it. I see a glow inside you . . ."

Sheryl . . .

"There's no middle ground in your world, no restless spirits wandering the earth. Except for these Soul Searchers and . . . zonbies."

Jake swallowed. At least he knew when Laurel had invaded his mind.

Abby's breathing increased. "Angels and demons. I never accepted the Bible as anything more than an attempt by primitive minds to rationalize life and death and impose whatever moral standard suited them, but you've broken bread with Cain and Abel." Her eyes widened with equal parts fear and awe. "You touched an angel just this morning when you kissed your dead wife."

You're talented, Jake thought. "If I've learned anything in the last year and a half, it's that different beliefs and forces don't necessarily rule each other out. It's a big universe."

Realizing that her cigarette had become ash, Abby lit another. "True. But you've been up close and personal with so many things. Not just spirits but actual monsters."

"Then you know that's why I'm here."

Abby's expression reflected consternation. "I don't know what the hell those things are, but in my opinion, your mayor and those old power brokers are much more dangerous than the creatures that attacked you."

"Those things are the key to this whole mess. Laurel was sure you'd be able to identify them for me."

Abby's eyes glassed over and she stopped blinking. She spoke in a slow cadence. "*The key will save your life.*" Then she blinked several times and shook her head. "Laurel misled you, though her heart was in the right place. I've never seen a monster in my life. Sitting here, reading your vibrations just makes me want to hide under my bed and never come out. Laurel knows I settled here for a reason. This region is home to powerful, ancient forces. I've spent most of my adult life trying to understand them, and after speaking to you for fifteen minutes, I feel closer to the truth now than in all the expeditions I've made around the state. Reichard and his cronies are here for the same reason. So was Nicholas Tower. These men are real bad apples." Setting her cigarette in the ashtray, she interlaced her fingers. "We're all tied together somehow."

"What about Marla Madigan?"

"I can't say. But I think your instincts are right. Those bastards took her."

"I was hoping for something more concrete than that."

Abby exhaled a stream of smoke. "Did you bring anything that belonged to her?"

Jake took out his cell phone. "Just her voice."

She nodded in a thoughtful manner. "That's perfect."

Jake searched through his messages, selected one, and pressed the speaker button.

A moment later, they both heard Marla's voice. "This message is for Jake Helman. I'd rather not give you my real name. Just call me Mrs. White. I'd like to engage your services. Please call me back so we can arrange a meeting."

Abby made a rolling motion with her cigarette-free hand. "One more time."

Jake repeated the command and set the phone in Abby's open palm.

The psychic narrowed her eyes as Marla's voice came out of the speaker. She seemed to focus on every syllable. Then she handed the phone back to him. "She's alive but scared. Terrified. I want to say she's somewhere underground, but I'm not positive."

"Somewhere in this state?"

"Very close to New York City."

Reichard's mansion, Jake thought.

Abby wagged one finger in the air. "I don't think so. Somewhere more industrial."

"Is there anything else you can tell me?"

"Oh yes. Laurel didn't waste your time sending you to me. I don't know what those monsters are, but I do recognize their vibrations. Maybe she did, too. They're very similar to vibrations that linger in this area." She took a business card from the table and wrote on its back. "See this man before you leave. He shares my passion for local lore. Maybe he can tell you more than I have. Laurel knew I could direct you to someone like him. I'm like a road map that way."

Jake looked at the name *Daniel Whitefish* and an address on the back of the card. "Thank you."

"Don't bother. I'm glad I met you. Not many people are lucky enough to glimpse the truth about what this world of ours is all about. Tell Laurel I said hello."

Jake stood. "I will."

Abby rose as well and led Jake through the house without her walker. "And you be careful. I get the feeling that the extra bit of soul you're carrying around will get you into trouble as often as it will get you out of it."

"Thanks."

When Abby opened the door, Jake glimpsed a silver SUV parked out front. Abby spun around, facing him and blocking his view at the same time. He didn't need to be psychic to see the panic in her eyes as she pushed him back.

"Get ins—"

The soft hiss of a silencer ripped the afternoon quiet, and Jake's face turned wet and sticky even as Abby's forehead opened up. He closed his eye and turned his head for only a second, and when he looked back, Abby's eyes had rolled up in their sockets, and she collapsed into his arms, pulling him to the floor. A second shot whizzed above Jake's head in the space where he had just stood, and he heard the bullet's impact in the stairs behind him. He dragged Abby's heavy body away from the open doorway. Looking at the golf ball–sized exit wound in her forehead, he knew she was dead even before her soul flickered and rose, illuminating the dark interior before fading.

Outside, an engine roared and rubber peeled.

Adrenaline pumping through his veins, Jake reached for his Glock and remembered he had left it at his office. He sprang to his feet and bolted through the doorway as the SUV sped away. He stomped across the wooden porch and sank into the grass along the walkway, then sprinted into the empty street.

That bullet was meant for me.

Abby had sensed the killer's presence and had thrown herself into harm's way to save Jake's life.

The SUV careened around the corner at the intersection ahead and disappeared.

Damn it!

Jake ran full speed after the vehicle, pumping his arms and legs, and stopped in the middle of the intersection as the SUV turned left at another intersection a block away. He looked from side to side, uncertain where he had parked his SUV, then ran back to Abby's house and slowed to a stop when he saw a man standing on his porch two houses away.

A woman exited her house across the street. Faces appeared in windows. More men and women emerged from their homes, all of them staring at Jake.

The gunshots had been muffled by a silencer. Had they come out to investigate the sound of the SUV's squealing tires?

His body offered an involuntary shudder in response.

No, they had sensed Abby's murder and knew he bore responsibility for it. With an almost casual realization, he touched the cooling blood on his face, then wiped it with both hands. His palms and fingers came away slick with blood and spackled with pieces of brain and skull.

Looking at the gray-haired woman on the porch next door, he said, "Call the police."

CHAPTER
9

A crowd of fifty people had gathered by the time the first Chautauqua County Sheriff's Department patrol car arrived. Jake stood on Abby's walk with his hands visible as two uniformed deputies got out of the vehicle. He had wiped as much of the gore off his face with his sleeve as he could. Holding his wallet, he watched the residents swarm around the deputies.

One woman who wore a winter coat over a purple dress gesticulated in his direction.

As the deputies approached him with grim faces, he heard additional sirens in the distance.

"Jake Helman. I'm a private investigator from New York." He offered his wallet.

The lead deputy took it from him and examined his licenses. "This *is* New York," he said. Both men were Caucasians who appeared to be his age.

"New York City. I used to work homicide for NYPD. I had a consult with Ms. Fay and was leaving when someone shot her through the open doorway. She's dead. The shooter took off in a silver SUV. There's no one else in the house."

The deputy handed Jake's wallet back to him. "Wait here."

Both men drew their weapons and entered the house. Jake saw them looking down where he knew Abby's corpse lay.

Another patrol car, followed by an unmarked sedan, pulled up to the scene. A moment later, an ambulance joined them. Two paramedics hurried into the house. The crowd swelled, and other members of the assembly appeared on the sidewalk up and down the street.

The deputies emerged from the house, and soon four uniformed men and a balding man in a green suit surrounded Jake.

"I'm Sheriff Gudgino," the man in the suit said. He wore a star on his lapel.

Jake introduced himself again and repeated what had occurred.

"You just happened to be present when a sniper shot Miss Fay."

"That bullet was probably meant for me. Abby just got in the way."

"Why would someone want to take you out?"

"Because I'm investigating the disappearance of Marla Madigan."

The sheriff let out a slow whistle.

Jake sat alone in the interview room after the two detectives had left. The room felt cold and professional, the overhead fluorescent lights painting everything a subtle shade of green.

One of the deputies who had first arrived on the scene opened the door. "Sheriff wants to see you."

Jake stood and followed the man through the Chautauqua County Sheriff's Department to an office.

Gudgino nodded at the chair before his desk. "Have a seat."

Jake made himself comfortable.

"Quite an afternoon."

"For you and me both."

"We found two shell casings in the street outside Miss Fay's house. The tire marks and statements from witnesses who saw that SUV driving away from the area confirm that part of your story, so I can't really charge you with anything. But Lily Dale is a quiet hamlet. We're not used to trouble over there. And we don't like it when someone kills our psychics. Not only is it morally offensive, but it's bad for tourism, of which there is precious little in this area. Most of those dollars get spent in Niagara Falls, with more and more going to Canada each year."

"I didn't expect anything like this to happen. I had no idea I was being followed. If I could go back and change things, I would." *And I'd kill the son of a bitch who did this.*

Gudgino sat back in his chair. "You think whoever's responsible for Mrs. Madigan's disappearance sent a hired gun to put you out of commission?"

"I can't be sure, but that's the only theory I have. I don't believe Abby was the target." *No one just happened to decide to kill a friendly old psychic when I was visiting her.*

"Who do you believe is behind these depraved acts?"

"I don't know. That's what I came here to find out."

Gudgino gestured at the air between them. "You came all the way from New York City to ask Miss Fay what happened to your mayor's wife?"

"That's right."

"You don't have psychics in the big city?"

Don't mention Laurel. "We're lousy with them. And they're lousy con artists. I knew Abby had helped out on a few murder cases. She seemed like my best bet."

"So you made an appointment to see her?"

They'll check her phone records and mine. "No, I just flew out here today."

"You must be a gambling man. A lot of Lily Dale's psychics leave town until the summer season starts."

"I didn't know that. I figured that even if she wasn't here, I'd find someone more reliable than some tarot card reader in Greenwich Village." He liked the lie even before the words came out of his mouth. Straight-arrow cops from upstate would view the village as a den of kooks.

"Was she any help?"

"No."

"Too bad. If your theory's right, you got her killed for nothing."

No shit. "It looks that way."

"What will you do now?"

"I have a flight booked for tomorrow morning. If you don't need me to stay, I'll head home to New York."

Gudgino smiled. "This is New York."

Jake returned the smile. *Play the game.* "Right. Sorry. No offense intended."

"And you'll continue your search for the mayor's wife?"

"If I can. The FBI will be all over this by the time I get back."

"Well, we don't need you here. We've got your statement and your personal information. You live in your office, eh? Sometimes I feel like I do, too. But I'm glad I got a home, where I can tip back some beers and watch TV. You go on back to your city, Mr. Helman. Try not to get anyone else killed. If we catch Miss Fay's killer, I'll see you when you return to testify. But something tells me that triggerman is already a hundred miles from here."

Jake stood. "Thanks for your hospitality."

"Oh, it wasn't hospitality. Just professionalism. I run a professional department. You might want to sit back down, though. I have someone on hold who has been waiting to speak to you."

Jake sat.

Gudgino pressed a button on his telephone. "Thanks for waiting, Lieutenant. Mr. Helman's right here. I have you on speakerphone."

"Helman?" Jake recognized Geoghegan's voice.

On hold, my ass. He heard the entire conversation. "Present."

"I thought I told you not to leave town."

"*Town* is a relevant term. Everyone keeps telling me I'm still in New York, so this little day trip never really felt like I'd left home."

"What the hell are you doing upstate?"

"Looking for Marla Madigan." He tried to keep the sarcasm out of his voice.

"It doesn't sound like you found her, but someone sure found you."

"They missed, unfortunately for Abby Fay."

"You're not a very hard man to find; just follow the bodies. But you sure seem like a hard man to kill. This is at least the second time you dodged an assassination attempt."

You don't know the half of it. "Has Marla turned up?"

"Not yet. I'm beginning to think she won't. Why don't you come home so we can compare notes?"

"I'll be home tomorrow morning. Maybe we can do lunch."

"You have my number. No funny business. Come straight back to our favorite city. No side trips."

"I've done enough sightseeing, Teddy."

Sitting in the rental car, Jake programmed the address Abby had given him into the GPS. Twenty minutes later, he knew he had reached the Chautauqua reservation when he passed an enormous wood carving of an Indian, complete with moccasins and feathered headdress, standing with one hand raised as if saying, "How?"

He crossed the reservation border and saw a complex of nondescript one-story buildings surrounding gas pumps. A simple sign read, "Gas and Cigarettes—Cheap." Several cars waited in line for the pumps, so he supposed there was truth in advertising. He followed the road past a tribal police department and a volunteer fire department and then school grounds. Teenagers loitered outside the brick building, their fashions as current as those he had seen in Manhattan.

The GPS's female voice guided him along three connecting roads into a neighborhood consisting primarily of ranch houses: a slice of small town, USA that just happened to be located on an Indian reservation. Numerous men and women tended to their yards and gutters. Jake located the address he sought, which belonged to a white ranch house with a minivan and a Chevy Impala parked in the driveway.

After knocking on the door, he waited for a minute before an attractive woman with straight black hair and a wide nose stood before him, a chubby infant cradled in her arms.

"Yes?" the woman said, surprise in her voice.

"I'm looking for Daniel Whitefish."

She eyed him with suspicion. "Just a minute." Leaving the door half open, she withdrew inside.

Jake glimpsed a cartoon playing on a color TV.

A moment later, a short man wearing glasses, his black hair pulled back into a ponytail, opened the door the rest of the way. "I'm Daniel."

"My name's Jake Helman. I'm a private investigator from New York . . . *City*. Did you hear the news about Abby Fay?"

Daniel frowned. "Yeah, I did."

"I was with her when she was murdered. I just spent three hours at the Chautauqua County Sheriff's Department in Mayville. Can I come in?"

Daniel stared at Jake, as if trying to read him.

"I came to Abby for help on a case I'm working on. She pointed me in your direction."

"Me?" Daniel glanced behind him. "I'm a family man. If your case got Abby killed, I don't want you anywhere near my wife and child. We can talk right here."

Smart man. "I don't care where we talk. I'd just like a few minutes of your time. Then I'll be on my way, and you'll never hear from me again."

Daniel stepped outside and closed the door behind him. "Abby was a good woman. Who would kill her?"

"Someone who meant to kill me. I think she sensed what was about to happen. She pushed me out of the way when she could have saved herself."

"Did you know her long?"

"I never met her before today."

"But she was willing to die for you?"

Jake nodded.

"Then this case of yours must be pretty important. Why did she give you my name?"

"That's what I'm here to figure out. Don't you . . . *sense* anything about me?"

Daniel grunted. "I'm not a psychic or a shaman or anything remotely connected to the stuff Abby was into. I teach cultural studies at Buff State. I don't know anything that could possibly be worth getting killed over. Why don't you tell me about this case?"

"The New York City mayor's wife disappeared."

"I heard something about that."

"She was my client. She hired me to dig up some dirt on her husband. While I was doing my job, she disappeared. I feel obligated to find her."

"And that brought you to Abby?"

"Let me tell you something I didn't tell your sheriff."

"He isn't *my* sheriff."

"During my investigation, I saw something unnatural. Something most people would find impossible to believe exists."

"You've got my interest."

"Without going into too much detail, I saw a monster. Some sort of half man, half fish. It walked erect, like you and me, and it wore a cloak. But I saw that thing up close. I touched it. I smelled it. And there's no way on earth it was human. Worse, I know there are more of them."

Daniel raised his eyebrows, then let out a laugh. "I'm sorry. I don't mean to laugh under the circumstances, but Abby knows I'm a man of science. I'm interested in my culture's myths and leg-

116

ends but purely from a historical perspective. I don't believe in the supernatural."

Jake felt himself turning red. He'd always expected someone to laugh at him someday. *Maybe I didn't go about this the right way.* "You don't have to believe in the supernatural. You don't have to believe me. But Abby believed you were the only person who could help me. She said there's a concentrated power in this state, possibly in this area. Is there anything you can tell me about any local legends?"

"Between Niagara Falls and Lily Dale, there are a lot of ghost stories around here."

"You're thinking in terms that are too general. Try something that only you—of all the people Abby knew—would know. Call me guilty of racial stereotyping, but to me that suggests something to do with Native American mythology. Are there any stories of monsters from this area that wouldn't be common knowledge?"

Daniel's expression grew serious. "Wait here."

Jake watched the man go inside, and then he faced a closed door. He glanced around the neighborhood. The sun had started to set.

When Daniel emerged from the house, he wore a denim jacket and carried a plastic garbage bag stuffed one-quarter full. "We'll take my car."

Daniel tuned the radio in his Impala to a sports station as he drove Jake across the reservation. They circled a park, and Jake saw the sun close to the gray surface of Lake Erie, the sky around it pink. He saw Indians on the beach, which appeared to be rocky and strewn with shale. They drove along a grassy stretch covered with picnic tables, the trees and bushes obscuring Jake's view of the lake. The road angled upward, taking them above the lake's water level.

Daniel parked in an asphalt lot near a playground, and they got out.

"You have a camera?"

"I never go anywhere without one."

"Then follow me."

Daniel led Jake toward the road and the trees beyond it. They walked along a chain link fence until they were hidden from the people on the beach and in the park. Daniel handed the garbage bag to Jake, then set his palms on the top bar of the four-foot-high fence and vaulted onto the grass on the other side. Jake handed the bag back to him and followed suit. Daniel guided him onto a craggy dirt path that afforded them a panoramic view of the lake, and Jake realized they stood near a cliff's edge.

"We're thirty feet up and the water below is only four feet deep, so watch your step."

"I intend to." Jake gazed over the curved edge at the murky green water.

"You can see Canada on the other side," Daniel said, pointing at the water.

Jake squinted, and the hazy image of a skyline came into view on the horizon. Then a horizontal bolt of lightning ripped the sky.

"We can see their storms, and they can see ours. I guess that brings us closer together. Come on, this way."

Daniel led Jake up a steep dirt incline until they stood on grass again, looking down at two rock walls angled to form a giant *V* in the wet, rocky sand. Powerful waves smashed the shale embankments and the sand, then receded.

"Where are we going?" Jake said.

"I'm taking you to the only monster I know."

Jake glimpsed what appeared to be a large five-foot-high opening at the bottom, facing the lake itself.

A cave.

Daniel hopped onto a ledge below them and then onto another below that. Jake did the same. Halfway down, Daniel took out his wallet and set it on the rocks, then peeled off his clothes to his underwear and shoved everything into the bag. "Stuff anything you don't want to get wet in here."

Jake stripped to his briefs and deposited his clothing inside the bag with Daniel's gear. He followed Daniel down to the last level of shale, where they watched the water recede.

"We can run almost to the entrance," Daniel said, "but the waves will catch us before we can climb in. Keep your hands in front of you, or you'll get all scratched up on the shale. Ready?"

Jake looked above them. The limbs of trees growing beyond the cliff's edge obscured the darkening sky.

"Just a minute." He scrambled back to the top and crouched behind the edge. Tree roots and thick clumps of grass dangled around him. He scanned the park in the distance. Two different groups—one family and half a dozen teenagers—cooked food on communal brick grills. Four vehicles besides Daniel's Impala occupied the parking area. A twenty-something couple walked hand in hand alongside the fence they had scaled.

"What are you doing?" Daniel said beside him.

"I got Abby killed today. I can't take that chance with you, especially after seeing your family. I want to make sure we weren't followed. If we go into that cave, we'll be sitting ducks when we come out."

Minutes passed. No other vehicles entered the park. Jake

detected no movement in the trees.

"Come on, man," Daniel said. "There's no one out there but us injuns."

Nodding, Jake said, "Roger that."

They climbed back down, and Daniel handed the garbage bag to Jake. "You carry this," he said.

They waited for a wave to crash into the rocks, and as soon as the water receded, they leapt onto the sand and sprinted across the shale base. They reached the cliff face, and Daniel clambered up the shale. Jake heard the roar of rushing water behind them. He threw the garbage bag over Daniel's head and shoved the man forward. Daniel scurried up the four feet of rock into the cave's mouth just as cold water slammed into Jake, smashing him against the rocks. Shale scraped his chest and face, but the cold water numbed the pain. The water jerked him back, and he clawed at the shale in vain. Daniel turned and reached out with one hand, but the water dragged Jake fifteen feet away from the rocks. Odors he'd never smelled before clogged his nostrils, and he realized that he reeked of Lake Erie.

The water buffeted him, and he rose on the crest of another wave, which rushed toward the craggy rocks. He flailed his arms and kicked his legs, trying to control his trajectory, which proved as useless as trying to control his velocity. Jake felt himself being turned sideways and glimpsed Daniel's frantic expression as the water hurled him at the rocks. He absorbed the initial impact with his left shoulder and cried out. The water hammered at him, rolling his body, and he fell into the cave at Daniel's feet and expelled lake water from his lungs. Coughing, he pulled long strands of mucus from his nose.

"You're okay," Daniel said.

"If you say so." Jake's throat ached as he spat foul-tasting water.

Daniel helped him to his feet, and they stood silhouetted in the dying sunlight. Daniel picked up the garbage bag and took out two flashlights. "You'll want your camera for this."

Jake fished in the garbage bag for his cell phone and found it.

Daniel powered on his flashlight, and the intense beam played over the moist walls. "Come on."

Jake followed him once more, and as they penetrated the darkness, the stone floor rose and the ceiling grew higher. He aimed his flashlight at stalactites and black shapes clinging to them: bats. "How do you know about this place?"

"Everyone on the reservation knows about it. This is part of our heritage." He aimed his beam at a section of flat rock wall covered with colorful markings. "As kids, me and my friends used to come here to drink beer and smoke cigarettes. As an adult, I have far more interest in it."

Jake stepped closer to the flat rock and stared at the mural on its surface.

"The original artwork is carved into the rock," Daniel said. "The colors faded a long time ago, but artists on the reservation restore it every few years."

The mural started at their knees and ended above their heads and stretched ten feet from side to side. On the left-hand side, Jake saw the cliff they had just stood on. A muscular Indian warrior rode a white stallion that reared up on its hind legs. A woman with white skin and yellow hair was draped over the horse in front of the warrior, her hands bound.

Jake moved to his right, revealing more of the painting with his flashlight. Lake Erie stretched before him, its gray-green water unmistakable. He stopped moving and gazed at the artwork's central feature: an enormous sea monster—a cross between an octopus and a bird—that beckoned to the warrior with massive tentacles and wings. Its eyes were black and rimmed with blood, its sharklike teeth the size of the warrior's head.

"Say hello to Avadiim," Daniel said.

CHAPTER
10

Jake studied the mural. "Avadiim?"

"Yes," Daniel said. "I guess you could call him the great god of Lake Erie."

Jake gestured at the Indian warrior. "Who's the dragon slayer?"

"He was called Horned Sparrow. I take it you're no expert on the Seneca Nations?"

"That's a bet you'd win." Jake photographed the mural from several angles.

"The Senecas were great warriors in this area. Great *conquerors*. During the Seven Years War, they helped the British take Fort Niagara from the French, and during the American Revolution, they raided colonial settlements. One of their fiercest chiefs was even known as Red Jacket because he wore the jacket of a British officer he served under. General Washington sent General Sullivan with four thousand men to solve the Seneca problem. Sullivan's Expedition drove the Senecas back to Fort Niagara, where they were defeated. Ironic, isn't it?"

"Would it be politically incorrect for me to say that what goes around, comes around?"

"The Senecas signed treaty after treaty and settled along the Buffalo Creek, Tonawanda Creek, and Cattaraugus Creek, which all became reservations like this one. Horned Sparrow didn't want to settle down on a reservation. He took pride in his heritage as a Seneca warrior, and he remembered the stories he heard as a boy— of Avadiim, the great war god of Lake Erie. Late one night, he snuck into Jamestown, where he kidnapped the daughter of a grocer. He brought her to the cliff above us on horseback and called for Avadiim to accept her as his sacrifice in exchange for aiding the Senecas in a war against the United States. Some believe that Avadiim rose from the lake's bottom and accepted the sacrifice. Others think Horned Sparrow just threw her into the water, where she drowned."

"What happened to Horned Sparrow?"

"He never got to lead his campaign against the whites, and Avadiim didn't do much to help him. The soldiers caught him praying on the cliff the next day. They tied him up and dragged him all the way to Fort Niagara. When they arrived, he had no skin on his bones, and they left his corpse outside the fort's walls for the dogs to eat. The body of the grocer's daughter was never found."

"How old is this painting?"

"I don't know. Like I said, it was here when I was a boy. And it was here when my father was a boy. And when my grandfather was a boy."

"So maybe a hundred years. This may not even be the cliff where the soldiers found him."

Daniel shrugged. "True."

"How integral is Avadiim to actual Seneca lore?"

"It doesn't exist in our written legends, just as part of our oral history. I guess you could say it's the equivalent of the bogeyman: a phantom designed to frighten children, possibly to keep them from venturing too close to the water."

Jake gestured at the monster. "This looks like a hybrid of an octopus and an eagle. I'm no geologist, but I doubt very much that octopi ever lived in Lake Erie."

"I'm sure you're right."

"So it's likely that whoever painted this had seen an octopus somewhere else. Which makes me believe the painting was created long after Horned Sparrow's death. Something else puzzles me. I've seen plenty of drawings and paintings of similar creatures attacking sea vessels, but they were always giant squids, I assume because it's easier to draw five tentacles than eight. Why did this artist go for the full monte? And why did Abby think it was important for me to see this?"

"I don't remember ever telling Abby about this painting, and I'm pretty sure she never crawled into this cave."

Jake returned his cell phone to the garbage bag. "I don't believe she knew this painting existed, just that she had a sense it did, and she connected it to my investigation."

"You mean she connected Avadiim to the things you say you saw, without knowing there was a legend about Avadiim?"

Jake nodded. "The creatures I saw weren't octopi; they were humanoid. But they did have suckers on their fingers." He faced the mural again. "I'm wondering if this isn't somehow a metaphor for what she wanted me to discover."

"A metaphor for what, though?"

Eight tentacles. Eight old men. Avadiim. He looked at Daniel. "I have no idea."

The sun had set when they hunched at the cave's mouth, and the water that splashed on them felt even colder in the evening breeze.

"You still worried that someone might be out there?"

"Yes," Jake said. "Let me go first."

"You'll get no argument from me."

Jake waited for a wave to crash against the rocks and recede, and then he jumped onto the wet shale bottom and ran across the rocky sand. The water struck his feet as he reached the point where the two rock faces formed the point of the *V* and quickly rose to his thigh, but with none of the ferocity with which the waves pummeled the cave. Holding the garbage bag, he climbed the embankment and waved to Daniel, who made the same journey. They climbed halfway up the cliff, where Daniel removed two towels from the bag, and they dried themselves off and dressed in the cold air.

On the drive back, Daniel said, "I sure hope Abby didn't get killed over that mural."

"She wasn't killed for anything more than being with me at the wrong time. Nothing personal, but the sooner I get away from you, the better I'll feel."

"Nothing personal, but the sooner you get away from me, the better *I'll* feel."

Daniel pulled into his driveway and they got out.

Jake handed him a business card. "I don't know if that painting will amount to anything as far as my case goes, but I owe you

126

one. Anytime, anywhere—anything I can do to help you, give me a call. I mean it. And I'd like you to do something else for me."

"What's that?"

"I want to cover Abby's funeral, whatever the expense. Look into the details and get in touch with me, if you don't mind. If I'm not around for any reason, speak to my assistant."

Daniel held out his hand. "You got it."

Jake shook the man's hand, then got into his SUV and left the reservation.

✳

Jake ate at a McDonald's and drove back to the inn. He didn't see how his trip to Western New York had been anything but a waste of his time and Abby Fay's life. He intended to have a long talk with Laurel about the wild-goose chase she had sent him on and its repercussions. One thing was certain: Reichard and Madigan wanted him dead badly enough to send a hit man after him. He didn't know the identity of that assassin, and maybe he never would, but he would force the kingmaker and the mayor to pay for Abby's murder and Marla's disappearance. And the murder of the woman Madigan had sacrificed.

Sacrifice.

Horned Sparrow had sacrificed a woman to Avadiim, and Madigan had sacrificed one to join Reichard's club.

Jake pulled into the inn's parking lot and went inside. No one manned the front counter, but he heard a woman speaking on the phone in the room behind it. He found the stairway before he found the elevator, which was fine by him. Unlocking his door and entering his room, he felt anxious for a good night's sleep. Moving past the bathroom, he followed the narrow hall to the main room, where he flipped the light switch. A rifle with a silencer on its barrel lay across one of the two beds.

Jake sensed a man moving through the darkness behind him even before he glimpsed him in the mirror over the desk on his right. He instinctively raised his hand before his face in a swatting motion as the wire garrote whistled through the air and caught on his palm. Jake jerked the wire forward even as his assailant attempted to draw his hand to his face. With only seconds to free himself from his assailant's death grip, he pivoted on one foot and ducked at the same time.

The two men stood five feet apart, crouching like wrestlers poised to strike, and Jake measured his opponent: six feet tall, military crew cut, hard eyes and body, dressed in loose-fitting black clothes. An assassin.

The man who killed Abby.

Jake had made a serious miscalculation in assuming the man had fled the area after the publicity Abby's murder had no doubt generated.

With his steel-gray eyes betraying no emotion, the man discarded his garrote on the floor and drew a hunting knife with a gleaming, serrated blade from his belt. In that moment, Jake vowed never to travel without firepower again.

The assassin moved in on Jake, swinging the knife in a blur of motion, forcing him into the space between the two queen-sized beds. With limited room to maneuver, Jake backed up against a bedside table. Reaching behind him, he seized the lamp and hurled it at his attacker, who deflected the lamp with his knife. Jake dove onto the far bed, rolled over it, and landed on his feet on the other side. The assassin ran around the bed at a terrific speed. Jake waited until the man rounded the foot of the bed, then dove across the bed once more. As soon as his shoes touched the carpet, he ran for the desk, feigning to his right so the killer would think he was trying to escape through the front door.

The man appeared behind him with lightning speed, and Jake grabbed the wooden chair at the desk with both hands and swung it at the man with all his might. One leg of the chair struck the man's knife hand, sending the weapon across the room. As a bonus, another leg struck the side of his head.

Luck of the Irish, Jake thought, pulling the chair back for another swing.

The assassin shook his head and focused on Jake. He did not shake the hand that had held the knife. In fact, he did not move it at all but kept his wrist and fingers still.

Maybe I broke it, Jake hoped.

The man turned his body sideways, good hand and feet poised for attack.

Martial artist.

Jake didn't know what kind—kung fu, karate, tae kwon do. He had never studied any of the techniques but had learned plenty of hand-to-hand combat skills as a cop.

The man cocked his arm and fired his fist at Jake's head. Jake swung the chair hard, smashing the cherrywood down on the man's knuckles. The man's face turned scarlet, and Jake hoped he had broken this hand as well.

As Jake pulled the chair back for another swing, the man aimed a powerful kick at the underside of the seat that shattered the furniture and left Jake holding nothing but the chair's back and hind legs. Using both hands, Jake drove the remaining wood straight into the man's face, shattering the chair's frame and the man's nose at the same time.

While the assassin appeared dazed, Jake threw the two pieces of the chair aside and leapt onto the closest bed. He seized the rifle in both hands, threw his back against the wall, and aimed the gun at Abby's killer.

The assassin leapt snarling onto the bed, and Jake knew the rifle was unloaded even before he squeezed the trigger and heard nothing but a hollow click. The man dropped low on his right leg and used his left leg to sweep Jake's feet out from under him, dropping Jake. The man lunged for Jake's throat, and Jake raised the rifle sideways in both hands to hold him back. Protecting his fingers, the man pressed his palms against the rifle's barrel and stock, close to Jake's hands, and forced the rifle against Jake's Adam's apple.

Jake pushed back but the man was too strong. Feeling intense pressure against his throat, Jake tried to twist his body, but the man had pinned him to the bed's headboard with such force he could no longer breathe.

The man's face filled his vision, his eyes blazing with anger and his ruptured nose bleeding. He gritted his teeth, his own breathing coming out in deep bursts, and Jake watched a bubble of blood in the man's nostril expand and shrink, expand and shrink, threatening to burst but never reaching that climax. Desperate to look at anything besides the man's terrible face, Jake raised his gaze to the stucco ceiling, which went out of focus. Why did he have to die before he had a chance to figure out the key to the cabal of old men behind Marla's disappearance?

The key . . .

Abby had said, "The key will save your life."

With his eyelids twitching, Jake released the rifle with his right hand, which allowed the man to press the rifle against his throat with even greater power, and reached into his pants pocket. His fingers opened and closed in a spastic fashion beyond his control, but he managed to drag free the key to his rented SUV. He stroked the key's shaft, two and a half inches long, then drove it straight into the man's left ear until it would go no deeper, and turned the ignition.

The man's body shuddered, and he released the rifle as he sat erect, eyes wide. With a trembling hand, he pinched the inside of his ear and drew the key out of his ruptured canal, which spewed clumps of waxy blood.

Jake gasped for air, his swollen throat throbbing. He threw the man off him and onto the floor and crawled across the bed. He set one foot on the carpet and staggered forward into the desk. In the mirror's reflection, he saw the man lurching after him, the hunting knife clutched in his hand once more. Jake swiped a complimentary pen from the desk, spun to face the man, seized the wrist of his opponent's knife hand, and buried the pen in his left eye. The man screamed until Jake punched him in the throat, rendering him mute.

The man sank to his knees. He tilted his head back, gazed at Jake with his remaining eye, and opened his mouth to speak. Then his eye rolled up, and he fell backwards on the floor. His body shook, farted, and stopped moving.

Gasping, Jake massaged his throat.

Dark light rose from the man's corpse, seemed to congeal above it, and faded.

Jake sat on the edge of the bed, uncertain which of his assaults had killed the man and not really caring. He had no intention of allowing an autopsy to solve the riddle.

Self-defense, he thought.

It didn't matter. If he reported the man's death to the police, his search for Marla would grind to a halt as he subjected himself to the slow turning wheels of justice. And he believed Reichard and Madigan could make sure he was found guilty of murder and did serious time. He was not going to let that happen without a fight. This corpse had to disappear.

The telephone rang, causing him to jump.

CHAPTER
11

Jake stared at the ringing telephone. No one knew he had checked into this hotel except Carrie, and she would have called his cell phone.

The front desk?

The dead man on the floor had screamed before expiring.

Or maybe he isn't a lone gunman and his partner's checking to see if I answer . . .

Allowing the phone to ring out, he took the plastic liner out of the wastebasket beside the desk, pulled it over the man's head, and tied it to prevent the jellylike substance oozing from his eye and the blood from his nose and ear from pooling on the carpet. Blood had already collected on the fabric, so he ran to the bathroom, wet some tissue, and scrubbed the slick spots.

Thank heaven for stain-free hotel carpeting.

He ripped the comforter from the bed, ascertained that blood had not stained the sheets, and tossed the comforter into the bathtub. He had just grabbed the dead man's ankles and was in the process of dragging the corpse into the bathroom when he heard a knock at the door.

Damn it!

Jake continued the heavy lifting. Inside the bathroom, he draped the man's legs over the bathtub and ran the water. He closed the bathroom door as he opened the front door.

A young woman with short dark hair and a pierced nose stood before him. The name tag pinned to the lapel of her blazer identified her as Beth. "Is everything all right? Another guest complained he heard screaming in here."

Jake recognized her voice. Beth was the young woman he had heard in the room behind the counter when he had returned from the reservation. "Everything's fine. I didn't realize I was so loud. I sat down in the desk chair, and it completely fell apart underneath me."

"Oh, my God, are you hurt?"

"No, I'm fine. I was just startled. I didn't mean to disturb anyone."

"I should call an ambulance."

"Please don't. I just want to take a hot bath and get a good night's sleep before checkout."

"Are you sure? I need to have you fill out an accident report."

"Really, that isn't necessary. I'd rather keep this between us. It's kind of embarrassing."

"My manager would want to comp your room at least."

"He doesn't need to know about it. Just don't bill me for the chair, okay?"

Beth tried to get a better look inside. "I tried calling you but there was no answer."

Jake nodded at the bathroom door. "Sorry. I was running my bathwater."

"Okay. Promise me you'll call the front desk if you need anything."

"I will."

Beth walked away, and Jake closed the door and returned to the bathroom, where he shut off the water. He turned the dead man's pockets inside out but found no wallet or ID, just keys and a remote for a rental car.

✳

Jake slipped out one of the hotel's side exits. Circling the parking lot, he aimed the dead man's remote control at every silver SUV he saw until one beeped and flashed its headlights. He walked to the vehicle, unlocked it, got in, and searched it. In the glove compartment he found a wallet. A New York driver's license identified the man as Kiel Kove. A Virginia license named him as Ashley Martin. A Florida license identified David Willard. And a California license listed Henry Klepparek. Then Jake found a corporate security card.

What have we here?

The ID read, *Ashby Morton, White River Security.*

Jake tapped the card in his hand. He had heard of White River Security. The company sent security contractors all over the world, from South America to the Middle East: highly paid corporate mercenaries. White River won no-bid contracts from the Pentagon and made a profit wherever war or instability wreaked havoc. He had no trouble imagining a connection between the outfit and Karlin Reichard.

Climbing into the backseat, Jake rifled through a rolling suitcase until he found round-trip tickets for Ashby Morton from West Virginia to Buffalo. The return ticket was for the next day, just like Jake's. He also found a room key for a Best Western located on the same strip.

In and out, wham, bam, you're dead, man.

He had a long night ahead of him, and he didn't foresee sleeping on the plane.

Jake drove his own rental vehicle along the strip until he located a twenty-four-hour home supplies superstore. He dropped two hundred dollars in cash on the materials he needed, then located a pay phone in the parking lot because he did not wish to use his cell phone unless necessary. God only knew if White River had the ability to listen in on his calls. Plying the phone with quarters, he called Carrie.

"Hello?" a man's low voice said over music in the background.

Ripper, Jake thought. "Can I speak to Carrie? This is Jake."

Ripper did not answer him.

A moment later, after some rustling on their end of the line, Carrie took over. "What is it, boss?"

"I'm sorry to do this, but I need you to go into the office."

"*Now?* It's Saturday night. We're at a party on Long Island."

"Sorry, kiddo. Call me when you get there."

"Jake, Ripper isn't going to be very happy about this. It's his drummer's birthday."

"Leave him there. I don't want him in the office anyway."

"He'll never let me travel alone."

"Then bring him along, but make him wait downstairs. Remember, I can access the security cameras from my laptop."

"Yeah, yeah. I can tell you right now he isn't going to leave right this minute just because you say so."

"Do what you can."

"Are you in trouble?"

"Always."

"That's what I thought."

Returning to his room at the inn, Jake pulled on clear plastic shoe covers, a jumpsuit with gloves and a hood secured by a drawstring, and a pair of goggles. Then he lined the bathtub and bathroom floor and walls with plastic drop cloths. He used scissors to cut away Morton's clothing, rather than struggle to undress the corpse, and deposited the items in an industrial-sized garbage bag. Arranging the corpse in the bathtub, he took out the handsaw used for tree trimming. He would have preferred a power tool, but that would have created chaos with other hotel guests.

Raising Morton's left leg, he cocked the knee and placed the saw's teeth against it. He had never disposed of a body before, and he wished he didn't have to now. Life would have been so much easier if he could have just rolled Morton's corpse out of the hotel on a luggage cart, but the chances of him being seen were too great. He thought about everything he could to take his mind off the grisly task at hand: Sheryl. Marla. Martin. Edgar. Joyce. What would any of them think if they saw him now?

Sheryl could be watching me right now.

He was glad he had rented an SUV.

Jake drove along the highway through the darkness, tuning the radio until he came across a news station. He got off at the exit he wanted, and this road was even darker, with trees flanking each side of the road and no streetlights in sight. The headlights illuminated the wooden statue of the Indian at the trading post, but this time Jake turned right before he reached it and followed a road along the edge of the woods. There were no other vehicles or houses or other signs of civilization, and as Jake got out, he glanced at the sky and marveled at the visibility of the stars, which he rarely saw in the glare of New York City.

Watch the stars, brother!

He opened the SUV's hatch, took out a flashlight, a shovel, and one of the bulging garbage bags and walked into the woods, snapping twigs beneath his feet and brushing branches away from his face with the flashlight. He located a small clearing dusted with pinecones. After dropping the shovel and the bag onto the ground, he positioned the flashlight in the crook of a tree so it served as a spotlight. Then he picked up the shovel, cleared away pinecones, and used his foot to drive the shovel's blade into the ground. An owl hooted somewhere in the trees as he dug.

After fifteen minutes, he stepped into the hole up to his thighs and piled fresh dirt along the edges. His goal was to dig a hole three feet deep and five feet wide, but his body ached, and he doubted his ability to see his task through to its conclusion. Climbing out of the hole, he threw the shovel into the dirt and rotated his shoulders.

Jake returned to the SUV without the flashlight, which wasn't too difficult since the clearing was just a hundred yards from the road. He opened the hatch, took out two more bags—leaving the one with Morton's trunk for last because it was heaviest—and headed back for the woods. Before he reached the trees, he heard an engine and saw white light come around the bend. Operating on blind instinct, he charged into the woods and turned around.

A pickup stopped next to the SUV. Several figures leapt out of the truck bed and circled the vehicle. Some of them carried rifles.

Shit!

Jake hurried to the clearing, easy to spot with his flashlight in the tree. He thought he had seen four men jump out of the truck bed, which meant two more men rode in the front. A six-man assassination squad. Throwing the heavy garbage bags into the hole, he snatched the flashlight from the tree and turned it off. Then he grabbed the shovel and jumped into the hole.

Peering over the mound of dirt, he saw half a dozen flashlight beams swarming through the woods, some of them moving in his direction. He tightened his hands on the shovel's handle, knowing he could take out one, possibly two of the men, but no more, not if they were trained like Morton. He had to run, but he also had to circle back to the SUV or he'd be trapped like a wild animal, hunted by the White River assassins.

The killers fanned out, expanding their hunting area while closing in on Jake.

Realizing he had made a mistake by hiding in the hole with Morton's body parts, Jake turned his back on the men and climbed out the other side. Still clutching the shovel, he hid behind the pile of dirt, which prevented him from seeing his pursuers. Now he wished he had called Gudgino and taken the heat for killing

Morton. He had a terrible feeling that he and Morton were going to spend a lot of time together in the hole he had dug.

A circle of light illuminated the pinecones on the ground twenty feet from his head. He scanned the trees in the opposite direction. He would have to run as fast as possible to stand a chance of escaping, but the faster he moved, the more noise he would make, creating an audible target for the shooters.

A bird called out from the trees. A similar bird responded.

I don't like that.

Gathering a deep breath, Jake leapt to his feet and spun on one foot, his other leg reaching for the ground. The butt of a rifle stock slammed into his face, and he flailed his arms and fell into the hole. Lying on his back with both knees raised, he batted his eye at the sky above but saw only spots of pulsing light. He massaged the aching left side of his face.

"Over here, I got him!"

Jake heard running footsteps above, and as the spots of light in his vision vanished and he saw the sky through the treetops, one figure after another appeared atop the dirt surrounding the hole. Six men aimed flashlights and rifles down at him, making it impossible for him to see them.

"Get up," a deep voice said.

Forgetting about the shovel, Jake got to his feet.

"Don't you know how this works? Raise your hands."

Jake squinted at the speaker. "Don't you mean fold them behind my head?"

"Raise your hands or you're losing a kneecap."

Jake raised his hands.

"What's your name, Joe?"

"If I tell you it's Frank, will you let me go?"

The speaker dropped his flashlight on the ground and held out one hand and snapped his fingers. "Gimme your wallet."

The discarded flashlight lit one of the other men from below. Out of his peripheral vision, Jake glimpsed gold jewelry and a Mohawk haircut.

This isn't what I thought. He took out his wallet, and as the speaker leaned forward to take it, Jake saw the man was an Indian.

Another man, standing on the speaker's right-hand side, aimed his flashlight at the wallet. Spilled light illuminated other faces from underneath, causing them to glow like jack-o'-lanterns. Jake guessed the Indians were all in their midtwenties, which didn't make them any less dangerous.

The leader thumbed through Jake's cash before looking at his ID. "What's a Jake Helman?"

"This one is a private eye. My PI license is in there."

The man studied Jake's documentation. "This guy's from the twenty-four-dollar city."

Jake heard chuckling all around him.

"What are you doing on our land?"

How do I explain this? "I was driving back to my hotel and I got lost."

"Oh yeah?" the man said. "Looks like you got lost in a hole. Good thing you found a shovel to dig your way out. What's in that bag? You dumping your garbage on our land? We don't need your garbage. We have our own."

Jake stayed quiet, sweating in the cool night air. *Think, think, think.*

"Usually people don't bury their garbage unless they're taking a shit. Are you taking a shit?"

Jake swallowed. "Not yet."

"Show us what you brought us."

Jake saw there was no talking his way out of this situation. Getting down on one knee, he grabbed the industrial liner in both hands, tore it open, and pushed it over. Morton's head rolled out.

"Oh, shit!" one of the Indians said, laughing.

Closing Jake's wallet, the leader aimed his rifle, which lay across his forearm, at Jake. "Stand up."

Jake obeyed, several rifle barrels following his progress.

"I bet you think we're scared now. We aren't scared. We've all seen bodies before. There are bodies all over this reservation. Someone wants to hide a corpse, they bury it here on protected land. No police or feds can come looking. The Mafia in Niagara Falls does it all the time. It's the perfect spot—unless you get caught."

"There's five hundred dollars in that wallet. What do you say you just take it and let me go?"

"You gonna take your garbage with you?"

He knew the man was playing with him. "Sure, whatever you say."

"We could take your money and leave you cold in this hole. Buy some firewater and go gambling and shit, you know?" He tossed the wallet at Jake's feet. "We don't want your money."

Jake's cell phone rang, causing him to flinch.

The Indians laughed.

"You expecting a call?"

Carrie. The ring tone continued. "Yes, actually. It's kind of important. Do you mind?"

The speaker raised his rifle, aiming it straight at Jake's face. "Go ahead."

Jake answered the call. "Go ahead, Carrie."

"I'm in the office. Sorry it took me so long. Ripper didn't want to leave the party. He's downstairs now."

142

Jake stared at the barrel aimed between his eyes. "I want you to go to the safe in my office."

"Okay, I'm walking now. I'm opening the door. Now I'm turning on the light. I'm standing at the safe."

"I'm going to give you the combinations for all three locks. Then I want you to open the safe door." He read her the combinations one by one. "Now throw the lever. You'll probably need to use both hands."

"Jeez, you aren't kidding," Carrie said, grunting.

"There's a laptop on the shelf in there. Take it to my desk and turn it on. *Do not hook it up to the Internet.*"

"Okay, I have the laptop. What about these CDs and files?"

"Don't touch them. Forget you ever saw them."

"Right, boss."

The lead Indian cleared his throat. "How long is this going to take?"

"Just a couple of minutes, and then you can shoot me."

"What did you say?" Carrie said.

"Nothing. Stay focused."

"It's booting up. It's asking me for a password."

"*Sheryl.*"

"Uh-huh. Okay, something is happening. It says, 'Tower International—Building Better Life.' That's kind of creepy, huh? 'Tower makes monsters,' right?"

"There's a search window. Key in *Avadiim*. That's A-v-a-d-i-i-m."

The Indians turned their heads to each other in apparent surprise.

That's got their attention, Jake thought.

"A file opened," Carrie said. "Only it's spelled differently here:

A-v-a-d-e-m-e."

Interesting. "All right, listen. There are blank CDs in the drawer. I want you to burn this file—*just this file*—to a disc. Then I want you to stick the laptop back in the safe and lock all three locks again. Understand?"

"I am a college grad, remember? What do you want me to do with the CD after I burn the file?"

"Just take it with you. Don't read it. If I can, I'll call you back. If you don't hear from me in twelve hours, give it to Maria Vasquez and tell her to discuss its contents with that psychic who works downstairs."

"Boss, what the hell have you gotten yourself into?"

"I can't talk anymore. Just do what I said and maybe I'll see you soon." Jake pocketed his phone.

The leader of the men maintained his rifle's aim. "What do you know about Avadiim? And who did that head belong to once upon a time?"

Sensing the worm had turned, Jake lowered his hands. "I only know what Daniel Whitefish told me about Avadiim, and I saw the cave painting out by the lake. This man worked for White River Security. You've heard of them?"

The man nodded. "I read newspapers."

"Earlier today, this man killed a woman in Lily Dale. He was trying to kill me. He tried again in my hotel room, which is why he's in his current state. I have my reasons for not wanting the police to know about any of this. Most of them have to do with a group of very powerful men who are behind a lot of very bad shit."

"White men?"

"To the one."

"What do they have to do with Avadiim?"

"That's what I'm trying to find out."

144

The man lowered his rifle. "Avadiim's nothing but a monster in a children's bedtime story. You're wasting your time."

Jake relaxed. "Maybe, but it's the only lead I have."

The man grunted. Whether in approval or disapproval, Jake couldn't tell. The other men lowered their guns.

"We didn't see you here," the man said. "And you didn't see us. Finish burying your body, get the hell out of here, and don't ever come back."

"Deal."

"One more thing: you're missing an eye. I must have knocked it out. Sorry about that."

Feeling himself turning red, Jake touched the edge of his empty eye socket. The pain on that side of his face had prevented him from sensing the glass eye's absence. All six men aimed their flashlights at his feet, and he searched the ground for the orb.

"Here it is," said the man with the Mohawk. He bent down behind the dirt and held up Jake's eye, which he tossed to him.

Jake caught the eye. "Thanks."

Chuckling, the men returned to the darkness from which they'd come.

CHAPTER
12

Driving back to his hotel with his eye in one pocket, Jake pressed autodial on his cell phone.

"Good, you're alive," Carrie said.

"Thanks to your call. Where are you now?"

"We're in a taxi heading home. I'm charging it to petty cash."

Smart girl. "When you get there, upload the document on that CD to your computer and e-mail it to me at this address: shadow33@whozit.com."

"Anything else?"

"Delete the e-mail from your sent folder, remove the file from your hard drive, and destroy that CD. I mean, break it, burn it, and bury its ashes at sea."

"You realize I'm on overtime?"

"There will be a bonus for you on top of that."

"You're the best boss in the world when you're desperate."

Jake pulled into the inn's parking lot and got into Morton's rented SUV, which he drove one mile along the strip to the Best Western. He locked the doors, took the keys with him, and walked back in the direction of his hotel. Since the highway exit wasn't far, there was more traffic on the street than he would have liked, and he walked with his head down. Outside the inn, he chucked the keys into a storm drain and popped the glass eye back into his socket.

When he entered the lobby, Beth looked up from behind the counter with a quizzical expression.

"Forgot my toothbrush in my car," Jake said, patting his jacket pocket.

Outside his room, he removed the Do Not Disturb sign from the door and confirmed the hair from his head he had stuck across the doorframe remained there.

Once inside, he checked the room for visitors anyway. Odors from the cleaning chemicals he had doused the bathtub and bathroom with assailed his senses. The bedside clock displayed 1:17 a.m. He needed sleep but had other priorities.

First, he washed his glass eye and reinserted it into his socket, then he brewed coffee using the "gourmet blend" in the bathroom. Next, he powered up his laptop, accessed his e-mail account, and found the attachment he wanted from Carrie. He regretted having given her the combinations to the safe and making her burn the CD. Although he trusted her, he did not wish to endanger her, and Marla's disappearance and Abby's murder confirmed just how dangerous his enemies were. He couldn't wait to get back to Manhattan to check Afterlife himself. Time was critical.

He opened the attachment, and the familiar typography of the file appeared before him. The heading *The Order of Avademe* appeared at the top of the page, with the Indian spelling below it in parentheses. A list of seven numbered names appeared next.

So much for my "eight men equal eight tentacles" theory.

He did a double take when he came to the last name.

1. Karlin Reichard
2. Norman Weiskopf
3. Silas Coffer
4. Bruce Schlatter
5. Richard Browning
6. Simon Taggert
7. Benjamin Bradley

The founder of Sky Cloud Dreams. Jake sat back in his chair. Benjamin Bradley, Sky Cloud Dreams, and the Imago movement were connected to Karlin Reichard, the Reichard Foundation, White River Security, and an ancient Indian monster named either Avadiim or Avademe.

Martin's in deeper trouble than I realized.

He did a search on each name, matching the faces in the images with those he recalled seeing in Reichard's party room when Myron Madigan murdered the drugged woman. Norman Weiskopf headed the largest defense contractor in the US. Silas Coffer owned the largest independent oil company. Bruce Schlatter was the CEO of the top ranked health insurance company in the nation. Richard Browning ran the leading bank. Simon Taggert owned White River Security. Except for Benjamin Bradley, all of the men served on the board of directors of the Reichard Foundation.

Myron Madigan makes eight.

Industry. War profiteering. Health care insurance. How the hell did the head of a wacky space cult fit in with these power brokers?

Religion. Money.

And Myron Madigan provided politics.

Poor Marla.

Jake checked out of the hotel four hours later after an abbreviated sleep cycle.

"Are you sure you're okay?" Beth said.

"I'm fine. I just got some bad news and need to catch an early flight back to New York."

"I hope you had a nice trip," she said.

Jake drove past Buffalo and its airport. Two hours later, he had breakfast at a roadside diner. As he listened to two New York State troopers discuss sports over coffee, he wondered how much time would pass before the car rental agency Morton used reported his SUV missing, or before the hotel where the man had stayed connected the vehicle in the parking lot with the man who had failed to check out. Jake had wanted to snoop around the killer's room but considered the risk too great.

His soul was dark, he told himself. *I killed him in self-defense.*

How many more times could Jake place himself in these situations before he killed an innocent man or his own luck ran out? If he did kill an innocent, he would taint his soul, and he knew a certain demon that looked forward to getting his fiery hands on it. If Jake got killed, at this point, he believed he might ascend to the Realm of Light. The same fear and hope he had lived with for seventeen months, ever since the nightmare at the Tower when Sheryl's soul had saved him from Cain. He sighed, and the server refilled his coffee cup.

He spent two more hours driving, then pulled over to a rest stop, reclined his seat, and took a two-hour nap. After grabbing lunch, he got back on the highway and drove for another hour, formulating a shopping list in his mind.

"Hi, Joyce. How's Martin?" Jake enjoyed the view of Pennsylvania's Pocono Mountains, an hour away from New York City.

"Sullen."

"Has anyone attempted to contact him?"

"Not that I can tell. Even with his grandmother helping, it's impossible to keep an eye on him every minute."

"You have to try. Call in another relative if necessary, just for one more week or two."

"What's got you worried?"

"Benjamin Bradley, the head of Sky Cloud Dreams, is involved with some very unsavory gentlemen."

"Is Martin in danger?"

"I don't think so, but we can't take a chance. Maybe Bradley's all about fleecing the Dreamers out of money, or maybe everyone in that wacky cult is at risk. I'm not saying this to make you worry needlessly. I just want to make sure nothing happens to your son."

"I'll do whatever you say."

Jake reached the road that ran parallel to Reichard's estate just before 3:00 p.m. Marla had told him that Mayor Madigan always stayed for lunch on Sunday when he went away on his retreats before returning to Manhattan. Although Marla's disappearance had forced Myron to return ahead of schedule, Jake hoped Reichard's other guests had not left early as well. He pulled into the access road opposite the estate, turned around, and backed up with the trees providing cover. He stopped short of the security gate, just in case the men assigned to it had been ordered to pay closer attention to the woods across the street. At least he was driving a different vehicle. Getting out, he located the same spot where he had sat before and trained his binoculars on the mansion.

Nothing to see yet. Sunlight gleamed on the bricks.

Lowering the binoculars, he observed that two men now occupied the booth. Half an hour later, a black stretch limousine stopped at the gates, which swung open. The limo pulled up to the booth, and the chauffeur presented the uniformed guards with his ID. A moment later, they waved him through.

As the gates closed, Jake raised his binoculars again and watched the limo climb the hill, navigating the winding turns with great care. At the top, the limo parked in front of the mansion, and the chauffeur got out and stood at attention.

A few minutes later, the mansion's double doors opened, and an old man Jake recognized as Silas Coffer stepped past the butler.

The chauffeur opened the back limo door for Coffer and helped him into the luxury vehicle. A steward carried the man's suitcase to the trunk, which the chauffeur opened. With Coffer and his luggage secure, the chauffeur slid behind the wheel and drove the limo downhill.

Jake tapped his foot on a stump. Twenty minutes later, the second limo—white, this time—came for Richard Browning.

But the third limo, a long black vehicle, came for the man Jake wished to see. His target, Simon Taggert, exited the mansion with greater speed than his cohorts had before him. Jake remembered seeing the man's cold eyes and widow's peak on the night when Madigan had killed the girl. He believed it was Taggert who had drawn his gun, intending to shoot him in the back. Reichard had made the mistake of stopping him. Taggert walked with the confidence of a man ten years younger than his sixty-two years. When his muscular chauffeur opened the door for him, the old man ducked inside.

Cocky bastard, Jake thought as he jogged back to his SUV and got in. He remained on the service road but pulled up another two hundred and fifty yards, parking behind a thick oak tree and dense bushes. He popped the hatch, climbed out, and drew Morton's rifle from the hatch, which he closed. Kneeling between the SUV and the bushes, he positioned the rifle and waited.

The limo came around the bend, as Jake knew it would, heading in the direction of the nearest highway ramp. Lowering his aim, he calculated the vehicle's speed. He knew he had only one shot. As the limo neared him, he trained the rifle's mounted scope on the front left wheel, followed the wheel until it was directly ahead of him, then held still, waiting for the rear wheel to replace the front wheel in the scope's crosshairs. He squeezed the trigger.

The sound of the wheel's tire blowing out obscured the suppressed gunshot, and the limo swerved like a shark before pulling over to the side of the road. Killing one hundred zonbies had made Jake an expert shot. Tossing the rifle through the window he had left open in the SUV, he darted around the bushes so they hid him but offered a clear path to the road.

The chauffeur got out of the limo and walked its length to the flattened tire. Chunks of rubber marked the limo's trail like skull fragments.

Jake waited for the broad-shouldered man to get down on one knee to inspect the rupture or go to the trunk.

He went to the trunk, turning his back to Jake, who bolted from his hiding place and sprinted across the road. The chauffeur popped the trunk, and Jake closed in on his quarry. When the chauffeur turned his head at the sound of approaching footsteps, Jake clamped a rag drenched in chloroform over the man's mouth.

The chauffeur tried to turn his head away, but Jake's body smashed into him, knocking him into the trunk. The man groped inside his jacket with a hand that turned limp and flopped down as he lost consciousness.

Jake tucked the man's legs inside the trunk in case a car passed. He opened the man's jacket, revealing a Beretta in a shoulder holster. Plucking the weapon free, Jake closed the trunk and circled the limo's rear, then jerked the passenger door open. Taggert gasped as Jake slid beside him and trained the Beretta on him.

"Who the hell are you?" the old man said, reaching inside his suit jacket.

"I'm the guy who's going to blow out the back of your skull if you don't get your fingers off that gun."

Taggert raised his hands. "I have money—"

Jake clamped the rag over Taggert's mouth and pressed the Beretta against his chest.

The old man's eyes widened with panic, then fluttered and closed.

Mission accomplished, Jake thought.

CHAPTER
13

"You can open your eyes now," Jake said. "That chloroform should have worn off ten minutes ago."

Taggert opened his eyes and raised his head. Jake had bound his wrists, waist, and ankles to various parts of a heavy office chair with metal legs. A shaft of sunlight cut through a gash in a sagging ceiling. The barn reeked of damp, rotting wood.

"Where are we?" The old man looked around.

"You don't need to know that," Jake said, circling the shaft of light from the shadows. "I get that all the time. It's nice to be the one playing things close to the vest for a change."

"Who are you?"

"You sent a man to kill me last night. Does that narrow down the list of possibilities?"

Taggert said nothing.

"Ashby Morton killed a psychic named Abby Fay in a village called Lily Dale, with a bullet meant for me. It was sloppy. Maybe you need to conduct better background checks when you hire people to do your dirty work."

Taggert seemed to regulate his breathing.

Meditation, Jake thought. "Are you planning to give me the silent treatment?"

Silence.

"I know you served in the marines before you joined a private contracting company that did wet work for the CIA and started your own company, so I bet you've been trained not to talk." He stood before his captive. "But you were younger then."

One side of Taggert's upper lip curled. "I could kick your ass right now if I wasn't tied up."

Jake looked him over. The old man had a tight body, all right. "You probably could. Too bad you *are* tied up."

"What happened to Morton?"

"If I told you that, I'd have to kill you, too."

"What about my driver?"

"He's fine. At least he was the last time I saw him." Jake had driven the limo deep into the woods, along the service road near Reichard's estate, then hauled the chauffeur out of the trunk and set him in the front seat. He kept the man's Beretta in case he needed it. "I'd think twice about giving him a Christmas bonus, though."

"You're guilty of kidnapping."

Jake shrugged. "Who's going to know? I doubt your man will call the police. He's either gone straight to Reichard or called your company, in which case *they've* called Reichard. And if Reichard

156

calls the police, it will be someone very high up, who will deal with this in a very quiet, very unofficial manner."

"You're acting like a lunatic."

"What choice do I have? I can't return to my office. I'm sure I can't use a credit card without your people knowing about it. I can't pull money out of the bank. If I lie low, you and your cronies have the resources to find me. I had to strike back fast and hard."

"Morton's body—"

"—will never be found."

"If you're going to kill me, do it now."

Jake shook his head. "We both realize that just killing you won't serve any purpose. There are six more of you old bastards, plus Madigan. I'd have to kill every one of you before I could sleep at night. That's a lot of work."

"That only leaves negotiation."

"Uh-uh. None of you serpents are trustworthy."

"Then what do you want?"

"Information."

Taggert snorted.

"Where's Marla Madigan?"

The old man stared at him. Jake thought he saw a hint of a smile.

"I guess you farts think someone like her doesn't matter. Well, she matters to me. Who was that girl that my esteemed mayor murdered while you watched and clapped? She matters, too."

Taggert's smile grew more defined.

"Let's try a different tack. Tell me about Avademe."

The smile vanished from Taggert's face.

"I've always wondered what would happen if one of you sons of bitches who advocate torture was tortured yourself. I've been tortured. It's something I've always wanted to do to some deserving soul."

"I'll die before I tell you anything."

"We'll see." Jake gestured at the gold ring on Taggert's right hand ring finger. "That's a very interesting ring you've got there. What is that squiggly shape? A serpent? A sacrificial dagger?"

Taggert smirked.

"It looks like a tentacle to me. I'm willing to bet the ring Reichard slipped onto Madigan's finger was identical, and every one of the other greedy parasites has one just like it. The eight of you *are* Avademe."

Taggert clenched his fists.

"Easy there, tiger. You might lather yourself into a heart attack, and I haven't figured out whether or not I want you dead yet. What I do want is that ring."

"Fuck you."

Jake raised his eyebrows. "Ah, now that got a response. You don't want to part ways with your bling? Too bad."

As Jake moved closer to Taggert, the old man sucked in his breath and his body turned rigid. Jake seized the wrist of the man's right arm and pressed down on it, pressuring it against the chair's armrest. With his right hand, he pried at Taggert's fist, trying to separate the ring finger. He glanced at the old man, who glared at him, jaw set, sweat beading on his forehead. At last Jake worked the finger free, but Taggert crooked his joints, making it impossible to remove the ring.

"Have it your way." Jake jerked the leathery finger back until it snapped.

Taggert scowled but did not scream.

Jake stood staring at the broken finger, which turned purple. He tried to pull the ring free, but it didn't budge. "Damn. Now it's too swollen."

Taggert's sneer revealed an air of triumph.

"I guess I'll have to cut it off." Jake strode over to a dusty wooden workbench upon which he had set a new tool kit. Throwing the latches on the kit, he opened its lid and took out a pair of pruning shears the size of pliers, with rubber-coated handles and short, curved, gleaming new blades. Without saying a word, he returned to Taggert, gripped the broken finger, and positioned the blades on either side of the finger, just below the gold ring. Taggert held his breath and Jake squeezed the handles. The blades bit halfway through Taggert's finger, and the old man's rigid body shook. Closing both hands around the pruning shears, Jake squeezed harder, and the blades did their duty with a wet snipping sound.

The finger fell in the dirt at Taggert's feet, and blood squirted out of the remaining portion of the finger. Bowing his head and squeezing his eyes shut, his face turning a deep shade of scarlet, Taggert grimaced.

Jake got down on one knee and reached for the severed finger. Taggert rocked forward, tipping over in the chair, and snapped his jaws at Jake's face. Jake jumped back with the finger in hand and Taggert landed on the dirt smudged floorboards where Jake had just stood. The old man unleashed a howl of frustrated anger rather than pain.

Jake glanced at the finger, then at the old man lying on his side. "If you don't want to bleed to death, you'd better hold still." He walked over to the bench, set the finger down, then returned with gauze and adhesive tape. He bent over, grabbed the chair, and righted it with a groan.

Tears streamed down Taggert's ashen face. "Give me back that ring!"

Jake wrapped the bandage around the bloody digit. "Not

gonna happen. It's mine now."

"No!" Taggert rocked back and forth in the chair, thrashing like a wild cat.

"If you fall over again, I'm leaving you in the dirt." Jake returned to the bench and examined the finger. He squeezed it above the ring, forcing blood out of the open wound. The swelling disappeared, and the ring slid right off. Walking back to Taggert, he raised the ring between his thumb and forefinger. "Now I think I have something to bargain with."

"Giveitbacktomeyoupieceofshit!"

With calm deliberation, Jake peeled off the latex glove on his left hand and slid the ring over his finger.

Taggert screamed.

"It fits just right. See?" Jake displayed his hand, palm out. "It's kind of ugly, but I think I'll keep it."

Taggert groaned and rocked like a baby, mucus dangling from his nose.

Jake crouched low to the floor, sitting on the balls of his feet. He looked into the old man's eyes. "Taggert?"

Taggert screamed again, a furious bellow, his eyes wild like an animal's. He threw himself forward at Jake, who sprang back. Taggert landed facedown on the floor this time. Jake set one foot on the man's shoulder and rolled him over onto his back. Dirt streaked Taggert's face.

"Now that I'm engaged, tell me where they've stashed Marla."

Taggert spat at Jake but the saliva fell short. "I don't have to tell you anything."

"Don't members of the Order of Avademe share information with each other?" He hoped they did, anyway.

Taggert spoke in starts and stops, emphasizing each syllable.

"That's the catch. As long as you've got my ring, I'm not a member. I don't have to tell you anything."

Jake rested one foot on the old man's chest. "Then I guess I'll have to talk to someone who's obliged to fill me in. Here's what's going to happen: I'm not going to kill you. I'm going to leave you right here. Don't bother trying to wiggle free; even if you smash the chair to pieces and get loose, you're in the middle of nowhere. I'll let Reichard know exactly where you are. If you want to be found, stay here."

"If you tell them where I am, I'm finished. Without that ring, I'm a dead man."

"Do tell."

Taggert's head sagged back in resignation. "You're right: the eight of us comprise Avademe. Our companies are tied together. We share profits. We influence world affairs to ensure maximum growth. All of us are fully aware of everyone else's activities. The alliance the rings represent prevents us from moving against each other or interfering with each other's enterprises. With that ring, I'm a key member of the group, protected from my associates. Without it, I'm just someone who knows too much."

"But you're the head of White River Security, with an army at your disposal. Surely you can protect yourself."

Taggert shook his head. "All eight members have equal stock in each other's businesses and ventures. With their combined interests, my fellows own more of White River than I do, and I have no resources without them. White River isn't the only security firm we control."

"But it must be the biggest and most powerful. They must need you."

Taggert swallowed. "If I disappear, someone else will just take my place." Tears welled in the old man's eyes. "Please give me back that ring. I'll make you rich beyond your wildest dreams."

Jake studied the gold on his finger. "Are you saying this ring grants me your stake in all of those companies? Including yours? That already makes me richer than I'd be if you shared your fortune."

"With a very steep price to pay."

Jake smiled. "I guess I'll play it by ear whether or not I tell them where you are."

"At least tell them you killed me. Give me a head start!"

"We'll see."

Jake returned the pruning shears to the tool kit, which he latched and carried out of the barn.

Behind him, Taggert wailed like a baby.

Jake exited the barn and slid the door shut. He had chosen the rickety structure because it stood surrounded by fields and trees. Rusted farm equipment had sunk deep into the ground. He walked around to the side where he had parked his rented SUV, and as soon as he saw the vehicle, he froze. Two men he knew stood leaning against it: Gary Brown and Frank Beck, former detectives from NYPD Narcotics, murdered by Katrina using vodou.

"'lo, Jake," Gary said.

Frank just stared, which Jake found unsettling.

"You guys look pretty good for corpses," Jake said. This is what his life had come to: two dead former colleagues appeared before him, and he took it almost in stride.

Until they stepped closer to him in unison and a familiar panic spurred his heart.

"You look pretty shitty for someone who's still alive," Gary said.

Jake swallowed. What the hell did they want with him?

"Gotta thank you for whacking that voodoo cunt after what she did to us," Frank said with his usual charm.

"That was Edgar's doing," Jake said.

"Whatever. You had a hand in it. I listen to that bitch's screams all day long, and let me tell you, it's music to my ears."

Jake's gaze moved from one man to the other.

Minions.

Dread and Baldy, two lowlifes he had killed during a tavern robbery he had foiled, had also paid a visit to him once. Actually, they had chased and beaten him.

"What can I do for you fellas?" He tried to sound casual despite his creeping unease.

Gary smiled. "There's nothing you can do for us, pal. We're burning the midnight oil long and hard. Who knew that shit was for real?"

I know what you mean.

"And who would have guessed that a fuckup like you would take down the Cipher, Old Nick, Prince Malachai, *and* Katrina? You've got moves, man. No wonder he wants to see you."

"He?" Jake felt the blood rushing from his head to his toes, and he focused on the SUV behind the minions.

"Don't even think about running," Frank said.

Gary gestured at the trees surrounding the field. "Like you just told that codger, you're in the middle of nowhere."

A terrified scream inside the barn made Jake jump.

Taggert!

Jake ran around the barn and pushed the door open. He took a single step inside and gasped.

The demon stood seven feet tall, his body naked and muscular, with transparent skin revealing fiery veins and organs. The red and orange light burning inside his body shone on the barn's walls.

A black soul rose from Taggert's corpse: a sphere of cancerous energy. The dead man appeared ten years older than when Jake had left him: frail, almost mummified, with agony frozen on his features.

Cain raised his hands before his face, his fingers opening and closing with fierce anticipation. Taggert's soul rolled through the air toward him like a basketball rebounding to a player. But the moment the dark energy seemed to settle within Cain's grasp, it exploded like a bomb, the concussion knocking Cain to the ground.

Jake felt nothing, not even a mild tremor, and the chunks of rotten energy vanished before they could strike anything.

Cain leapt to his feet with a deafening roar and groped the empty air for Taggert's soul, like a child jumping for bubbles. Then he seized the old man's corpse by its arms and jerked it and the chair off the floor. He shook the corpse with such force that Jake heard Taggert's neck snap. "GIVE IT TO ME."

That booming voice had given Jake countless nightmares.

When Taggert's empty husk failed to reply, Cain hurled it at the floor, which coughed up dust amid the sound of breaking bones.

Cain turned in Jake's direction for the first time, the two pinpricks of light suspended in his gaping eye sockets flaring at the sight of him. His chest rose and fell with frustrated anger, which only increased Jake's dread. "I TOLD YOU WE WOULD MEET AGAIN."

Jake's knees buckled. Facing Cain again was his greatest fear. He turned to run, but Gary and Frank blocked the doorway. Jake tried pushing his way between them, but they shoved him back.

"Don't make us hurt you," Gary said. "We don't want to hurt you."

"Speak for yourself," Frank said. "Why should we be the only ones to suffer?"

Jake charged at them again, but they slid the door shut.

"Good luck," Gary said as the door latched.

Jake pounded on the door. "Open up! *Open up!*" The fiery light on the door intensified, and he felt heat on his back.

"Turn around."

With the muscles in his neck resisting, Jake turned to face the entity Old Nick had called the Reaper. Cain: the first killer, brother of Abel, son of Adam and Eve, emissary for the Dark Realm. The demon stood still as a statue, just as Jake remembered him from their last meeting at the Tower. The temperature inside the barn climbed at least ten degrees.

Cain snapped his fingers, and Jake heard Gary and Frank screaming outside. He knew they were burning, just as Dread and Baldy had under similar circumstances. "There is no escape."

Jake pressed his back against the door. When he spoke, his voice sounded like the croak of a boy experiencing puberty. "Remember, Sheryl gave me a piece of her soul. Abel said you couldn't harm me."

Cain did not speak for a moment. Jake found the silence disconcerting. He searched for some indication of a response in the fire in Cain's veins.

"I have no wish to harm you . . . at this time."

Jake felt a ray of hope. "You don't?"

Cain shook his head, the movement subtle.

"Then what do you want?"

"I need your help."

Jake's brows arched so high he feared his glass eye might pop out of his socket. "How the hell can I help you?"

Cain sat on the floor, next to Taggert's broken corpse, with his arms wrapped around his raised knees. "MY BROTHER IS MISSING."

"Abel? I know." Jake knew better than to try to hide his thoughts from the demon.

Cain looked up at him. "TRUST NOTHING THAT WOMAN TELLS YOU."

Jake's mouth opened while he searched for a rebuttal. "I was married to that woman for two years. I owe her my life, remember? She saved me from you."

"DO HER BIDDING AT YOUR OWN PERIL."

Jake did not like the sound of that. "Is she really an agent of Light?"

"YES. SO WHAT? THAT MEANS NOTHING."

"From where I'm standing, it does."

"DO NOT LET YOUR EMOTIONS CLOUD YOUR JUDGMENT."

The only emotion Jake felt was terror. "What do you want from me? And why did you kill old Taggert here? He deserved to die; I'll grant you that. But he was helpless."

"I DID NOT KILL HIM. I SIMPLY APPEARED BEFORE HIM. HE TOOK ONE LOOK AT ME AND HIS HEART EXPLODED."

Jake believed that. "I doubt it was that simple."

"I DID POSE A QUESTION TO HIM."

"Which was . . . ?"

Cain sat in silence.

Son of a bitch! Jake stepped forward. "If you want me to help you do God only knows what—"

"NEVER MENTION THAT NAME TO ME!"

"Sorry. I forgot. If you expect my help, you'd better share some useful information."

"I asked him the location of Avademe."

You too? "And that scared him to death . . . which should have allowed you to claim his soul, which would have provided you with any answers he knew. How convenient. Too bad his soul had other plans. Why couldn't you take all of his thoughts before he died?"

"The same force that consumed his soul also protected his thoughts from me."

Jake clenched his hands, hoping to hide the ring.

"I know you took his ring. Your efforts to conceal the truth from me are pathetic."

"But you want my help?"

"As the woman explained to you, there are fields in this world that are invisible to both the Dark Realm and the Realm of Light."

"Sheryl called them blind spots."

"Do not trust her."

"You already said that."

"Some of the invisible fields are growing. In one of them, the Destroyer thrives. It has consumed many souls. I fear it has consumed my brother."

He believes Avademe is the Destroyer of Souls. He thinks it's a living creature. "So? The two of you aren't exactly close. You did kill him, and the last time I saw you, you were smashing his head apart on the floor of Old Nick's Soul Chamber."

"Abel and I are linked together for eternity. He was the first agent of Light, and I was the emissary of the Dark Realm. If his energy has been consumed—"

"Then yours can be, too."

Cain buried his face behind his knees. His shoulders shook, and steam hissed out from around his skull.

Jake stood mute. Was Cain *crying*?

The great demon's voice quivered. "IT'S HOPELESS. EVERY-
THING IS SO BLEAK. WHAT'S THE POINT? THE END IS NEAR. FIRST,
THE DESTROYER WILL CONSUME HUMANITY. THEN IT WILL TURN
TO THE LIGHT AND THE DARK."

"If what you're saying is true, and based on the rate at which
this Destroyer has consumed souls so far, it will take centuries for
him to devour every soul on earth. Maybe a millennia. By that
time, the sun will go supernova anyway. Maybe you should live—
or whatever it is you do—for today and not tomorrow."

Cain leapt to his feet, gripped Jake's throat in one hand, and
charged across the barn, slamming Jake against the door, his feet
dangling above the floor. "YOU DON'T UNDERSTAND!"

Staring into those pulsing points of light that served as Cain's
eyes, Jake thought *his* heart would explode. He felt tremendous
heat radiating from Cain's body and, remembering how the demon
had burned the faces of two security officers at the Tower, worried
that his neck would sizzle. But his flesh did not burn.

Cain jerked his arm back, allowing Jake to land gasping for
breath on his ass. Cain took three giant steps away, giving Jake
space. Jake examined his throat: no damage done, despite the
demon's supernatural strength.

"THERE IS A NATURAL ORDER TO THE UNIVERSE THAT WAS
DICTATED BY THE CREATOR. LIGHT AND DARK COEXIST, LOCKED
IN THE ETERNAL STRUGGLE, EACH SEEKING TO CONQUER THE OTH-
ER. THE DESTROYER IS NOT PART OF THIS NATURAL ORDER. IT IS
UNDERMINING EVERYTHING. IT MUST BE STOPPED."

Jake cleared his throat. "How?"

"I DON'T KNOW." Cain turned and paced.

Jake rose. "What is it you expect me to do?"

"You can go where I cannot, where my minions cannot, where the Light cannot. You must find Abel, or, if he has been consumed, identify where he fell."

"And then?"

"Summon me as you did before."

Jake pondered the scenario. "Suppose I trace Abel to one of the 'invisible fields' of yours. If you can't see it, how do you expect to materialize within it?"

Cain touched the center of his chest. His hand penetrated the glassy skin, through muscles and bone, and touched his glowing heart. He pulled a piece of the lavalike organ out and closed his fingers around it, his hand shaking with effort, smoke rising between his fingers. "Take this."

When Cain uncurled his fingers, Jake saw the demon had transformed his tissue into something entirely new: a glass eye with a blue iris. Jake blinked at the replacement sphere. "You want me to stick that inside my head?"

"It will allow me to see what you see, and that will enable me to materialize where necessary."

Jake reached for the eye with his forefinger and thumb. Though warm, it did not burn. He took it from Cain's palm. "I think all you're going to see for the time being is the inside of my pocket."

Cain did not respond.

"Let's get something straight. I generally don't work for free. I do make exceptions but not when the stakes are this high."

"What do you want?"

"You know the bokor Katrina?"

"I have devoured her many times. Delicious."

Jake paused before speaking, allowing the image of Cain eating Katrina alive to sink in. "Then you know she transformed my friend Edgar into a raven. I want him back as he was."

"IMPOSSIBLE. I CANNOT INTERFERE WITH THIS WORLD IN THE MANNER YOU SUGGEST."

Jake gestured at Taggert's corpse. "I'd say you interfered with him pretty directly."

Cain spread his hands apart in a gesture of innocence. "I NEVER TOUCHED HIM WHILE HE WAS ALIVE."

"Why did you wait until now to interrogate him?"

"I CAME HERE TO SEE YOU, NOT HIM."

"But you still questioned him. *Why now?*"

Cain's skin rippled and grew red. "HE WAS INVISIBLE TO ME UNTIL NOW."

Jake glanced at his ring. "The rings generate the blind spots, making the activities of this Order of Avademe impossible for you to observe."

Cain stood silent, his body giving off so much heat that Jake felt sweat pouring over his skin.

"But you see me now."

"THE RING ON YOUR FINGER HAS NOT BEEN TUNED TO YOUR PHYSICAL BEING. ANY POWER IT GENERATES MEANS NOTHING TO ME."

But it meant plenty to Taggert.

"WHAT ELSE DO YOU DESIRE FROM ME IN EXCHANGE FOR YOUR HELP?"

Jake frowned, then rubbed his chin. "How about a clean slate between the two of us? If I find Abel, or discover what happened to him, you forget I set those souls in the Tower free. I want a total pass on that one. There's to be no retribution, even if I wind up in the Dark Realm for some future act of insanity."

Cain extended a grisly hand. "DEAL."

Jake stared at the hand. He had caused Old Nick's death rather than allow the man to shake that hand and seal his deal with Cain. Now it was his turn to shake hands with the devil, which he did.

A rip appeared in the air behind Cain, and the demon vanished through it, allowing hundreds of tormented screams to escape in the process. The rip closed over itself, leaving behind the acrid stench of sulfur.

Jake allowed himself a deep sigh, then pocketed the eye. He had finally gleaned some useful information from one of his supernatural contacts.

CHAPTER
14

Jake stood Taggert's body up in the chair at the edge of a wide hole in the barn's floor, then gave the corpse a sharp kick and watched darkness swallow it. Outside, he saw no signs that Gary and Frank had ever materialized. He got into the SUV, started its engine, and called Carrie from the road. She had nothing new to report and assured him she had deleted the Afterlife excerpt from her computer and had destroyed the CD.

He drove straight to Reichard's estate. Although he saw no signs of police activity on the road as the sun set, he knew he had gotten all the use out of the service road possible. When he stopped at the front gates, the security officers gave him curious looks but opened the gate and allowed him to present them with his driver's license.

"Tell Reichard that Jake Helman wants a word with him."

"I'm sorry, sir," the guard closest to Jake said. "Mr. Reichard sees no one without an appointment."

"He'll see me. Call up to the house."

Frowning, the guard turned to the telephone in the booth. A minute later, he handed Jake's license back with a surprised look. "You're cleared."

"Thanks." Jake felt odd driving up the hill after watching so many other vehicles do it. He followed the winding brick driveway to the mansion's entrance.

The butler he had seen over the last three days answered the door. "May I take your jacket, sir?"

"No, thanks." At least the jacket hid how dirty his shirt had become.

"I need to pat you down."

Jake upturned his right hand so the butler saw his ring. "Really?"

The butler showed no sign of recognizing the ring. "Really."

Just a lackey. Jake raised his arms, allowing the serious-faced man to frisk him. He had left the Beretta under the front seat of the SUV.

"Follow me to the den."

Jake followed the manservant down a corridor and through a room filled with antiques and musical instruments. The ceilings were fifteen feet high. Jake felt as if he were passing through a museum more than a home, and he wondered if Marla was one of the chief exhibits. The butler slid two dark wood doors apart, revealing Reichard in his study. The billionaire sat behind a desk as wide as a small car, with intricate carving in the wood. Leather-bound books filled glass bookcases. Jake entered the sanctuary and the butler closed the doors, leaving the men in private.

Reichard peered at Jake over his reading glasses. "I hope you don't mind that I'm both surprised and disappointed to see you here."

"I'm pleased to disappoint you."

"Taggert's man bungled the job."

"Twice."

The old man removed his glasses. "And you kidnapped Taggert right out from under our noses?" His voice revealed a hint of admiration.

"Desperate situations require desperate actions."

Reichard rose. "Where's Taggert now?"

"Let's just say he won't be attending any more dinner parties or weekend soirees here."

Reichard shook his head with a resigned smile. "Where's the body?"

"What's it worth to you?"

Reichard shrugged. "I'd gladly pay one million dollars to verify his death."

Raising his hand, Jake showed Reichard the ring on his finger. "Just a million?"

Reichard's eyes expanded, the ring reflected in his pupils. "Only a ghoul would rob a dead man of his jewelry." He gestured to an upholstered sofa. "Have a seat."

Jake sat down and Reichard settled beside him.

"You've got balls marching in here like this after what you pulled today," the billionaire said. "What's your angle?"

Jake nodded at the ring on Reichard's finger. "I want to join the Order of Avademe."

Reichard constructed an innocent expression. "I don't know what you're talking about."

"Taggert said otherwise."

Reichard raised his white eyebrows. "I never believed that Taggert, of all of us, could be made to talk."

"I can be very persuasive when I need to be."

"Yes, I gather."

"Which seems to have paid off. I understand I'm now a very wealthy man."

"Wealthier than you can possibly imagine. *If* we accept you into our organization, that is."

Jake sprang to his feet so fast Reichard pulled himself into a defensive posture. "Uh-uh. Don't even try it. I have the ring. This makes me part of your group whether you want my company or not, and there's nothing you can do about it. I know this protects me. You can't kill me, you can't order someone else to kill me, and you can't sic the authorities on me. I've just become a very important man in your life."

Reichard offered a tight-lipped smile. "I wonder what Taggert *didn't* tell you."

Sitting again, Jake crossed his legs and folded his hands over his lap. "Taggert isn't my only source of information."

"You have my full attention."

"I assume that when the eight of you decided to have me killed you did a background check on me."

"Yes. It wasn't very impressive, as I recall."

"Maybe you missed this small detail: for one week, I was Nicholas Tower's director of security at the Tower."

Despite Reichard's efforts at maintaining a poker face, Jake saw a glimmer of reaction at the mention of Tower's name.

"We didn't miss that. Your tenure just seemed inconsequential, except that Nicholas died on your watch."

Nicholas. "He kept extensive notes on all of his activities.

They're mine now, just like this ring." He saw no reason to mention Afterlife.

Reichard's eyes narrowed. "You're bluffing."

"I have a list of your names, businesses, and affiliations before Tower's death—a complete dossier on your activities and misdeeds. Old Nick practically wrote a whole book on you guys. You probably don't know it, but he had a lot of free time on his hands, holed up in that fortress."

"What else do these notes say?"

"I haven't finished them yet, but they back up what Taggert told me and then some."

Reichard seemed to weigh Jake's words. "If you really wish to join our order, you have to follow certain protocol. You can't just take a ring off a dead man's finger and become one of the world's grand masters."

"I think I can."

"We may not be able to eliminate you, but we do require certain assurances before we can admit you into our circle. Like it or not, you have to earn our trust."

"Trust takes time. I have the ring. I want to be included now."

"It isn't that simple. We're talking about a great deal of power and responsibility."

Jake stood again. "I'm talking about a great deal of *money*, and I want my cut of it right now."

"How mercenary of you. If money is all you're interested in, we'll pay you seven million dollars for that ring."

"One million from each surviving member? That's a nice sum but not nearly as much as I'll make as a full partner. And Taggert made it clear that without this ring, he was not only expendable but undesirable. He was more afraid of you partners than he was of me. So I think I'll keep the gold *and* the green."

Reichard got to his feet. "You're playing a very dangerous game."

"This kind of payday is worth the risk."

"There are two very large elephants in this room." Jake glanced around the study.

"You witnessed Myron sacrifice that young lady two nights ago, and you tangled with our watchers. You killed four of them."

Watchers, Jake thought. He gave Reichard his most threatening stare. "Madigan killed that girl as an entry fee into your club. I'm sure you videotaped it, just like I did, as an insurance policy in case he changed his mind about staying in the group. As for those watchers, as you call them—I don't know what the hell they are, but they sure aren't human. But then, you should see the things Tower created."

"'Tower makes monsters,'" Reichard said.

"Exactly."

"You leaked those files to the media."

"Indirectly."

"You think you know what you're getting into, but you don't have a clue."

"I'm a big fan of on-the-job training."

Reichard showed Jake his own ring. "You don't say a word about this to anyone. If you do, that's the one exception in which we do have the right to kill you. In fact, it becomes our obligation. Breathe one word about this to a single soul, and we'll make you wish you were in hell."

Sensing this was no time for flippancy, Jake said nothing.

"Come back here tomorrow night for dinner. I believe you know what time we eat. I'll summon the others for an emergency meeting. We'll decide then what to do about you."

Jake offered a subtle bow. "I look forward to it."

Then he exited the lion's den.

Free to use his credit card again, Jake returned the SUV to a branch of the car rental agency located in Lower Manhattan, then took a taxi to Twenty-third Street, where he knocked on the door to Laurel's parlor. Night had fallen and the city lights glowed.

When Laurel opened the door, a look of relief spread across her features. Jake stepped inside, provoking a caw from Edgar, who lighted on the round table. He hadn't realized Laurel allowed Edgar out of his cage, but he supposed this was a good thing since the cage was so small. Laurel made a move to embrace Jake, but he raised one hand, gesturing for her to stop.

"I don't think you want to touch me," he said.

Her face turned grim. "I know Abby's dead."

"Knowing it isn't the same thing as experiencing it."

Her eyes watered. "Was it terrible?"

"Murder usually is. But it was fast, almost instantaneous. She died saving me."

"I sent you to her. That makes me responsible for her death." She extended one hand straight out. "Let me see."

Jake closed his fingers around hers. Laurel immediately recoiled. Jake began to release his grip on her, but she seized his wrist with her other hand. With their faces inches apart, Jake felt her breath on his face and inhaled her perfume. If not for the crazed look in her eyes, he might have been turned on.

Laurel searched his face. "Sheryl . . . Cain . . . What are you doing?"

Jake turned red, as if she had caught him with his drawers down.

She lifted his hand and stared at the ring on his finger. She brushed the gold tentacle with her thumb. "What are you *doing*?"

"Whatever it takes to bring them to their knees."

Releasing him, Laurel raised both hands to her temples, then brushed her long hair out of her eyes. She appeared ready to faint, as Abby had done. "I don't think you *can* stop them."

Jake helped her over to the table, where she half collapsed into her padded chair.

"They're just men."

She gazed at him with concern in her eyes. "Not seven men: an army. And you're *one* man."

"That's why I'm going to attack them from the inside, instead of going at them from the outside. I can't just wipe them out like I did Katrina's zonbies. I have to find their heart and destroy it."

"This isn't an undercover police assignment. You've uncovered something bigger than you realize. And Cain seems to think this Avademe is a living entity."

Jake sat opposite her. "I don't believe in sea monsters."

Laurel closed her hands into fists. "I'm only picking up secondhand vibrations through you, but that's enough. Don't underestimate these people. Combined, they have greater resources than Tower did."

He studied her eyes, searching for a glimmer of untruth. "What do you know about Avademe?"

"I swear to you, I've never heard it before."

He considered her words. *Maybe.* "I know you're in hiding. Is it from Reichard and his group?"

She stared at him for a moment without answering, and he noticed her bosom rising and falling. "No," she said.

Jake glanced at Edgar. "Sheryl and Cain both described areas on earth hidden from heaven and hell. Sheryl called them blind spots. Cain called them invisible fields. When Abel appeared to me seventeen months ago, he was able to read my thoughts. Sheryl knew that Edgar had been transmogrified into a raven, but she didn't know that I had moved him here, and she seemed unaware that you even exist. Abby went on and on about how New York is a focal point for psychics and spiritualists because it has a long history of supernatural activity. I think that activity is directly linked to these blind spots, and Sheryl and Cain don't know you exist because this parlor"—he looked around the room—"is a blind spot to them. You've created some sort of seal around yourself that renders this space invisible to these higher beings. You're afraid of something, and you've made yourself a prisoner here to hide from it. What I don't understand is why neither of them saw you in my mind."

Laurel tapped her fingernails on the table, through its cloth, and Edgar returned to her. "I can't answer the questions you're asking me. Not without endangering both of us."

Jake jumped to his feet, knocking the chair back. His sudden movement caused Laurel to flinch and Edgar raised his wings in protest.

"Oh, not you, too! I'm sick of everyone around me keeping important information from me. If you won't tell me, I'll tell *you*. You used your powers to heal me when Katrina put that hex on me, and you healed me again after Reichard's fish men burned my skin. But you didn't just heal me, did you? You worked more than one kind of magic on me. Whatever you do to make this place invisible to certain forces, you also did to my thoughts and memories of you, so none of these higher powers can see you."

Laurel rose, her movements even. "If I did do anything to you, it was to protect both of us."

Jake ran one hand up his face, pushing his hair back. "Jesus Christ. I've already got some of Sheryl's soul inside me, and now I've also got some of whatever it is you have and do. This isn't even my body. It's just a vessel for you two—"

"You're overreacting. You've seen and touched things no other man has. Did you ever stop to think that Sheryl's energy is the only thing keeping you sane after everything that's happened to you? Other men would have crumbled from the knowledge you possess. I've felt her in your body. Pure energy. She didn't just save you; she's *still* saving you. And in my own way—miniscule compared to hers—I'm trying to protect you, too. Even from her."

Laurel's comment made Jake recall Cain's warning not to trust Sheryl. He sagged into his chair, and Laurel circled the table and stood before him. He spoke in a forceful tone. "Does your situation have anything to do with Marla Madigan, Myron Madigan, or Karlin Reichard?"

Laurel shook her head.

"What about this Destroyer of Souls?"

"No."

"Abel?"

"I've never met, seen, or had anything to do with any angel or demon. My situation has no bearing on you or your cases. I'm just trying to help you."

Jake grabbed her biceps for emphasis. "There's nothing you can tell me about these bastards?"

"Nothing. I sent you to Abby, and she sent you to this Daniel Whitefish. I don't know anything about him, or I'd have sent you straight to him instead of her, and maybe she'd still be alive."

"But maybe Daniel would be dead instead. Or me."

"Perhaps."

He felt the heat in her arms, an odd sensation. She had once told him that she was trying to atone for past actions, just as he was. Maybe they were two of a kind. He let go of her to shield his thoughts and emotions. "I need you to keep watching Edgar until this is all over."

"Of course."

He turned and left her without saying good-bye.

CHAPTER
15

Jake took the stairs to his suite. Flicking on the lights, he hung his jacket on one of the chairs in the reception area. Carrie had left no notes on his desk.

It's still the weekend, he reminded himself.

He took a Diet Coke from the fridge and entered his office. Opening the blinds, he glanced at the Tower. Was Old Nick finally coming home to roost? He had felt the megalomaniac's presence ever since first visiting Reichard's estate.

He sat cross-legged on the floor behind the safe and turned the combination dials. The safe unlocked and he swung the door open. The Afterlife laptop rested on its shelf. He took it to his desk, plugged it in, and waited for it to boot up.

Jake drummed his fingers on the desk. He couldn't be certain that Carrie had only copied the one file and that she had destroyed all traces of the copy she had made, but he had to trust her. A greater uncertainty at the moment was whether or not to trust Laurel, who possessed his memories and thoughts. And Cain had warned him not to trust Sheryl.

Tower International—Building Better Life . . .

After keying *Avademe* into Afterlife's search engine, Jake saw the same page Carrie had sent him, with no additional information, so he shut the system down. He stood, reached into his pants pocket, and took out the glass eye that Cain had given him. He held it close to his real eye and rolled it between his thumb and forefinger.

Screw this.

He set the eye on the desk, took a tool bag from his bottom desk drawer, and returned to the safe. After returning the laptop to its rightful place, he opened the tool bag and used the screw gun to remove the steel plate from the inside of the safe door. With the plate gone, he faced the mechanisms for each combination lock. Next, he removed a slender gray plastic case from the back and unsnapped it, revealing his precision locksmith tools. It took him half an hour to reset the combinations and reattach the plate.

Abracadabra. The world is safe again.

"You shouldn't have made that deal with Cain," Sheryl said behind him.

Jake jumped off the floor. When he settled again and his heart had stopped pounding, he clenched his teeth. "Why don't you appear outside the front door and use the doorbell so you don't scare the hell out of me?"

She crossed the office to him. "I'm sorry. Since ascending, I've forgotten what it's like to be flesh and blood."

He looked her up and down. She had changed into a little black dress. He approved.

Bending sideways, she peered at the glass eye on the desk. "Cain is the enemy, the emissary of evil. He tortured you and tried to steal your soul."

Jake found himself admiring the shape of her ass. God, he missed her body. "I could never forget either of those things. Or that you saved me from him."

Sheryl faced him again, her eyes reflecting the overhead light. "You can never trust an emissary from the Dark Realm. *Never.* Do you understand?"

"That's pretty obvious. The real question is, can I trust the Realm of Light?"

Her expression turned serious, a trace of anger simmering beneath her features. "Do you trust me?"

"I don't know." It hurt him to speak the words.

"Don't allow Cain to sow seeds of doubt. The Dark Realm has always tried to divide and conquer."

"As far as I can tell, you and Cain want the same thing: to find Abel. Maybe you should team up and leave me out of this."

The light in her eyes changed. "That's impossible. We can never work together. Don't take anything that monster says at face value. He doesn't care about Abel. You don't know his true motives."

"I'm beginning to realize yours."

She said nothing.

"Do you believe in true love?" Sheryl had spoken those words to him in the past, both as a living person and as a Soul Searcher.

She held his gaze. "Yes. Now more than ever."

"Tell me again why the Realm of Light sent you to enlist me."

"No one sent me. We think as one, for the good of the Sphere.

We *are* the Sphere: a single body of energy."

"All merged together. Your thoughts, as you say. What about your feelings? What about your love?"

She remained still.

"It all sounds very trippy in heaven, very hippie."

"It's beautiful there. If you could just experience it, you'd understand."

"It sounds like a cult to me."

"You're wrong."

"Let's get back to your motives. I thought the higher-ups sent you here to take advantage of my feelings for you, but that isn't the case, is it?"

"No."

"You came here all on your own. You're the one using me."

"I'm only asking you to help me, and don't forget the outcome of this will impact every living creature on earth and every sentient being in the higher dimensions."

"You neglected to tell me that with all that *sharing* going on up in the clouds, you managed to fall in love with Abel."

Sheryl turned transparent for a moment, allowing him to see the wall behind her, as though her concentration had broken. "You don't understand. You can't."

"Because I'm such a primitive life-form?"

"And because you're blinded by your feelings for me. You're clinging to a ghost. The Sheryl you knew and loved stopped existing when the Cipher killed her. I've evolved to a higher plane. I know and feel things you can't possibly comprehend while your energy inhabits your body. When you ascend, you'll know what I'm talking about."

"*If* I ascend. I'm jumping through hoops here, and there's a pretty good chance I'll screw up and damn my soul trying to navigate this maze. But you don't even care about that as long as I find Abel, do you?"

She caressed his cheek, her touch making his heart ache. "That isn't true. I love you and I always will. That's why I kept track of what you were doing when you went up against Katrina. But Abel and I share energy now. We exist on the same plane. I need to know where he is, not just because of my bond to him, but because the agents of Light need to know what he learned about the Destroyer of Souls. There are much more important things at play than you and me or me and him."

"The problems of two people don't amount to a hill of beans, right?" Closing his fingers around her wrist, he removed her hand from his cheek. "Here's the thing: you want me to help you, want me to lay my life on the line for you and Abel and the Realm of Light, but you won't help me to help you. You won't identify the blind spots where this Destroyer might be hiding."

Her eyes grew shiny. "I can't tell you anything. But you've already located some of them on your own."

"Maybe I only want to help those who want to help themselves."

A single tear trickled out the corner of one eye. "I *can't* help you . . ."

He touched the tear with the tip of his finger and examined it. "This tear is just energy, right?"

Now Sheryl sobbed. "Jake, please . . ."

"Cain cried, too. I have no reason to trust either one of you—do you hear me? I won't be anyone's sucker again ever. Not even yours."

"I *need* you."

Jake stepped back from her. "For a year and a half, I've fooled myself into believing we could be reunited someday. I lived my life according to that slim hope. That's how much I love you."

"When I came here the other day I explained you need to move on. I haven't misled you."

"Yeah, you warned me. I was just too thickheaded to hear what you were saying. I should have kicked you out then. Can I do that? Kick you out?"

She shook her head. "Please don't . . ."

"Since you won't tell me anything useful, I want you to leave. It's breaking my heart all over again just to look at you, knowing what I know. Don't worry. If I come across your boyfriend, I'll be sure to part my lips and whistle. But don't you ever show up like this again unless I call you."

Sheryl looked at him, and he realized that she had stopped blinking and breathing. She had become little more than a life-sized photograph, which only reinforced that she was no longer human. And then she disappeared.

"Goddamn it!" Jake kicked his desk so hard that he put his foot through a wooden panel. Jerking it free only caused more damage. At least he knew his tears were real.

With his emotion spent, Jake opened the door to his bedroom. The cramped space had never more resembled a jail cell. Stripping his clothes away, he had no desire to climb onto the narrow bed and sleep alone again, but that was exactly what he did.

The next morning, Jake showered and shaved and ate breakfast alone at a diner he favored. Marla's disappearance remained on the front page of the *New York Daily News.* The FBI had been called onto the case, and several of Myron's organized crime targets had fallen under suspicion of kidnapping Marla in retaliation for his actions against them as the city's district attorney. Jake wondered when the FBI would call him in for questioning, just to rule him out as a suspect. He'd never had the pleasure before, and staring at someone besides Geoghegan would come as a welcome relief.

After breakfast, he walked to the garage and got into his Maxima. It felt good to sit in his car. He drove downtown and crossed the Brooklyn Bridge. Driving over the bridge and along Flatbush Avenue, he could not help but remember the nights he had spent fleeing and attacking Katrina's zonbie hit men and pushers. Just thinking about them made gooseflesh rise on his arms. Soon he passed the decaying ruins of the Brooklyn Navy Yard, which the city had purchased after the navy decommissioned it. Businesses occupied some of the small buildings, a few were in the midst of restoration, and others appeared to be completely abandoned. Rusted cranes jutted up from patches of trees like ancient Mayan temples.

Jake turned into a long driveway that led him into a wide parking lot filled maybe 10 percent to capacity. He got out and hiked across the grassy property, passing buildings that lacked windows and even basic upkeep. Nearing the boundary, he gazed at the property next door, which stood in marked contrast.

Reichard Shipyard, the large sign on the other side of the

fence read. Jake scanned the enormous buildings, docks, and ships. Karlin Reichard owned the largest shipping fleet in the world, with shipyards or piers in every corner of the globe. His grandfather had developed the Brooklyn location and built it into a thriving national business, which Karlin's father took international. The size of the enterprise—and the fact that he saw just one component of it—made Jake appreciate the ambition required to make such a venture successful, let alone dominate its market. Raising his binoculars, he studied the structures: sleek, modern, fortified. He saw glass brick windows, steel doors, and security patrols, some on foot and others in vehicles. The foot patrolmen wore side arms. In the Age of Terror, he knew, precautions were necessary. How fortunate, for the sake of appearances. Who could question the need for so many armed men?

Blind spots, Jake thought, studying the hangars, docks, and pier. Each member of Avademe had a base of operations. For Campbell Bradley, it was the Dream Castle; for Taggert, it could have been any one of White River Security's compounds around the world or several of them. For Karlin Reichard, it was right here and probably on his estate as well. Cain had said the invisible fields were multiplying. What better form of multiplication than corporate expansion?

Avademe.

Abby had said that Marla was imprisoned underground, possibly someplace industrial. Jake took out his camera and lined up the first photo.

Jake waited until he knew Martin would be home from school to make the drive to Jackson Heights. When the old woman—iron-gray hair, wrinkled brown skin, bright eyes despite her age—answered the door, he wondered if she remembered him.

"Hi, Miss Wood."

"It's Rosemary, Jake. Come on in." She spoke in a slow, tired voice.

Jake had met Joyce's mother at barbecues and parties when Edgar and Joyce were still together. Happier times.

"Joyce is at work," Rosemary said as Jake entered the house, a box in one hand. "You want to see Martin?"

"Yes, I do."

"Well, go on upstairs." She made her way to the couch. A magazine lay open on the coffee table, and a talk show played on the TV.

Jake went up the narrow staircase and knocked on the only closed door.

"What?" Martin said in an irritated voice.

"It's Jake."

After a moment of silence, Martin opened the door wide enough to accommodate his head. "Yeah?" The boy sounded defiant.

"Can I come in?"

"Suit yourself." Martin opened the door, crossed the room, and hopped onto his bed. He picked up an open paperback and settled against the bed's headboard.

Jake entered the room. Posters for science fiction movies covered the walls. Comic books hid the desk. Dirty laundry lay piled in one corner. He grabbed the desk chair, positioned it before the bed, and sat down.

Martin stared at the pages of his book, though Jake knew he was too distracted to read.

"What are you reading?"

Martin looked at him with disdain in his eyes, then raised the book high enough for Jake to see the cover: *Babel-17* by Samuel R. Delany. Neither the title nor the author meant anything to him.

"Is it good?"

Martin shrugged. "Hard to tell. I just started it. It was my father's. I have to clear anything I read with my mom."

Jake had never known Edgar to be a science fiction reader. His ex-partner liked to quote such poets as Robert Frost and Emily Dickinson. *I guess there's a lot about him I don't know.* "Your mother's just looking out for you."

Martin lowered the book to his lap. "Like you are?"

"That's right. You may not realize it, but that's the truth."

"I should be able to read anything I want, and I should be able to e-mail anyone I want, and I should be able to—"

"—do anything you want? Get real, kid. There's plenty of time to screw up your life when you turn eighteen. Until then, your mother's responsible for you. So is your father. You have to live by their example, not someone else's."

"Benjamin Bradley says not to be afraid of ideas. He says we need to open our minds up. He warns us that other people are afraid of what we believe, that they just want to control us and stop us from spreading the truth."

Tread carefully, Jake thought. "I want to ask you something. Do you *really* believe in the Imago? That some space alien that colonized earth is going to return, and when he does the people

192

who believe in him are going to shed their human forms like the laundry on your floor and become like him?"

"It sounds stupid when you say it, but that's why you say it the way you do, to change my mind. Dreaming isn't any crazier than any other religion. It's all about faith."

"Benjamin Bradley is a fraud. His father was supposedly a good writer. I don't know. But Benjamin tried his hand at writing, and he was a complete hack. He made a fortune off his father's work, and when he couldn't make any more money off it, he found a new way to make money: religion. Why do you think no one ever heard of the Imago before? Because Benjamin only made it up two years ago. Think about it: the Bible is thousands of years old. So are the Kabbalah and the Koran. Scholars and religious leaders have devoted their lives to studying them. The Book of Imago isn't ancient. *You're* older than it is. Because Benjamin made it all up. The only thing separating Sky Cloud Dreams from every other dime-a-dozen cult out there is that he had a fully realized plan to suck people into his scheme, and millions of dollars to put that scheme into effect, and men and women on his payroll to help him meet his goal. I know they got to you through HyperSpaceBook. They *own* HyperSpaceBook. It's one big con game, and Benjamin is the grifter in chief."

The emotions ranging across Martin's features fell somewhere between anger and grief. "You're just saying that. He's a great man!"

"No, he's not. He's not even decent. He's taking advantage of you and the other Dreamers. You've all kept him rich, and that's all he cares about. You want to believe he cares about you, that he understands you in a way no one else does, but I promise he doesn't give a damn about who you really are. I'm sorry, but if your father was here, do you think you'd have given these people the time of day?"

Martin's lower lip quivered. "But he's not here . . ."

"Just for a minute, pretend he is. What do you think he'd say about all this?"

When the first tear broke free, Martin dabbed it with the back of his hand.

"He'd set you straight; I know that. He'd make you look into your heart"—he tapped Martin's forehead—"and into your brain, so that you'd see what you already know to be true. I wish I could do that, but I don't know how. I'm not lucky enough to be a father. But if I was, I'd want a son like you, and I'd do everything in my power to protect him from creeps like Benjamin."

When Martin looked up again, he made no effort to hide his tears. "Do you really wish you had a son like me?"

Jake gave Martin's shoulder a reassuring squeeze. "You'd better believe it."

Martin sobbed and Jake took the boy into his arms. Jake wanted to cry, too. God, he missed Edgar. And he really did love Martin.

When Martin pulled back and wiped the tears from his eyes, Jake looked away to ease his embarrassment. Then he raised the box for the boy to see. "Speaking of your father, I brought you something."

Martin sniffled. "What is it?"

"Open it and see."

Martin set the book down again, swung his legs over the bed, and took the box. "My birthday was a month ago."

"I know. I'm sorry I missed it."

Martin shrugged, then opened the box. Separating the crumpled sheets of newspaper Jake had used to pack the gift, the boy removed the stone statue and inspected it. Jake gave him credit for masking his disappointment.

"What is it?" Martin said.

"The Maltese Falcon. A reproduction of it, anyway."

"What *is* it?"

"*The Maltese Falcon* is a book and a movie. More than one movie, I think, but the one with Humphrey Bogart is a classic. I took my wife to see a revival of it on our first date."

"Black and white, right?"

Jake smiled. "Yeah, but trust me, it's a good one. It's about a private eye named Sam Spade who tangles with a bunch of nefarious creeps who all want to get their hands on the Maltese Falcon. Your father gave that to me when I opened my office." He saw no point in adding that he had used the statue to kill the Black Magic junkie who stabbed him in the eye. *I guess I wouldn't make a very good father.*

"Don't you want it?"

Jake liked the way Martin thought. "I *do* want it. I like the way it sort of looks over me and reminds me to stay out of trouble. But I think you might like that, too. Let's do this: you hang on to it for me until I find your dad. Once everything gets back to normal, you can return it to me. Deal?"

Martin cracked a smile. "Deal."

Jake stood. "I have to get going. I'm working on a case."

"Like Sam Spade?"

"Yeah."

"With nefarious characters?"

"Nefarious like you wouldn't believe. But I'm going to come out here and see you just as soon as I settle up with them, okay? Maybe we'll catch a movie."

"I'm grounded, remember?"

"I think your mother will make an exception in this case." Jake hoped he remained alive long enough to keep his promise.

CHAPTER
16

Jake had grown accustomed to the drive to Reichard's estate. He didn't own a tuxedo, but he wore a black suit for the occasion. It wasn't every day he was sworn into a cabal of rich powerbrokers who named their group after an ancient Indian lake monster. The estate's security gates swung open, and Jake presented his ID to the guards, then steered his car up the driveway. The sun had set, and the Maxima triggered motion detectors and floodlights. He scanned the dark woods along the property for any sign of the robed watchers, but the trees hid any movement beyond them.

Instead of parking the Maxima outside the mansion's entrance, he followed the driveway to a small parking area that overlooked the tennis court and the swimming pool. Cool air greeted him as he got out and headed to the mansion. When he looked around, he felt a prickling sensation on the back of his neck, and he did not know if his body shivered from the chilly temperature or his fear that the fishlike creatures could tear him to pieces before he even reached the front doors. He walked faster, only slightly reassured by the knowledge that his Glock was in his car if he needed it.

The same butler who had admitted him on the previous visit opened the doors and gave him a slight bow. "Good evening, Mr. Helman."

Jake stepped inside and raised his arms. "Good evening to you."

The butler frisked Jake and led him down a different corridor that ended before two sliding doors. He knocked on the doors, which he then opened one at a time. Seven men, all dressed in tuxedoes, occupied the room. Some sat in leather chairs, while others stood near the oversized fireplace, drawing heat from the flames. Cigar smoke wafted through the air, and glasses containing alcohol reflected the orange firelight.

"Mr. Helman," the butler announced.

Jake strode inside, aware that everyone in the drawing room was sizing him up. He recognized each man from the research he had compiled on them, and he immediately locked on Myron Madigan.

The doors slid shut behind him, and Reichard rose from his chair and crossed the room. "Come in, Jake. I'm glad to see you're punctual. What can I get you?"

"I don't drink."

"Then you'll never fit in around here," said the man Jake recognized as Richard Browning.

The others laughed, including Reichard, who put one arm around Jake and guided him deeper into the room, where the other men circled them.

"Allow me to introduce you to Norman Weiskopf," Reichard said.

Weiskopf had a growth on one side of his round face and a lazy eye on the other. He held out his liver-spotted hand, and when Jake shook it, he said, "You don't look like much to me." Then he winked with his good eye. "But appearances can be deceiving. Look at me!"

"Thanks for giving me the benefit of the doubt," Jake said.

"And this is Bruce Schlatter," Reichard said.

The insurance king clapped Jake's shoulder. "It's nice to see a young face around here for a change. Myron's younger than the rest of us, but he's so damned ugly it doesn't matter."

The men laughed again. Jake had not expected such jocularity.

Reichard gestured to a tall man with gaunt features. "Silas Coffer."

"Pleasure," the man said with a half smile.

Reichard brought forward a man Jake had no trouble recognizing. "Benjamin Bradley."

"Pleased to meet you," Bradley said.

Jake did his damnedest to hide his contempt for Bradley. *The prick who hoped to brainwash Martin.* He shook Bradley's hand. "Same here."

"And finally," Reichard said, "allow me to introduce our newest member, who I know you're familiar with: Myron Madigan."

Jake stood toe to toe with the mayor, which meant he had to look down his nose at the pudgy little man to make eye contact with him. Madigan held a glass of liquor and a Cuban cigar in his left hand and gave off an air of corrupt entitlement that repelled Jake.

"Helman," Madigan said.

"Mr. Mayor."

"Just Myron in here. You've caused quite a stir." He smiled and offered his free hand. "I hope we can still be friends."

I've *caused a stir?* Jake wanted to strangle the man on the spot. Instead, he shook his hand. "Anything's possible."

Reichard motioned to a chair. "Have a seat. Let's talk before dinner."

Jake sat in the chair and crossed his legs. The other men took their seats, completing the circle. Their studious looks made him feel like an animal in a zoo.

"I've already told everyone that you rejected my initial offer in exchange for the return of our ring," Reichard said.

"*My* ring," Jake said. "I took it fair and square."

"That's highly debatable. In any case, we're prepared to double that amount, plus offer you 1 percent of the net profits from our respective companies for the remainder of your life."

Jake considered the numbers. *Fourteen million dollars.* In theory, he could live like a king for the rest of his life. "Is that your final offer?"

"I'm afraid so. We think it's excessively more than reasonable."

"*I'm* afraid I'll have to pass."

Reichard's cheerful expression drew tight.

"You see, as I've already explained, I know that once I take this ring off my finger, there will be no rest of my life. You'd have me killed immediately. Some people look down on the life I live. I'm sure all of you do, if you give it any thought at all. But it's the only life I have, and I'm determined to make the most of it. Besides, fourteen million bucks and a share in seven of the most lucrative companies in the world may be a lot, but you forget I have Nicholas Tower's notes. You gentlemen are worth a lot more than that. Over one hundred companies support the Reichard Foundation. I'm sure you have much deeper pockets than you're letting on."

Rising, Reichard fixed Jake with a hard stare, then grinned at his fellows. "You see what I mean? He's impossible to deal with! Jake, you're not only hard to kill; you're also ambitious as hell. I like that. Come on. Let's eat!" Turning his back on Jake, Reichard headed for the doors, which he slid apart.

Madigan extinguished his cigar in an upright ashtray and joined the old men following Reichard.

Jake brought up the rear. The evening was proceeding in a much different manner than expected.

The eight men filed into the dining room, which was larger than Jake had surmised from his vantage point outside the mansion. The table accommodated twenty people, and the place settings had been arranged four on each side of the table. Jake sat beside Madigan, who sat beside Bradley, who sat beside Browning. He supposed the arrangement was a pecking order, with the most recent members on one side of the table and the senior partners on the other.

Two servers dished out the food, a selection of roasted meats, sautéed vegetables and potatoes, with side dishes of caviar and calamari.

When the servers poured drinks, Jake covered his glass. "Water is fine," he said.

"I find your reluctance to imbibe unsettling," Weiskopf said. "Karlin has the best booze in the country." He raised his glass. "This is hundred-year-old scotch. If you're going to join our board, you need to learn to appreciate the finer things in life. Otherwise, what's the point?"

Jake smiled. "We each have our own standards of quality."

When the servers left and closed the doors, Reichard said,

"You have us at a great disadvantage. We're unaccustomed to men forcing their way into our midst. We generally spend a good deal of time and effort recruiting our members. You've proven to be much more resourceful—and troublesome—than your records suggest."

Jake savored his food. "It's a knack I have."

"Understand, you've created a dilemma for us. Our arrangement has existed for more than a century. During that time, every member who's been inducted—except one—has obeyed our constitution to the letter. It's something we take very seriously. As you rightly pointed out, we can't eliminate you, nor can we knowingly allow someone else to do so. That ring guarantees your inclusion in our activities as well as your protection."

Jake gestured with an open hand. "So what's the problem?"

Weiskopf leaned forward. "The problem is that every man sitting here is worth billions of dollars. If we accept you, our law requires us to give you a cut of our holdings. What do you bring to the table? We own entire private investigation firms. Munitions. Security contractors. You have nothing to offer us."

Jake nodded at Madigan. "I don't believe the mayor here has nearly the kind of dough you're talking about."

"He has other value," Schlatter said. "We shepherded his career into Gracie Mansion, and our expectation is that he'll eventually sit in the Oval Office. We've played a role in every conflict this country has engaged in since World War I and reaped the benefits. Do you have any idea what an advantage it will be to receive no-bid contracts for White River Security and our other interests? We've never had one of our own elected to the top office. The closest we've ever come has been vice president."

"Not that we've ever needed a president," Reichard said. "We own all the politicians we need, thanks to my foundation. We have no real regard for politics beyond our bottom line. It doesn't matter which party is in power, provided we can influence it to serve our purposes. And that's been the case for almost four generations. We don't care what laws are passed, as long as they contain enough loopholes for us to operate as we see fit."

"*We* run this country," Weiskopf said. "We have for one hundred years. Every critical social and financial decision has been made or approved by us to enhance our profit margin."

"We *are* the United States," Reichard said with obvious pride.

Jake looked around the table. "Forgive me for saying so, but I don't see any women or minorities here."

Reichard smiled and Weiskopf chuckled.

"And you never will," Schlatter said.

Jake chewed on their words along with his food. "What does that make the rest of us?"

"A worker force and a consumer base," Weiskopf said.

"Which brings us back to our problem," Reichard said. "I'm sorry, but you just don't measure up. If we spent two decades cultivating you, you still wouldn't deserve to keep our company. And yet, you seem to have given us no choice in the matter."

"Bully for me," Jake said. "Who was the guy who broke the rules?"

"Your former employer."

Jake swallowed his food. "Old Nick?"

Reichard's good cheer evaporated. "Nicholas was one of our peers. Unlike you, he brought a great deal to the table. But he became obsessed with certain notions that led him astray."

"He wanted to live forever."

Reichard nodded. "He devoted far too much time and capital in his quest for eternal life, which is antithetical to our philosophy."

"Which is?"

"To live for today, not for tomorrow, and to amass as much treasure and power as possible. We don't concern ourselves with the afterlife."

"How pragmatic of you."

"Religion and morals are for lesser men," Coffer said.

"Nick and his obsessions," Browning said with obvious disappointment. "Genetic engineering and the Reaper."

Jake tried to hide his surprise. "You know about the Reaper?"

"We know all about the Dark Realm and the Realm of Light. Where do you think Nick learned about them? The difference is, we don't give a damn." Weiskopf clucked his tongue. "You know about Cain from Nick's notes?"

"Yes," Jake said with a straight face.

"We should have killed Nick," Schlatter said. "Screw the rules. We should have bombed the Tower from below or had a plane flown into that penthouse. Then we wouldn't have to worry about his *memoirs* opening Pandora's box." He focused on Jake. "We can get to anyone, you know."

Reichard sipped his wine. "But then we'd never have recovered his ring. Nicholas left the reservation, so to speak. He sealed himself in the Tower and had enough power that he knew we could never reach him to take back our ring. We pressed him to reconsider his position, but he broke off all communication with us. The last thing we heard from him was his vow to return his ring if he died. For ten years, we had only seven active grand masters. In one sense, that was good because it prevented deadlock when we had disagreements. Upon his death, true to his word, we took delivery of his ring, which Benjamin now wears."

Bradley's grin made Jake ill.

"We got our ring," Coffer said, "but Nick's death cost us a fortune. The son of a bitch didn't just cut us off; he cut us out of his genetics enterprises. And when the feds broke up his company, it was the last straw for the economy, the one time since the Depression when we lost control."

Reichard's voice iced over. "And we blame you for that, Jake. 'Tower makes monsters.' You admitted you were responsible for leaking the information that resulted in Tower International's dissolution."

Jake sipped his water. "It seemed like a good idea at the time."

"It's that reckless attitude that concerns us. It took tremendous effort and financial sacrifice for us to get the economy back on track. You cost us billions, far more than the government spent. And now you expect us to welcome you into our organization with open arms and hand you Taggert's share in our operations. I'm sure you appreciate why that prospect doesn't sit well with us."

"I'll grow on you," Jake said.

"You don't deserve that ring," Weiskopf said.

Jake shrugged. "And yet here I am."

"You haven't earned it, damn it."

"I beg to differ. I survived two attempts on my life."

"You have to make a sacrifice to be a member. We all did."

Jake set down his fork. "Is that what's bothering you?" He reached inside his jacket, took out an object wrapped in a handkerchief, and placed it before Weiskopf. "Here."

The old man looked at the handkerchief with curiosity, then unwrapped it. His good eye widened at the sight of Taggert's severed finger, which had yellowed.

"That doesn't prove anything," Bradley said. "For all we know, Taggert suffered a heart attack during your interrogation of him, and you just cut off his finger after he was dead. The man had three heart surgeries."

Jake did not like how shrewd his companions were, but he felt a little indignant. "I promise you, he was alive when I snipped this off. He cried like a baby. His corpse has several broken bones."

"Show us the body, then."

"I don't think I care to incriminate myself like that."

"We all incriminate ourselves," Weiskopf said. "That's the whole point of committing sacrifice. It's an insurance policy."

"I killed Morton, too," Jake said.

"Where's *his* body?"

Jake smiled.

"We need Taggert's body," Reichard said. "He wasn't some contractor like Morton. He was the head of a multibillion-dollar company with international dealings. He testified before a senate committee. He can't just disappear. An investigation will lead the FBI here."

"Can't you kill any investigation?" *Let's see how powerful you guys really are.*

"We can control the investigation's ultimate outcome, but we don't wish for anyone to know that we even meet here. That's why we get together only once a month under normal circumstances. You've obviously disrupted that schedule. And then there's the underground media. Give us that body so we can avoid suspicion."

Jake felt he had to give them something as a show of faith. "All right, he's in an abandoned barn an hour away." He gave them directions. "Tell whoever you send to look in a hole in the floor. They'll need rope. Is Morton really so insignificant that you're not even concerned about an investigation into his disappearance?"

"Completely."

"I'm glad I killed him. Abby Fay didn't deserve to die like that."

"Regrettable, but you have to share part of the blame."

Jake felt himself growing hot.

"How did you kill him, anyway? He was skilled in such matters."

Jake glanced around at the faces staring at him. "I used my bare hands. I didn't need a dagger."

"That doesn't count," Weiskopf said. "It was self-defense."

"What would you like me to do, cut the throat of a drugged-up hooker while you all watch?"

"No," Reichard said. "We have something else in mind. We want you to kill Raymond Santucci."

Jake blinked. For a moment, he was speechless. "You want me to assassinate the governor of New York?"

"We want Myron to become the next governor of this state," Reichard said. "That will be the perfect stepping stone to the presidency."

Jake glanced at Madigan. "If he's such a talented politician, let him run for the office."

"We will. Just not against Santucci, who's extremely popular. If we kill him, he'll be succeeded by his lieutenant governor, Mark Fryer, who's a walking time bomb. The man has a checkered past and is incapable of running this state. He's doomed to failure and ridicule, and Myron will beat him handily. Taggert had planned for Morton to do the job, and since you killed both of them, this seems like the best alternative."

"Not from where I'm sitting."

"We've already arranged for the governor to have dinner with someone in our employ at a quaint little restaurant in Albany to-morrow evening. You need to arrive before them and shoot Santucci between the eyes. Our witness will describe someone who looks nothing like you. Wear a disguise, if you prefer. Just be sure you don't shoot the witness, too. The restaurant has no security cameras, and the lighting is low. The perfect location for a hit."

Jake smelled a setup even over the exquisite aromas rising from the gourmet food. "This is crazy. What about the governor's security detail?"

"We'll handle them."

"That isn't very reassuring."

"We have to trust you, and you have to trust us."

"You're asking an awful lot."

"Hardly. The minute you pull that trigger, you'll belong to Avademe. The next morning, seventy million dollars will appear in an offshore bank account we'll set up for you. That's ten million from each one of us. Myron will confirm it's that easy."

"Your entire world will change overnight. You'll be richer and more powerful than you ever dreamed possible, and we'll know that you truly belong at this table." Madigan seemed displeased at the thought of sharing his newfound wealth so soon after acquiring it.

Jake knew that if he refused the assignment, his time in the cabal would end before it started. If he accepted the proposal, he would at least buy time. "Seventy million is a lot of money," he said.

Reichard winked at him. "Tax free. You can buy your own mansion with that kind of money. New cars, the best clothes, the finest women. You'll never have to work again in your life. Even better, you'll draw profits from every one of us in this room each quarter. You'll be a full-fledged member of the circle. There's no better feeling in the world than *running* the world."

I bet. "That's a lot to digest over one meal. Can't you have another long arm from White River Security do the hit?"

"We have literally hundreds of men and women stationed around the world who will kill anyone we tell them to without question. But we want you to do this. We *need* you to kill someone *for* us. A sacrifice."

"Couldn't I just sign my name in blood somewhere?"

"You belonged to a brotherhood once. Now you're an independent operator. An outcast. Our assemblage is also a brotherhood. We need to know you're a team player, that you won't turn rogue on us like Nicholas did."

Jake felt dumbfounded that he and Tower shared similar traits. "Before I accept your offer, I need to know a few things."

"You don't set the terms."

"Myron's wife hired me to get dirt on him. I'd say I was successful. I didn't turn the evidence over to her, and I never spoke to her about what I saw. She's no threat to any of you."

"You're right about that," Reichard said in an ominous tone. "What else is on your mind?"

"I'm not satisfied with the answer I just got to my first question."

"Then you're not satisfied. What else?"

"I want to know what the hell those creatures—those watchers—were that attacked me the other night. They look nothing like anything I saw at the Tower."

Reichard sat back. "Kill Santucci and we'll tell you everything. Until then, you've learned all we care to share."

Surveying the faces at the table, Jake felt so close to the truth. "How can I say no to seventy million dollars?"

Reichard beamed. "Excellent! We'll furnish you with details after dinner. Now let's enjoy dessert. I had a German chocolate cake flown in from Germany just for the occasion."

CHAPTER 17

Jake drove back to Manhattan with his hands shaking and his knees knocking against each other. He had known from the minute he had taken Marla's case that he was dealing with men who would stop at nothing to carry out their plans, but he hadn't suspected just how powerful this nest of vipers would prove to be.

The most powerful men in the world, he thought. *Nicholas Tower multiplied by seven.*

Avademe ruled the world. Or at least it ruled the United States and influenced the rest of the world. Seven men whose greed and lust for power had resulted in evil on earth—and possibly elsewhere.

Blind spots.

According to Cain and Sheryl, the Dark Realm and the Realm

of Light were unable to observe Avademe's activities. Or were they? Cain had warned Jake not to trust Sheryl, and sure enough, Sheryl was using Jake to locate Abel because she loved him. Jake knew better than to trust Cain, and Laurel had secrets of her own.

He had no one to trust except Carrie, and she was no use to him. He felt more alone than ever. Not only because Sheryl's heart belonged to Abel, but because Edgar no longer existed as Jake had known him. In Hunts Point in the Bronx, while battling Katrina's zonbies, Jake had entrusted Edgar with his life, and Edgar had come through for him with flying colors.

His hands tightened on the steering wheel. He needed to learn more about the Order of Avademe. The bastards had done their best to convince him they were only interested in accumulating personal wealth, but he knew better. How were they destroying souls, and why?

Headlights from oncoming cars bounced off the windshield. He could not see the drivers, but he knew the men and women operating the vehicles were oblivious to the existence of the Avademe cabal, just as he had been until three days ago. All across the country, people worked low- and seemingly high-paying jobs, while Reichard and his gang grew fat on money acquired by ginning the system.

A system they created, he thought, fitting world events into a timeline that corresponded to the century Avademe had been pulling political strings. World War I. World War II. The Korean War. The moon landing. Vietnam. The Gulf War. Afghanistan. Iraq. All events and conflicts that had increased the personal wealth of each man in the circle.

War profiteers.

And no one else on earth but him had a clue.

✳

Walking to his building from the garage, Jake studied the faces of people moving on the sidewalks, then the buildings above him, and finally the Tower. He loved New York City, but he was beginning to view everything as an illusion: a country and world built on lies. He thought of the great technological advances since World War I and suspected Avademe had pushed them on a world unprepared for them. Pollution, global warming, warfare—these conditions either served the cabal's interests or resulted from them.

The entire world is dying so Karlin Reichard can fly chocolate cake in from Germany.

He clenched his fists.

Old Nick's ambition had resulted in thirteen murdered civilians as far as Jake knew. The number of people killed in wars that Avademe had either started, conflated, or prolonged over one hundred years was incalculable. All to keep the industrial war complex thriving and the cabal's bank accounts swollen.

He stopped outside Laurel's parlor and debated knocking on the door. He needed someone to talk to, and she knew him better than anyone else. That was part of the problem: she knew him too well. He couldn't even touch her without her absorbing his thoughts and secrets. But he intended to visit her before heading to Albany.

Jake entered his building and took the elevator to the fourth floor. Inside his suite, he searched all the rooms to make sure no one lurked about waiting to surprise him. The security system obviously didn't work where supernatural entities were concerned.

Satisfied that neither heaven nor hell intended to pester him, he sat at his desk and did some general research on his newfound prospective partners and their respective companies. It didn't take long before he pictured a giant spiderweb enshrouding the earth, with its many strands intersecting each other. The majority of the men owned several companies and sat on the boards of others, and that was just the public tally.

Sipping a Diet Coke, Jake searched *octopus god* and *octopus monster*. After sorting through dozens of line drawings of giant octopi clinging to tall ships and other vessels and a number of illustrations from Jules Verne's *20,000 Leagues Under the Sea* and stills from its movie adaptations, he found some text on a website devoted to world mythology that raised his interest.

> Na Kika, the octopus god of the Gilbert Islands, was the son of the first beings, Nei Teuke and Na Atibu. Na Kika used his great tentacles to raise the earth from the Pacific Ocean's bottom, creating the chain of sixteen atolls and islands. Na Kika's name means "Sir Octopus."

The names sound Indian, Jake thought. He cross-referenced Gilbert Islands and discovered the native population was Micronesian. *A long way from Lake Erie.*

> Kanaloa is the Hawaiian creator and the god of the underworld, who teaches magic in the form of an octopus. According to the Hawaiian Creation Myth, the cosmos are only the latest in a series of universes, and the octopus Kanaloa was the sole survivor of the previous universe.

Abel had described the Realm of Light and the Dark Realm as other dimensions. Could they have been *previous universes*, or could *previous universes* be the term used by ancient Hawaiians to define the higher dimensions?

> Tae-o-Tagaloa of Samoa is a human-octopus hybrid. Throughout southern Polynesia, magic connected to the numeral eight stems from the tentacles of Tae-o-Tagaloa.

Human-octopus hybrid. The thought of Reichard's creatures caused Jake to shudder. *Hybrid* made him picture Tower's Biogens. Pondering the Polynesian emphasis on the number eight, he studied the ring on his finger, turning it from side to side so the gold tentacle reflected the overhead light. The disparate myths tore his differing theories apart rather than unifying them. Pushing his chair back, he ran his palms down his face and sighed. None of this was going to help him before his deadline to assassinate Santucci.

The telephone on the desk rang, and Jake checked the caller ID. *Unavailable.*

He lifted the wireless phone from its receiver. "Hello?"

"Jake? Benjamin Bradley. Myron and I are sitting in my limo downstairs. Come join us."

Jake's body tensed up. What could Bradley and Madigan want with him so soon after the cabal's big dinner? It didn't matter. He would learn the answer soon enough. "I'll be right down."

He changed into dark slacks, a polo shirt, and running shoes, then put on his shoulder holster and Glock, which he concealed beneath a jacket. It felt reassuring to carry his gun again. He took the stairs so he would see sooner if anyone waited in the lobby. It proved to be empty.

A stretch limo idled at the curb outside, a chauffeur waiting for him. Exiting the building, Jake wondered if the man knew how he had treated the last chauffeur he had encountered. He noted the black SUV waiting behind the limo—Madigan's security detail.

The chauffeur opened the rear door for him. "Good evening."

Nodding at the man, Jake looked for a holster but saw none. As he climbed into the limo, he thought of mafioso going for late-night rides with comrades only to vanish.

"There he is," Bradley said.

Jake's right hand twitched, ready to grab the Glock's grip beneath his jacket.

Bradley and Madigan sat in the long seat perpendicular to him. Each man held a drink. The chauffeur closed the door and circled the limo.

"The bar's fully stocked," Madigan said.

Jake's gaze never left the two men as the chauffeur got into the front seat and closed the door. He felt a personal animosity toward each villain: Bradley for cultivating the Dreamers and Madigan for his criminal treatment of Marla. "I don't drink, remember?"

The limo crept forward, a real smooth ride.

"We'll have to cure you of that foible," Bradley said.

Jake felt his muscles tightening.

"Relax," Madigan said. "This is a social call."

"It's a little late for visitors."

"We're not visitors. We're hosts. That makes you our guest."

"Where are we going?"

"It's a surprise," Bradley said.

"I'm not a fan of surprises. They usually amount to trouble."

"You'll like this one," Madigan said, almost leering. "Trust me."

Not as far as I can spit, Jake thought. "I have a big day tomorrow.

I need my beauty sleep."

"Your assignment will go off without a hitch," Bradley said. "And our little diversion will relieve you of that stress you must be feeling."

Jake sat back in his seat. The limo headed uptown, got on the FDR Drive, and headed uptown faster. The men kept staring at him, which made him squirm.

At last Jake said to Bradley, "That's some business you've got. All tax free because of the religious angle, right?"

Bradley smiled. "We don't discuss business except when all of us are present. That way no one gets paranoid."

Jake turned to Madigan. "I'm surprised you're traveling with such a light entourage."

Madigan shrugged. "I pull what strings need pulling to draw as little attention as possible."

"Pretty ballsy, considering the attention your wife's disappearance is getting."

Madigan was about to respond when Bradley tapped his shoulder and shook his head.

They got off in Yorkville, Jake's old neighborhood. The limo turned up Second Avenue, then Eighty-sixth Street, and glided toward Carl Schurz Park. Jake wondered if they were going to Gracie Mansion. Instead, the limo pulled over to the curb of a narrow, three-story brick building with white trim. Jake had passed the building many times when he lived in the neighborhood but had never given it much thought. He always assumed a wealthy family lived there.

The chauffeur opened the back door and Jake got out, followed by Madigan and Bradley. Jake looked at his fellows, awaiting instructions, and Bradley led the way to the building's front door and rang the bell.

A muscular man in a suit, his hair cropped close to his skull, opened the door. His gaze darted from Jake to the old men. "Good evening, gentlemen. Won't you come in?"

As they entered the building, Bradley said, "Lionel, meet Jake Helman. He's a contender."

"Welcome," Lionel said in a voice that held thinly veiled contempt.

Who the hell is this guy to look down on me? Jake thought. "Uh, thanks."

Lionel closed the door, and Bradley and Madigan hung their coats on gold wall hooks.

"I think I'll leave mine on," Jake said, not wishing to explain his Glock.

"Not for long," Madigan said with a wink.

Lionel escorted them down the hall and opened a door at the end, admitting them into a deep room that resembled a nightclub, complete with a long bar, plush banquettes, European lamps, and pink and lavender fabrics dripping from the walls. Jake counted eight women luxuriating in the room, posed to perfection. By his estimate, they ranged in age from twenty to twenty-three. They had dark skin, porcelain skin, short hair, and long hair and were squeezed into outfits that revealed plenty of skin. Their full lips formed half smiles and half kisses.

"The most beautiful women in the entire city," Bradley said. "There's always eight of them on call around the clock to service us or people we want serviced: world leaders, rival tycoons, or just friends and business associates."

Jake measured each woman. They could have been models and probably were. "You guys run a brothel?"

"The best little whorehouse in Manhattan," Madigan said with a grin.

Jake found it difficult to mask his disgust with Madigan. The man had allowed the cabal to abduct Marla, and here he was prowling a cathouse. He didn't even pretend to be concerned for his wife.

"We don't run this place," Bradley said. "We own it. Or one of the subsidiaries of one of our subsidiaries does. We own private clubs all over the state for our own amusement. Call it quality control."

A woman wearing thigh-high leather boots and just enough black material to conceal her private areas crossed the room and stood before them. Straight, long dark hair spilled over her back. Jake found her stunning in every way, from her brown eyes and perfect cheekbones to her figure. She smiled at Bradley and Madigan but focused her attention on Jake. "Who do we have here?" she said.

"A new member," Bradley said. "Jake. He's to receive full benefits."

The woman caressed Jake's forearm with her fingernails. It had been a long time since a woman had touched him with the intention of arousal.

"I'm Lacy," she said. "Welcome."

"Lacy's one of the managers," Bradley said.

"She'll suck you dry," Madigan said in a mock whisper. "She has my highest recommendation."

Lacy smiled. "Thank you, Mr. Mayor."

"Take a look around," Bradley said. "Pick whoever you want. Take two or three, if that's your thing. Just not Lacy. She's with me tonight."

"Bastard," Madigan said in a jovial tone.

Lacy took Jake's hand. "Come on. I'll introduce you to the girls."

"Have fun," Madigan said as Lacy led Jake deeper into the parlor.

Jake felt a sense of excitement as Lacy squeezed his hand. Her perfume filled his nostrils and his heart beat faster. He didn't know why the old bastards wanted him to get laid, but he could think of worse ways to establish his cover. Sheryl had certainly given him permission to indulge in a little carnal pleasure.

Lacy guided him to a spot in the room that provided him with a close view of the other seven women, who sized him up with predatory eyes, leading him to believe they received bonuses for their services.

"Girls, I'd like you to meet Jake," Lacy said. "Treat him right and he just may become a regular."

"Hi, Jake," the women said in unison.

"Hello." Jake hoped his face wasn't turning red from the attention. He eyed a dazzling Chinese woman who sat on a banquette, one arm draped over the back to emphasize her breasts. Then he looked at a South American beauty with brown skin, the bangs of her straight black hair drawing attention to her feline eyes. And a Latina with curves in all the right places, her gold jewelry guiding his attention to her taut stomach. A leggy blonde standing at the fireplace cocked one eyebrow at him. A light-skinned black woman with coffee-colored hair only had to tilt her head to quicken his pulse. A brunette with short hair, decked out in red lingerie and a silken robe, crossed one leg over the other, pointing the toe of her stiletto shoe in his direction. Another black woman, with darker skin and long curly hair, regarded him over her shoulder, flexing her tight ass at him. Jake swallowed.

Lacy scraped the back of his neck with her fingernails, drawing an electric charge out of him. "They're yours for the choosing, dear. Every one of them will do whatever you want, so don't be shy." Leaning so close to him that he felt her breath in his ear, she whispered, "Remember, this isn't a onetime proposition. You can have all of them eventually, even me."

Despite his best efforts, Jake felt himself stiffening down below.

"Choose," Lacy said in a breathy tone.

Jake focused on the South American woman, and before he knew it he had moved in her direction.

Meeting his gaze head-on, she rose on toned legs and tossed her hair over one shoulder like a model in a shampoo commercial.

"Excellent choice," Lacy said behind Jake. "Bianca will make you feel like a new man. She'll teach you how the birds sing in Brazil."

Jake looked into Bianca's brown eyes, which flashed equal parts exoticism and eroticism. Her smile conveyed a sincerity that suggested more than role-playing, and he desired her.

Bianca—if that was her real name—slid her soft fingers between his. "Let's go up to my room, unless you'd rather sit at the bar."

Jake shook his head, and she led him past Bradley and Madigan, who stood leering. He found Madigan to be a particularly vulgar man.

Bianca opened the door, her every movement drawing Jake's attention to a different part of her body. He followed her along the corridor, past the man who had admitted him, and up the curved stairway.

On the second floor, Bianca opened a white-paneled door. She pressed her back against the doorframe, offering Jake a view of her breasts, and nodded inside.

Jake moved past her into the spacious room, which was dominated by a king-sized bed. Mirrors decorated the walls and ceiling. A Jacuzzi waited beside an open bathroom. A bureau with hand-carved wooden drawers served as a display for sexual aids and devices.

The door closed behind him, and Bianca's arms encircled his chest. "Tell me you want me," she said.

"You're very desirable." He searched the room for cameras. He saw no signs of any, but in the age of fiber optics, that meant nothing. The last time he'd had sex was with Kira Thorn in the Tower, and that had turned out to be for Old Nick's entertainment pleasure.

Bianca strode forward and stopped between Jake and the bed. "Do you want me to take my clothes off? Or do you want to undress me?"

Jake looked her up and down, from her firm calves to her tight waist and her full breasts. "You do it."

With a hint of a smile, Bianca disrobed. She peeled off her garments and discarded them on the floor until she stood nude except for her shoes. She posed for Jake, offering him several different views of her body, which she seemed to enjoy. "Do you like?"

Jake nodded. "Very much."

Bianca moved closer to him, and his gaze flitted to the wide areolas around her erect nipples. She slid her palms up his chest, then clawed at his pectorals and drew her fingernails down his abdomen, causing his body to shudder. Her right hand slid over the erection in his pants and stroked it, causing him to twitch.

"I take it you don't need Viagra," she said, leading him to believe that the other members of Avademe did, except maybe for Madigan. "What about other drugs? I have anything you want, except for Black Magic. Just enough for the clientele."

Jake's throat turned dry at the prospect of cocaine. *You don't want to go there*, he told himself, but standing before her, he did. "Just some music."

Smiling, she went over to the sound system, which afforded him a view of her curvaceous ass. "What would you like to hear?"

"You choose."

Bianca opened a menu on a touch screen attached to the music player and selected an entry. A moment later, opera music swept through the room. She glanced at him with raised eyebrows, as if seeking his approval.

"Louder," Jake said.

Bianca raised the volume, and he sat on the bed and took out his cell phone.

She circled the bed and stood before him, a disappointed look on her face. "What are you doing?"

"Checking my messages." Even as he spoke the words, he opened a menu and selected a video file. Glancing up at her, he read indignation in her pout.

"I hope you find me more interesting," she said.

Jake offered her a conciliatory smile. "Get down on your knees."

Now looking satisfied, Bianca kneeled on the floor in front of Jake and slid her hands along the inside of his thighs, kneading his groin.

Jake turned the cell phone so the image on its screen faced her. "Do you know her?" he said in a whisper barely audible over the music.

Frowning, Bianca stared at the image. She narrowed her eyes for a moment, and Jake knew that she did indeed recognize the woman on his phone. Then her face grew passive. "No," she said, with a lot less conviction than she had shown in gaining Jake's interest.

Jake unfroze the image of the woman Madigan had murdered, then rewound the footage to the beginning and allowed it to play at regular speed. He showed her the screen and studied her expression as she watched the murder play out. She gasped and the color drained from her features.

When she raised a hand to her mouth, Jake gripped her wrist and jerked it away. Then he gave her hair a sharp tug, pulling her head to one side, and whispered into her ear, "I'm pretty sure there are cameras and listening devices in every room in this building, whether you know it or not. I'm also certain the girl in that footage worked here, that the old bastards who finance this whole operation and others like it use this place as a farm to harvest women like you for scenes like the one I just showed you. If you're following what I'm saying, nod and smile as if I just made a very imaginative request."

Bianca nodded and smiled, despite the fear in her eyes.

"That was no staged performance. It really happened. I saw it in person. That girl is never coming back. They brought me here so I could choose someone I liked. Your life is now in danger, but I had to pick someone. When I leave, you better start thinking of a plan to get the hell away. Don't tell anyone else, because you don't know who to trust or who else might be listening. Take as much cash as you can tomorrow and disappear. Don't use your credit cards, and don't go anywhere you've been before, because they'll find you and they'll kill you."

Jake sat back, and Bianca looked at him with tears in her eyes.

"I'm sorry, but you'd better put on a good show now." Sliding the cell phone into his pocket, he laid back with his arms folded behind his head.

Bianca crawled over him, her hair hiding her face. "Thank you." She kissed him on the mouth, and he tasted the salt from her tears. She pulled his T-shirt up to his neck and kissed his chest, working her way down to his belt, which she unbuckled.

Jake closed his eye and tried to imagine Sheryl as Bianca took him into her mouth, but he saw another face instead.

When Jake went downstairs, he nodded good-night to Lionel, the muscle-bound doorman, who gave him a curt nod in return.

Outside, the chauffeur stood smoking a cigarette against the limo. Madigan's security detail remained invisible in their SUV. The chauffeur tossed his cigarette and reached for the car door handle.

"Don't worry about it," Jake said. "I don't know how long the others will be. I'll just take a cab."

On Second Avenue he hailed a taxi and instructed the driver to take him home, where he took a shower and then unlocked the safe.

A while later, Laurel appeared sleepy and surprised when she opened her parlor door. She wore a robe over her nightgown. "I know I'm stating the obvious, but it's late."

"This can't wait," Jake said.

She stepped back from the door, allowing him to enter. "You keep very irregular hours."

"Not by choice." Jake descended the steps into the parlor and set the metal attaché case on the round table where Laurel held her readings.

Laurel locked the door and joined him. "What's this?" She crossed her arms.

Jake thumbed the combination dials on the case and popped its lid, revealing the laptop, files, and discs inside.

She regarded the contents. "You asked me to hold that for you once before, and I said no."

"I realize that, but this is a different situation. Possessing After-life may have saved my life. I have reason to believe Reichard will send someone to retrieve this from my office. They can't find it."

Laurel traced the edges of the attaché case with trembling fingers, like an ex-junkie confronted with her worst bad habit. Drawing her hand back, she slammed the lid shut and spun the combination dials. "I don't want to be around this."

Jake moved closer to her. "You're the only person I can trust with it."

"Six months ago, you came to me right before you went to war with Katrina."

"Because you're the only person I can talk to about this crazy stuff."

"Then talk to me now. I'm here for you."

He stepped even closer. "I don't want to talk."

For the first time since he had known her, Laurel appeared nervous. "Then what *do* you want?"

Sliding his left hand on the back of her neck, Jake drew her close and kissed her on the mouth. Laurel responded with her tongue, and he squeezed one of her breasts. She arched her back, moaning. When they parted, Jake untied the sash of her robe. Laurel shed the fabric and wrapped her arms around his neck with greater passion than he expected, quickening his heart. He knew this simple contact opened his mind to her, allowing her to read his thoughts and feelings. At that moment, he didn't care.

Jake took off his jacket, revealing his Glock in its shoulder holster. "Where's Edgar?"

Laurel's breasts rose and fell. "In the bedroom."

He relocated the attaché case to a chair, intending to take her on the table, but Laurel shook her head.

"That table contains the vibrations of hundreds of my customers. It will be overwhelming for me and more than a little distracting." Unclasping her nightgown, she turned and receded into her living quarters, allowing the garment to fall to the floor in the doorway.

In the kitchen, Jake took off his shoulder holster and laid the gun on the counter.

Laurel emerged from the bedroom, naked and carrying Edgar in a cage. The raven cawed at Jake. "You're sleeping in the kitchen tonight," Laurel told the bird.

Jake admired her body. She wasn't a twenty-year-old like

Bianca or a genetically engineered fuck machine like Kira, but she was an attractive woman, maybe thirty years old, with a nice figure. A flesh-and-blood human being like Sheryl had been, except for her psychic abilities.

Jake raised one hand to the birdcage. "High five."

Edgar squawked and pecked at Jake's palm.

Jake followed Laurel into the bedroom, where she lit several candles on her bureau, the mirror doubling their output.

"Take off your clothes," she said, and he complied. "Now come here. I know just what you want."

Jake went to her and she stroked his erection, then kneeled before him and took him into her mouth. Sliding his hands over her head, Jake glanced at their reflection in the mirror. He saw the surprise on his face as Laurel worked him over, speeding up and slowing down her movements, running her tongue here and there, massaging his testicles with her hands at the same time. No sooner did it occur to him that he wanted her to do something differently than she adjusted her actions to fit his desires.

Like magic, he thought, and then he came with a loud moan and collapsed onto the bed. Laurel went into the bathroom and washed her mouth, leaving him to reflect on the experience they had just shared, which topped the hand job she had given him six months earlier.

Laurel returned and leaned over him, her hair whispering over his face. "Did you like that?"

Jake blew air out of his cheeks. "Copy that."

"More than what you got at that whorehouse?"

Jake's laughter hurt his stomach. "You've got special powers, lady."

"Then get up off your ass. I'm not some high-priced hooker. One hand washes the other in my world."

Jake rolled off the bed, allowing Laurel to lie on her back. She spread her legs wide apart, giving Jake a look at her shaved privacy.

"Let's see if you can read my mind," she said.

Jake lay across the bed on his chest, probing her with his tongue and fingers. It had been a long time, and as he went to work, he realized it had probably been a long time for Laurel, too. Her body shuddered and she clawed at his back, bucking her hips. Jake lost track of the time as he submerged himself in her essence, pleasing her repeatedly. Laurel cried out in tones that revealed near desperation and great relief, and when her body, slick with sweat, wilted, Jake's erection had returned.

They made love twice, the second time with more familiarity and boldness, their bodies moving as one, straining their muscles in unpredictable ways. In a single night Jake achieved the level of intimacy with Laurel that had taken him years to reach with Sheryl, and when their bodies lay spent and exhausted and sleep overcame them, they held each other with great tenderness.

For those few hours, Jake gave no thought to Avademe or his assignment to kill Governor Santucci. Then the sun rose and the darkness returned.

CHAPTER 18

Jake awoke in Laurel's bed to the aroma of hollandaise sauce. Sitting up, he looked around the room. One brick wall, no windows. *Like a prison cell*, he thought.

If only Laurel's powers *did* enable him to see into her mind.

He pulled on his briefs and jeans and padded barefoot to the kitchen. His groin ached and he felt drained. Edgar sat perched on the table, watching Laurel cook. She had put on Jake's polo shirt, and he studied her legs with appreciation.

Setting his hands on her hips, he said, "Good morning."

"Good morning."

"Mmm. Eggs Benedict. My favorite." Even as the words came out of his mouth, he thought, *Of course she knows it's my favorite . . .*

Laurel turned around in his hands. Draping her arms over his shoulders, she smiled. "Let's make this easy. Last night was great—"

"It was spectacular."

"Okay, spectacular. You needed it, I needed it, and it's been brewing since we met. But we're not meant to be together. I'm not looking for a relationship, and you're already freaking out over the idea of being with someone who can read your mind during sex."

"It has its advantages and disadvantages."

She moved her hands onto his chest. "It's okay. Believe me, I understand. You could pretend not to care that I have this ability, and I could pretend not to sense the things I do, but we'd both know the truth. How long could that last?"

Jake didn't realize his muscles had tensed until he felt them relaxing.

"See? You're already relieved. We both have bigger things on our minds than how to make this work."

"I guess you're right."

"I'm sorry about Sheryl."

"Thanks. I was really grasping at straws there."

"You may not want to admit it to yourself, but you already have feelings for someone else."

Maria. He opened his mouth to speak.

But Laurel touched his lips with one finger. "Don't apologize. You have nothing to apologize for. Last night I wanted you as much as you wanted me. It *was* spectacular."

Jake resigned himself that the truth had come out. "I don't think there's any chance of me and Maria getting together." He glanced at Edgar, who cawed. "Too much has happened."

"You never know. Sit down and eat your breakfast. For all we know, this could be your last meal, not counting whatever greasy food you pick up on your way to Albany."

Jake sat at the table and watched Edgar pace before him. "You and Edgar have developed quite a relationship."

Laurel served the food and sat down. "He's a good listener."

"So you do confide in someone?"

"Even a psychic needs to share what's on her mind sometimes."

Jake sampled the eggs Benedict. "You can always talk to me. I mean it."

She studied him before answering. "Thank you. It's best I not share my problems with anyone who can speak."

Jake chewed his food. "I want to help you with whatever your problem is."

"You have your hands full right now."

"Right now, yes. But in the future . . ."

"Maybe someday. If we live that long."

They finished their breakfast in silence.

✳

Jake emerged from Laurel's parlor in need of a shower. As she locked the door behind him, he glanced up at the cloudy sky.

"Jake!" Carrie stood a dozen feet away at the door to his building. A Korean man with long dreadlocks hovered beside her.

As Jake approached the couple, he registered the man's dirty black jacket and button-down white shirt. Standing next to Carrie, he looked like a giant.

Ripper, Jake thought.

With her eyebrows raised, Carrie clucked her pierced tongue.

She made no effort to conceal her surprise at seeing Jake exit the parlor so early in the morning. "You look like you had a late night."

"Good morning," Jake said, waiting for an introduction.

"Oh, this is Ripper. Ripper, Jake."

Jake held out his hand, but Ripper offered him a closed fist instead, so they bumped fists.

"'Sup?" Ripper said, revealing a gold tooth.

"Nice to meet you at last," Jake said. But it wasn't. Ripper gave off an odor and a vibe that made the hair on the nape of Jake's neck stand on end. He couldn't believe Carrie would associate with such an obvious lowlife.

"Ripper was just dropping me off," Carrie said. She stood on her toes for a kiss, and Ripper hunched over and complied with an open mouth.

Jake's stomach constricted, and he feared he'd toss the breakfast Laurel had cooked for him.

"Helman!"

Now what?

Detectives Storm and Verila joined the party, and Ripper melted into the background.

"Looks like we caught you just in time," Storm said.

Jake regarded the detectives. "Not really. I'm coming, not going. Let me guess: Geoghegan wants to see me downtown again."

"You read my mind." Storm glanced at Laurel's parlor. "You must be psychic or something."

"I need to take a quick shower before I go anywhere. You want to wait in my office, or do you want me to meet you downtown?"

Storm and Verila traded bemused looks, then said at the same time, "We'll wait."

Great, Jake thought.

✳

When Jake entered the interview room for Major Crimes in One Police Plaza, he saw two men in black suits sitting beside Geoghegan, who wore his customary snarl.

The men paid little attention to Jake. They appeared to be his age or younger, with short, professional hair that made them look like accountants.

Feds, Jake thought. "Teddy, I'm disappointed. I thought it was going to be just you and me again."

"Not this time. These gentlemen would like to have a few words with you. Special agents Dilman and Richter, Jake Helman."

Neither of the agents offered Jake their hand, so he kept his to himself.

"Why wasn't I invited to the FBI? I could use a change of scenery."

"Because the NYPD and FBI are working together on Marla Madigan's disappearance, and the task force is based here since we own the case. Have a seat."

Jake sat on the remaining chair and faced his inquisitors.

"Wasn't Buffalo enough of a change of scenery?" Geoghegan said.

"Lily Dale," Jake said. "It was lovely until Abby Fay took a bullet in her head."

"Meant for you," Geoghegan said.

"That would be my guess, but one never knows."

"Sheriff Gudgino seems certain of it."

Jake shrugged. "He's the expert. Can I have some coffee?" He faced the feds. "You'll have to forgive his manners. The job is tough on all of us."

Geoghegan rose with an uncharacteristic smile. "Tougher on some than others. How do you take it?"

"Cream and sugar, unless the cream is that powdered shit."

Geoghegan exited the room, and Jake waited for the show to begin. He had grown tired of these interviews and promised himself he would endeavor to avoid them in the future.

The feds shuffled some papers, then one looked up. "Mr. Helman, I'm Special Agent Richter. We've been going over your initial statement to Lieutenant Geoghegan, and we just have a few follow-up questions."

"Shoot. Unless you want to wait for Teddy."

"That's all right. We can start without him."

I bet we can. Joint task forces between NYPD and the FBI yielded competition more than cooperation. In this case, NYPD shared its information, and the FBI hoped to crack the case.

"You told Lieutenant Geoghegan that Mrs. Madigan hired you to prove her husband's suspected infidelities, and yet you say you were on another case the night she disappeared. You refused to divulge the details of this other case."

Jake raised his hands. "Okay, you got me. I lied to Teddy. I was on the Madigan case—*my* Madigan case, not yours—on the night in question. Boy, you guys are tough."

Richter showed no sign of emotion. "Why did you lie to Lieutenant Geoghegan?"

Jake leaned forward. "Can you keep a secret? I don't like him." He hoped Geoghegan was watching through the one-way mirror. "And it was just a white lie."

"So why are you speaking about it now?"

"Because Marla may not be alive anymore, which would make this a homicide case, not a missing persons case."

"It's a Major Crimes case," Geoghegan said as he reentered the room with Jake's coffee in a Styrofoam cup.

"Oh, Teddy—we were just talking about you."

Geoghegan set the coffee before Jake. "You said black, right?"

Jake smiled. "Right."

Teddy sat. "Now, where were we?"

"Mr. Helman was telling us how he was working the case Mrs. Madigan hired him for the night she disappeared."

Geoghegan acted impressed. "You don't say? That sort of contradicts your earlier statement, doesn't it?"

Jake shrugged again. "So arrest me."

"Don't tempt me."

Richter folded his hands. "Where did you go that night, Mr. Helman?"

Jake glanced at Agent Dilman, then back at Richter. "Doesn't he get to talk?"

Richter offered a humorless smile. "We do things differently than NYPD. We're not into that whole good cop, bad cop routine."

Jake nodded his approval. "I went out to Westchester that night to the estate of a gentleman named Karlin Reichard."

"Because . . . ?"

"Marla told me that once a month the mayor spends a weekend at Reichard's. According to her, Madigan said the weekends were political retreats, and Reichard was grooming his career. And on that weekend, our mayor was due for some career shaping. He wants to be president, you know."

"But Mrs. Madigan believed the mayor had other motives for visiting Mr. Reichard's estate?"

Smiling, Jake placed the tip of one finger on his nose.

"Let the record show that Mr. Helman just touched his nose.

Did your surveillance yield any results?"

Jake looked around for a recorder or a camera but saw none. "I'm afraid not. You should see that place; Reichard has some spread. I couldn't get anywhere near the mansion. Security was too tight."

"What time did you arrive at Reichard's, and what time did you leave?"

Jake exhaled. "I'd say I got there around 5:15 p.m., left around 10:00 or 10:30, and got back to my office by 11:45."

Geoghegan crossed his arms. "Prove it. Just so we know you were busy when Mrs. Madigan vanished."

Jake feigned hurt feelings. "You don't trust me?"

Geoghegan gave him a hard look.

Jake rose and pulled a handful of receipts out of his pocket. "Here are my bridge and highway toll receipts for that night." He tossed the receipts on the table. "They support everything I just said. You'll need to make copies. I keep the originals for tax purposes."

Richter moved the receipts around the table with one finger, examining them. "Mrs. Madigan disappeared shortly before midnight. This doesn't prove anything."

"I can provide you with digital security files that will show me entering my office building at a time very inconvenient for any theory you might have about me being involved with Marla's disappearance."

Geoghegan fumed. "What the hell were you doing in Lily Dale, wise guy?"

Jake turned to Richter. "Is he leading now?"

Richter shrugged, then scooped up the receipts and handed them to Dilman, who exited the room.

"Like I told you on the phone, I went to Lily Dale to find

a psychic who might be able to help me locate Marla. Abby Fay helped on several police investigations in the past."

"Who do you think killed her?" Richter said.

"I don't have a list of suspects."

"Guess."

Not wanting to implicate the cabal, Jake glanced at his watch.

"Are we keeping you from something?" Geoghegan said.

Yeah, I'm supposed to whack the governor. "Hm? No, I just like to pace my day. I read in the papers that you boys are pursuing the theory that one of the mayor's old Mafia enemies got revenge for Myron's work as DA. That works for me."

"You think the Mafia followed you to Western New York and shot a psychic in the head with a sniper rifle?"

"I admit it sounds far-fetched. Put me down for the mayor, then. I don't trust that ugly little prick."

Geoghegan's face reddened. "You think the mayor of this city sent a hit man to kill some psychic upstate?" ·

"I don't know who sent the hit man. You told me to guess so I guessed. I have no evidence or leads one way or the other. And I don't think anyone sent this hit man to kill Abby; they sent him to kill me."

Richter said, "Where does your investigation stand now?"

"With my client missing? Dead in the water. I'm looking for another assignment. Freelancing is brutal."

"I'm sure it is. Thank you for coming in. We have all we need. Special Agent Dilman will return your receipts on your way out."

Jake rose. "No problem. See how easy that was, Teddy? You could learn a lot from these guys."

Geoghegan glared at Jake.

Contrary to Laurel's speculation, Jake decided to eat lunch at the Cajun restaurant next door to his office. He considered grabbing takeout to share with her, but her last words to him had been *good luck* and he didn't want to say good-bye all over again, so he took Carrie instead.

"Administrative Professionals Day isn't for two more weeks," Carrie said as they sat in a booth in the back of the restaurant.

"I thought it was Administrative Professionals Day," Jake said.

"Is that what I am? Whatever."

Jake took an envelope out of his pocket and handed it to her. "Really, I just wanted to give you this and thank you for all your help this last year."

Carrie looked at the envelope with suspicion. "What is it?"

"My will. It wasn't drawn up by a lawyer. I did it myself. But it's notarized."

She left the envelope in his hand. "Are you planning on going somewhere?"

He didn't want to upset her. "No. But one never knows. It's best to plan ahead."

Carrie took a deep breath. "Why me?"

"You run my business. You'll know how to settle everything. It's pretty simple: I'm leaving almost everything to Martin Hopkins. If anything happens to me, I want you to set up a college fund for him."

"Boss, you're forgetting that I do your books. You don't have anything to give away."

Jake smiled. "I have a few accounts you don't know about yet. I'm making you my executor, so you'll get all the dirty details, and there will be a little money in it for your labor. I'm also leaving you six weeks' severance."

Carrie swallowed. "How serious is the trouble you're in?"

Jake made a noncommittal face. "Pretty serious."

"Then why don't you just drop whatever you're working on and get the hell out of Dodge?"

"It's not that easy. I owe it to someone—to two people—to see this through." There are others who could be impacted as well."

Her voice warbled. "Sometimes you have to worry about yourself first."

"You're right. But this isn't something I can run from. And sometimes there is no hiding." He shook the envelope. "Go on. Take it. There's another copy in the office."

Carrie took the envelope and stared at it. "I really don't like this."

"I'm touched. That being said, I don't want you to worry. I hope to be around for a long time to come."

Carrie stuffed the envelope into her handbag. "I want to help you with whatever you're working on."

"Thanks. There's nothing you can do."

"I don't believe that. I can be your lookout or your backup or your wheelman. Don't let my size fool you. I can squeeze a trigger as well as the next person, maybe better."

"I learned to fly solo. There's less chance of people I care about getting hurt that way."

Her eyes watered up. "You are so stubborn."

"I have to be me."

"All men are stubborn."

"Speaking of which . . ."

Carrie's expression turned defiant, as if daring him to speak his mind. "Yeah?"

"I can't help but wonder if Ripper is the right beau for you."

"Oh, not you, too. I get enough of that from my parents and my girlfriends."

"Surrounded, huh?"

"Let's put it this way: if Ripper turns out to be as bad as everyone thinks, I'm becoming a nun so I don't have to listen to all the 'I told you so's.'"

"Maybe these people are just looking out for your best interests. Maybe you should consider whatever they're trying to warn you about."

"Like you? What are you trying to warn me about?"

"I won't pussyfoot around. I got a bad vibe from him right away. Call it cop's intuition."

"Ripper's a musician."

"Did you see the way he disappeared as soon as Storm and Verila joined us outside the building this morning? He knew right away they were cops. Call it criminal's intuition."

"All right, look, Ripper doesn't like cops, okay? He did some time at Rikers."

"Now there's a surprise. What did he get pinched for?"

Carrie sighed. "Burglary. But he only did six months, and that was before we even knew each other. He's straight now. All he cares about are his music and me."

"You're a smart girl. I'm not going to lecture you. What's his real name, anyway?"

"So you can run a check on him? Forget it."

Jake grunted. "Okay, I tried. At least I told you what I think."

"Yes, boss."

Jake made a mental note to find a way to obtain Ripper's fingerprints if he lived long enough.

CHAPTER 19

Walking to the garage, Jake noted the heavy gray clouds that expanded overhead and wondered if Bianca had heeded his warning. Ordinarily, he would have doubted it, but the footage of Madigan slaying the prostitute was too shocking to rationalize. As his footsteps echoed in the garage, he scanned the parked vehicles and glanced over his shoulder. Shadows merged with oil spills on the cement. He stopped, waited, and listened. No movement except inside his chest. Was this how Marla had felt, dodging Madigan's security detail goons?

Using his remote, he unlocked the Maxima and got behind the wheel. With the doors locked and his shoulder strap pulled across the bulge of his Glock, he experienced momentary relief.

Then he realized how ridiculous that was; strapped in, he was little more than a sitting duck if a White River Security assassin wanted to take him out.

Shaking his head, Jake inserted his key into the ignition. Then he froze and his gaze locked on the key. He released his seat belt, popped the hood open, and jumped out of the car. Closing the door to silence the chiming alarm, he circled the front of the vehicle. He looked from side to side, checking the motionless shadows, then raised the hood. Although not mechanically inclined, he knew what the Maxima's engine looked like, and everything appeared normal.

He lowered the hood, the ensuing echo ricocheting around the garage like gunfire, then dropped to his hands and lowered himself just shy of the floor. Unable to see much of the car's underside in the dark, he pulled a Maglite from his pocket and used it to trace every groove, ridge, and texture he saw.

No bombs that I can see.

Exhaling, he stood and looked around the garage again, then got back into the car. He reached for the car key, hesitated, and turned it.

No explosion.

"You're getting paranoid," he told himself as he programmed the Albany address for Angeline's Old-Fashioned Italian Restaurant into his GPS.

Just like Marla was paranoid.

Driving through the Holland Tunnel into New Jersey, Jake

reassured himself that the ring on his finger would protect him from danger at the hands of the cabal. Taggert had been convincing enough for him to march into Reichard's den and then to break bread with the old men. They had more than ample opportunity to have him taken out if they'd so desired. Their rules regarding the ring had to be true.

He expected the drive to take just under three hours without any stops, and he planned to stop once for coffee and at least once to use a restroom. He had never been to Albany despite its close proximity to Manhattan, and he wanted to arrive at Angeline's early to scope out the neighborhood. Beyond that, he had no plan.

This is crazy.

Did he expect to pull a rabbit out of his ass when he found himself sitting at a table facing Governor Santucci? He had just over two and a half hours to think of something.

His fingers tightened on the steering wheel. *Anything.*

The cabal wanted him to kill Santucci. They guaranteed he would escape the governor's security detail. Did the detail work for them? They could just as easily shoot Jake immediately after he killed Santucci. Jake had no doubt he would one day suffer a horrible death, but he had never envisioned being gunned down after committing a political assassination. Of course, he had no intention of killing Santucci and intended to leave his Glock in the car just to eliminate the possibility of being shot if things got out of hand anyway.

Reichard could tip off the cops that I'm in the restaurant to kill Santucci. They could nab me on suspicion before anything goes down. That wouldn't violate the rules of Avademe.

Jake glanced in the rearview mirror and saw two cars. He had to assume that White River Security or some other personnel under the cabal's direction would follow him to Albany, even though they knew his destination. As long as they knew where he was, they knew where he wasn't.

The NJ-17 North became I-287, and he crossed back into New York State. Checking the cars behind him, he got off the thruway and pulled into a parking lot for several fast-food places. A blue Ford Taurus got off behind him. He used a bathroom and ordered a cup of Tim Hortons coffee, then drove to the ramp. The Taurus did not follow him. That didn't mean anything. A second vehicle could follow him once he got back on the I-287.

Jake took Route 17 North toward Albany, the sight of the city's name on road signs causing his stomach to tighten, and merged onto the I-87 North. As he paid the toll, a blue Ford Taurus with New York State plates drove through the booth ahead of him.

Son of a bitch!

He proceeded at a slower speed, allowing the Taurus to gain distance.

Doesn't mean anything, he told himself.

Ten minutes later, he saw no further sign of the Taurus. The soft rock music on the radio gave way to static, so he fiddled with the tuner until he found a news station with clear reception.

An hour later, at 5:30, he pulled over to another rest stop to stretch his legs and relieve himself of the coffee he'd downed. Gray clouds crossed the sky without rainfall. When he got back into the car, he removed his shoulder holster and stashed it in the side compartment of his door, where he could reach it if he encountered trouble.

Half an hour later, Albany's skyline appeared in the distance.

Damn.

He still didn't have a plan.

✳

With a population of just under 100,000, Albany was the sole remaining settlement from the Thirteen Colonies. Before that, the
Mohegan Indian tribe called the land *Pem-po-tu-wuth-ut*: the
place of council fire. In a sense, that tradition continued today:
Albany served as the capital city of New York, where lawmakers
engaged in absurd politics.

As the city's streetlights came on, Jake stifled a laugh. All of the
ridiculous behavior that had marked the state's attempts at legisla-
tion now seemed even more ludicrous than he had thought before.
They were mere dramas performed for the benefit of an ignorant
public; the lawmakers had no real power. They were just shadow
puppets performing for children, while the Order of Avademe
made the real decisions.

Jake exited the ramp and turned left on Broadway. The buildings were low enough to the ground to permit a view of the sky,
and few pedestrians walked the sidewalks. Cities entrenched in the
car culture seemed alien to him. The few people he saw appeared
to be college students. He located Angeline's with little difficulty.
The restaurant sat on a corner, just as his intelligence reported. He
circled the block twice before choosing a parking space two spots
away from the restaurant's side entrance.

"Santucci's security detail will be stationed outside the front
of the restaurant," Reichard had said. "This is the one place the
governor goes where he doesn't allow his security to follow. The
restaurant is too small for that kind of spectacle, and Santucci
is good friends with the owner. They were once lovers. Angeline

Saeli is the daughter of Big Tony Carpuzzi, head of the Carpuzzi family. With his political ambitions, Santucci had to break off the romance. He still carries a torch for the woman, even though he's been married to his wife for seventeen years. He likes to sit there and pine for her in private. Sometimes she joins him for dinner."

"Angeline is your employee," Jake had said. "She knows he's going to be taken out."

Reichard continued as if Jake hadn't spoken. "The curtains in the windows will be closed to prevent anyone outside from seeing in. You put two bullets in that son of a bitch's head, and as long as you use a silencer, the detail won't know anything until they hear the screams. Get your ass out that side door and into your car, and you'll be on your way before they can even radio for help. You just have to make one left turn and one right, and you'll be on the highway. It will take you less than five minutes."

And then I just have to be on the road for another three hours, praying the entire time that I won't be stopped.

Jake saw a number of flaws with this plan but kept his objections to himself. He knew from the minute he had accepted Reichard's proposal that he would never carry it out. He had pretended to embrace the scheme to buy himself time, but time had run out.

Half an hour passed, and Jake saw no signs of the security detail. Usually, one car would arrive in advance of the protected figure. At least, that's how they did it in the big city. He had to believe the governor, who ran the entire state, rated as much protection as the mayor.

Maybe Santucci isn't coming. Maybe he switched restaurants, or

Reichard wasn't able to—

Jake's cell phone rang and he jumped in his seat. Unbuckling his seat belt, he reached into his pants pocket and took out the phone. He did not recognize the number on the display. Scanning the street, he pressed the phone against his ear. "Yeah?"

"You can't do the job sitting in your car," said a man whose cold voice Jake didn't recognize. "Get your ass inside that restaurant."

Whoever it is can see me, Jake thought. But he didn't see anyone spying on him.

The phone on the other end went dead.

Jake pocketed his phone and readied himself. He took a can of styling mousse from his glove compartment and applied it to his hair, which he pushed straight back rather than parting at the side as usual. The mousse darkened and slicked his hair. Next he took a small, lightweight box and shook its contents into the palm of one hand: ten flesh-colored fingertips he had cut off latex gloves. He pulled the latex tips onto his fingers, ensuring he would leave no fingerprints anywhere in the restaurant. Even though he was not going to kill Santucci, he didn't want to leave any evidence he'd even been in the restaurant if he could help it. He got out of the car, searching the rooftops for anyone holding a scoped rifle.

He could take me out right now.

But the man who had called him could have shot him just as easily while he was strapped inside the car, unable to move.

Maybe.

Rounding the corner, he surveyed the surrounding buildings, most of them three or four stories high. As he pushed open the restaurant's glass door, he glimpsed his reflection, transparent like a ghost. After passing through a second door, he stood inside Angeline's and counted a dozen tables for two in the narrow restaurant, each one covered with an old-fashioned red and white checkered tablecloth. Gold fixtures gleamed on the dark wood walls, candles providing much of the limited illumination. Four couples occupied tables, spread out for privacy. Sheryl would have loved the place.

A young woman with nerdy glasses and a boyish haircut came over to him. She wore green slacks and a red apron over a white blouse with rolled-up sleeves. The girl couldn't have been more than eighteen. With a genuine smile, she clasped her hands. "Hi. Table for . . . ?"

"I'm alone. Can I trouble you for something in the back?"

"Sure, right this way."

Jake followed the girl to the rear of the restaurant and sat with his back to the wall, so he could observe the other diners. He ordered a diet soda and closed his hands into fists, so no one would see the latex fingertips as he perused the menu. When the girl returned with his soda, he ordered spaghetti and meatballs, not that he expected to be able to keep his food down. The knots in his stomach multiplied.

Jake stared at a round clock on the wall. Santucci was scheduled to arrive in twenty minutes. The front door opened and another couple entered. He glanced at the side door and could not see outside through the curtains. His shirt turned damp, but he avoided dabbing his forehead with a napkin because he did not wish to leave any DNA in the restaurant. What the hell was he going to do when Santucci arrived?

Finish my meal and leave as if nothing happened. Or finish my meal and bolt out of here like I completed my mission. Or warn Santucci to his face that Reichard and the cabal intend to kill him. When I don't do it, someone else will.

The clock ticked off another minute. Nine more to go.

Jake drummed his fingers on the table.

The girl brought his food and set it before him: two giant meatballs in a plate of spaghetti.

Seven o'clock.

No Santucci.

Sliding a fork he had brought from home from his pocket, Jake nibbled on his meatballs. Five minutes passed. He twirled spaghetti around his fork and tasted it.

Seven fifteen: the door opened. Another couple entered. No Santucci.

Jake's nerves gave way to anger and suspicion.

At 7:30, I'm walking out of here.

At that deadline, the girl took away his plate. "Would you like to see a dessert menu?"

He did not want dessert. "Yes, please."

At 7:40, he ordered carrot and almond cake. When it arrived ten minutes later, he asked for his check. He took two bites of the cake, pushed it aside, returned his fork to his pocket, and left a crisp $50 bill on the table.

Setup, he thought as he opened the side door and stepped outside. *Or maybe just a test.* He stood still for a moment, daring the man who had called him to shoot.

No gunfire.

He climbed into the Maxima, took out his cell phone, and called the man back.

The phone rang unanswered.

Probably a disposable burner that's already in a garbage can somewhere.

Jake shut his phone off and drove around the block. Still no sign of the governor's security detail.

They never intended for me to kill Santucci, he thought. *They just wanted to know if I would go through with it. As far as they know, I would have.*

He followed the ramp onto the thruway and headed toward Manhattan. For once, he felt lucky. The cabal had no reason to doubt his loyalty, and he had not been forced to break his cover. The worst that had happened was he had wasted the day on a wild-goose chase.

Half an hour later, the rain came. Jake listened to the staccato on the roof and the steady rhythm of the windshield wipers. He eased up on the gas pedal, then slowed down even more when howling wind buffeted the car. An hour after that, he turned on the radio. His next move depended on the cabal. He finally belonged to something again. Too bad he had to destroy it.

The voices on the radio droned on. The stock market was up. Six US soldiers were killed in two different wars. Simon Taggert, the head of White River Security, died peacefully in his sleep from natural causes. Tensions increased in the Middle East. All good news for the cabal members' portfolios. Jake felt relieved when a story came on about a Hollywood actress whose husband had been caught cheating on her with a stripper. At least Avademe hadn't been responsible for *that*.

The rear window filled with white light as a semitruck bore down on the Maxima. Jake swerved into the left lane so the truck could pass, but the truck did likewise and blared its horn. Jake returned to his lane, and the truck blasted past him like a leviathan, splashing the car with so much water Jake thought he was in a submersible. One of the wipers snapped, and the other one didn't clear the water from the windshield until the truck had pulled in front. As the truck melted into the rain, Jake felt claustrophobic in the car. He lowered his window, allowing cold rain to shock his senses back to life.

"It's ten o'clock," a male newscaster said, "and at the start of this hour we have breaking news. Governor Salvatore Santucci was reportedly aboard a yacht that sank off the coast of Long Island just a short time ago."

Jake flinched and nearly lost control of his vehicle.

"The *Nautilus VII* was owned by attorney Sheldon Dreier, who served as Governor Santucci's political advisor. The coast guard received a distress call from the captain of the 123-foot Heesen yacht half an hour ago, but rough seas prevented them from reaching the vessel before it sank. No survivors have been reported, and all hands are believed lost at sea. The cause of the vessel's sinking is unknown at this time, though the weather is believed to have been a factor. Lieutenant Governor Mark Fryer is expected to issue a statement in Albany momentarily."

Jake gripped the steering wheel in both hands, his knuckles turning white.

They did it. They fucking did it!

CHAPTER
20

The rain followed Jake to Westchester, where he barely discerned Reichard's mansion atop the hill as the security gates swung open to admit him. He waited for one of the two guards inside the booth to open its window before he lowered his.

"Mr. Reichard's expecting you, Mr. Helman." Water drizzled off the bill of the man's hat. "Go on up."

"Thanks." Jake drove forward, triggering the motion detectors on the way up the hill. The resulting light from the security floods slashed through the downpour. Water gushed down the brick driveways, splashing against the curved curb. Jake searched the woods for signs of the creatures, but he couldn't even see the trees through the rain. He parked in front of the mansion, shoved his

Glock into its shoulder holster, and got out.

The rain assaulted him, and he ran for shelter beneath the roof that extended over the entrance, supported by columns. Wind blew him sideways, almost knocking him over, and he was drenched by the time he reached the door, his hair plastered to his forehead. He ran his hand through the wet hair, then rang the doorbell and stepped back, ready to draw his gun.

The doors opened and the butler stood there, his face registering disapproval at Jake's waterlogged appearance, but no surprise. "Mr. Helman."

"Evening, Jeeves. Is the master in?"

Judging by his scornful expression, the butler's disapproval intensified into outright dislike. "Certainly. Won't you come in?"

"Don't mind if I do." Jake entered the foyer, dripping water all over the marble floor.

"Master Reichard is at his sanctuary."

"You mean that replica of an ancient temple out back?"

"Correct."

"Is he alone?"

"No, the other guests are with him."

Good.

"I'll have the chauffeur take you."

"Thanks but I'll walk." Jake had no intention of getting into a coffin on wheels.

"It's almost an eighth of a mile away from the rear of the mansion."

"I'm a New Yorker."

The butler took a long umbrella from a stand. "Then at least take this."

Jake accepted the umbrella and brandished it like a sword. "Thanks, Jeeves."

As Jake opened the door and stepped outside, he thought the butler said, "Good-bye, sir."

Halfway to the sanctuary, Jake glimpsed dim lights ahead through the downpour. The rain had not let up, and his shoes created puddles with every step. The umbrella protected his face, but from the sternum down, his cold, wet clothes clung to his shivering body. The wind changed direction and he walked into it, holding the umbrella as a riot control officer might a shield. Lightning flashed overhead, followed by thunder that seemed to come from every direction at once. Jake searched for any sign of the watchers. The trees and bushes in the woods, bowing to the wind, created movement he did not like. Then the gale force turned his umbrella inside out, and he discarded it rather than try to force it back into shape.

Jake stumbled the last several yards to the sanctuary, the structure offering shelter, and slumped against the door. He banged on the thick wood, then seized the golden French door handle and twisted it. The door swung open, and he staggered inside and caught himself.

The cabal members looked in his direction. None of them smiled.

"Shut that door," Reichard said, standing between Weiskopf and Coffer.

Jake turned to the door and closed it, grateful to reduce the chill.

"Why on earth didn't you have the chauffeur bring you?"

Jake wiped the water from his face. "I don't trust them since I beat down Taggert's driver." He glanced at the ceiling. "I see you've replaced the skylight." He gazed at the floor. "And the rug. No traces of Aquaman remain."

"We expected you sooner," Weiskopf said, chewing on his cigar like Winston Churchill.

Jake looked around at the men. Schlatter and Browning sat on a banquette, while Bradley, Madigan, and Coffer stood behind them. Madigan also puffed on a cigar.

"The weather slowed me," Jake said. "We never discussed me coming here tonight."

"Where else would you go?" Browning said in a taunting voice.

"You guys sure pulled one over on me," Jake said. "What was that, some sort of initiation prank?"

Reichard folded his arms behind his back. "We sent you on that fool's mission to keep you out of our way while we implemented other plans. I'm surprised you fell for it."

Jake aimed a finger in Reichard's direction. "You killed the governor!"

"*We* didn't do anything," Madigan said. "We never left this estate."

"Sure, sure. You had a button man do your dirty work. You ordered the hit, just like you ordered me to do it. What did you use, a plane or a submarine?"

"We ordered nothing," Reichard said. "And we had very little to do with the tragedy that befell Governor Santucci. Avademe killed him."

Jake opened his mouth to speak, but nothing came out at first. "Avademe?"

"Avademe is real," Bradley said, stepping around the banquette.

Schlatter rose. "Avademe is our god."

Browning stood as well. "Hail, Avademe!"

"Hail, Avademe!" the other men said in unison as they formed a half circle around Jake.

Jake blinked in confusion. "Your *god*? Avademe isn't real."

Schlatter's face twisted into a snarl, his eyes wild. "Blasphemer!"

"He *is* real," Bradley said.

"More real than any other god," Madigan said.

"Because he's flesh and blood," Coffer said.

Jake read each of their faces. "You're mad, every damned one of you."

"Avademe is real," Reichard said, "and has been for thousands of years. You won't find mention of him in any written history book, but he exists, and he sank that yacht."

"Avademe commands us," Weiskopf said. "He's ours to serve."

Jake stared at them. "You expect me to believe that some Indian sea monster—"

"Avademe doesn't belong to the Indians," Weiskopf said. "He doesn't *belong* to any men. We belong to him."

Reichard smiled. "It doesn't matter what you believe now. You'll believe everything soon enough. But by then it may be too late."

Jake swallowed. "Why is that?"

"You must be judged by Avademe, as all of us were judged. Regardless of whether or not you wear that ring, you must be deemed worthy of serving our god."

Jake did not like the sudden turn the conversation had taken. "I've killed two men since this all started—"

"Two of Avademe's servants," Bradley said in an admonishing tone.

Jake's gaze darted from man to man. "You sent me to kill Santucci. You should have allowed me to complete my mission."

"Avademe didn't want to take a chance on you and feared you might sabotage the kill," Reichard said. "It was Avademe's decision to let you play the fool. He's a very hands-on god—except that he has no hands."

The others chuckled.

"But I *would* have done what you told me to do."

"That remains to be seen. We have our doubts."

"I wanted the money. I still do."

"That I believe. And there's still a chance you may get it—after Avademe judges you. It's out of our hands, I'm happy to say. Let Avademe's wisdom decide."

"Hail, Avademe!" Schlatter said.

Reichard rolled his eyes. "That's enough."

Schlatter looked down at the floor and mumbled.

"You should have allowed me to prove myself," Jake said, trying to sound indignant.

"Do you mean that?" Reichard said.

Jake stood straight. "Yes."

"I'm glad."

Jake heard a low hissing sound. He tried to pinpoint its source, then realized he heard overlapping hisses coming from different directions. His heart beat faster, and the cabal members smiled at his fear.

Robed figures appeared in the doorways around the chamber that led to other rooms.

Jake felt his eye widening as the creatures stepped into the light of the fireplace. They all stood the same height, under six feet tall, with stooped shoulders. Occasionally, their clawed feet emerged from beneath their identical robes, and they flexed their webbed hands. The old men showed no sign of fear as the watchers stood interspersed between them. The hissing grew louder, and the creatures drew back their cowls, revealing feelers that undulated in the air before them, reminding Jake of the legs of centipedes. He tasted his dinner.

"You mistakenly surmised the watchers serve as our security

force," Reichard said. "In truth, they are here to watch over us. We serve them as we do Avademe, for they are Avademe's children."

The sick feeling in Jake's stomach expanded. From the moment he saw the cave painting of Avadiim, he had resisted the impulse to connect the monsters he knew existed to the one he wanted to believe was metaphorical.

"Each of us has a corresponding watcher, assigned by Avademe. There were eight of us. Now there are seven. You killed Taggert."

One of the creatures hissed louder.

"There were eight watchers. You killed four of them, one in this very chamber."

Now all four watchers hissed louder.

Jake summoned every ounce of restraint he possessed to keep from pulling his gun. He could take out all of the watchers and most of the cabal, leaving one old man to take him to Avademe. But what if that survivor refused to cooperate? To save Marla, he needed to see Avademe.

"What can I do to convince Avademe I'm worthy of serving him?"

"After you killed four of the children?"

"Sacrifice," Weiskopf said with relish.

The watchers reduced the level of their hissing so it sounded almost like human consent.

"Choose another target," Jake said. "I'm your man." *Anything to buy more time.*

"We already have chosen another target," Reichard said. "Or, rather, *you* have."

Bradley and Madigan disappeared into one of the back rooms and returned with a beautiful woman supported between them.

Bianca, Jake thought.

She appeared to be drugged, just like the woman Madigan had

slain, but remained fully mobile. She wore a see-through top and belly-dancing pants over the same lingerie Jake had seen her wearing the previous night.

"She's quite beautiful," Reichard said. "I can see why you chose her. We *all* see why you chose her."

Jake swallowed. He had doomed Bianca by warning her. Now they expected him to kill her. His suspicion about the brothel serving as a front for the cabal to harvest women was correct. He hated being right.

Bradley and Madigan guided Bianca toward Jake. Lightning flashed outside the glass block windows and the skylight. Thunder crashed, quieting the watchers.

Bianca focused on Jake, and he thought he saw recognition in her eyes. She slowed her movement, then resumed speed, stopping before him. Smiling, she drew her fingers up his chest, then put her arms around his neck. She pulled Jake's head down and kissed him on the mouth, her tongue pushing against his.

Responding to keep her calm, Jake eyed the cabal members. The leering old men came closer, the watchers following.

Jake's heart thudded in his chest. Bianca stroked his penis through his slacks, but fear prevented him from getting hard.

Reichard reached inside his tuxedo and withdrew the sacrificial dagger Madigan had used to slay his victim. Reichard held its pommel out to Jake, a devilish grin on his face.

Bianca stroked Jake harder, frantically seeking a reaction from him. The other men waited for him to take the dagger. The watchers stood silent and still, except for their feelers furling and unfurling in front of them.

Jake grasped the dagger, his tongue pushing back against Bianca's.

Wait . . . wait . . . wait . . .

Jake brought the dagger's tip close to Bianca's back and centered it between her shoulder blades.

Weiskopf sucked on his cigar. Madigan licked his lips.

. . . *wait* . . .

Lightning flashed.

Jake flipped the dagger in the air, caught its blade, and threw it. The dagger sank into a watcher's head with a soggy impact, the blade disappearing and the handle protruding from the middle of the feelers.

Thunder crashed.

The watcher emitted a high-pitched squeal and reached for the dagger. Bianca turned at the sound, and Jake sensed her growing confusion. The creature's claws closed around the handle. It pulled, squealed louder, and pitched forward, the impact of its fall driving the dagger deeper into its head.

Reichard gasped. The three remaining watchers shrieked and charged at Jake with outstretched claws.

Bianca pressed against Jake, who drew his Glock and fired twice into the head of the closest watcher, the gunshots deafening in the enclosed space. Green fluid spewed from between the quivering feelers, and the creature crumpled to the floor with a frog-like croak.

Jake aimed his smoking weapon at the watcher to his right, but before he could squeeze the Glock's trigger, the watcher on his left made a gurgling sound and shot its serpentine tongue into the air, and Jake felt the organ latch onto the back of his neck. He turned to fire at this creature, but a sudden injection of hot fluid into his body caused him to scream, drop the gun, and flail his arms. Numbness spread through his body, starting with his head, which rolled on his neck. The two surviving watchers stood motionless, waiting for the venom to take effect. Jake lost the feeling in his arms and hands. His heart and breathing sped up. The room tilted, and he realized the venom was getting him high.

Ignoring his fallen gun, Jake scooped up Bianca in his arms and threw her over his shoulder. He glimpsed the old men laughing as he turned away and staggered to the door, which he thought he reached in record time. He fumbled for the door handle and twisted it. The door swung open, and he charged into the freezing rain.

Jake had failed Sheryl. He had failed Carmen Rodriguez, who had hired him to prove her dead grandson was slinging Black Magic on a Brooklyn street corner. He had failed Edgar and failed Marla.

Failed, failed, failed!

As he sprinted through the rain with Bianca slung over his shoulder, he vowed he would not fail her.

The watchers' shrieks filled the night.

Jake stumbled forward, almost lost his footing, and regained his momentum. He heard footsteps bounding after him, so he ran faster. It was so hard with Bianca over his shoulder. Then he realized she was no longer there because he had dropped her.

Turning around, Jake saw Bianca struggling in the mud. She worked her way up onto her hands and knees but seemed unaware of why she was outside. Jake's point of view descended to ground level, and he slid over wet grass onto his back. He came to a stop and stared up at the rain falling on his face. It felt good to be alive, and he laughed out loud. Or he thought he did.

The surviving watchers' heads appeared above him, blotting out the rain, and reached for his face with sharp claws.

Jake wanted to scream. Instead, he blacked out.

CHAPTER
21

Water, rushing.

Submerged clanging.

Deep reverberations.

Breathe!

Jake sucked in his breath, scorching his lungs.

Where am I?

"You're in a world of trouble," Aunt Rose said. "Just like your father, God rest his soul."

He was twelve years old again. "I didn't ask to come here."

"None of us do. We have no say in the matter." Rose sat knitting a scarf before the TV.

"What does my father have to do with anything?"

"He killed himself. Stuck his off duty revolver in his mouth and pulled the trigger. He was hurting, and that hurt damned his soul. When you're older, you'll try to kill yourself, too. Like father, like son."

"I don't believe in destiny."

Rose smiled. "Everything is predestined." She held up the sweater for him to see. "What do you think?" The sweater had eight sleeves.

"I'm not a puppet." He felt older now, stronger.

"That's exactly what you are," Old Nick said.

They stood in the man-made park on the top floor of the Tower.

"See?" The old man raised his hands, showing Jake the strings that dangled from the marionette controls he grasped.

"Where's Kira?"

Tower winked at him with his discolored eye. "She's downstairs in your unit, screwing your brains out."

That didn't make sense. "But I'm not downstairs. I'm *here.*"

Tower grinned. "You're not even here."

"Stop playing games!" Jake drew his Glock and aimed it at Old Nick.

"You're too young to play with guns. Give that to me." The old man took the water pistol from Jake, who cried.

"You're a mean old man!"

Old Nick pointed the gun at him. "Of course I am."

"You go to hell!"

"I'm already there." Old Nick squeezed the trigger and Jake's world transformed.

Dread and Baldy lay facedown on the ground, screaming as Gary and Frank kicked and handcuffed them.

"Help us," Dread said, his pale face turning scarlet and spittle flying from his mouth.

Baldy sneered at him. "Motherfucker!"

Holding his Glock in both hands, Gary looked at Jake. "Don't worry, partner. We got this under control."

"I'm not your partner," Jake said.

"Fuck you," Frank said. "You're one of us."

"They're right," Edgar said.

Gary and Frank stepped back, aimed their guns, and depressed the triggers. The gun barrels flared, and shell casings struck the ground. Dread and Baldy stopped screaming as bullets ripped their bodies and spilled their blood.

"No," Jake said. "They're wrong."

Edgar clucked his tongue. "You took a wrong turn, buddy. I wish I could have helped you."

Jake shook his head. "I wish I could have helped *you*. Why aren't you a raven?"

"Sheryl set me free."

"Stop it. Sheryl's dead."

"You know better than that," Sheryl said. "I'm inside you."

Jake fought back tears. "I love you. I miss you."

Sheryl wiped the tears away. "Oh, honey, I know that. But I'm in heaven now."

"Heaven's overrated," Kira said.

"How would you know?" Old Nick said. "You have no soul. I know: I *made* you."

Kira squeezed Old Nick's hand. "Yes, Daddy. Can I eat Jake now?"

Old Nick covered his bad eye with one hand. "Of course!"

"I'll make you fly," Katrina said. She looked beautiful in the firelight.

"I don't want to be a raven," Jake said.

"You have no choice." She unbuttoned her blouse.

"Stop saying that!"

"Everyone has a choice," Sheryl said. "That's what it's all about: making the *right* choice."

"I want to make the right choice."

"Then you have to listen to me," Laurel said. "I give you good advice, don't I?"

"You got Abby killed."

"Only my body is dead," Abby said. "My spirit lives on."

"She's in heaven with me," Sheryl said.

Laurel tilted her head to one side. "You see? Everything worked out fine."

"Not so fast." Marla shook her head. "What about me?"

"Where are you?" Jake said. "I need to find you."

Madigan blew smoke in his face. "Forget it. She's going away forever."

"Forever is a long time," Jake said.

"Help me," Marla said.

"I'm trying . . ."

"Save me," Sheryl said.

"It's too late for that. The Cipher already killed you."

"Rescue me," Laurel said.

"You won't let me. Tell me what you want me to do."

"Fuck me!" Kira said.

"I don't want to do that again."

Kira turned into a giant spider. "I want to eat you!"

Standing behind Jake, Laurel slid her hands around his chest. "That was so nice."

Bianca kneeled before him. "I want to eat you, too."

Sheryl crossed her arms. "Remember, I watch everything you do."

Old Nick snapped his fingers. "I like to watch, too."

"I'm not putting on a show for you," Jake said.

Reichard grinned. "I beg to differ."

Jake summoned his resolve. "You'll beg for your life."

"That's what you think," Taggert said.

"I didn't kill you."

"Because you're soft," Weiskopf said.

Bianca unzipped his pants. "I'll make you hard."

Jake sucked in his breath.

"Maria likes you," Edgar said.

"Who's Maria?" Katrina said, frowning.

Laurel whispered into Jake's ear while Bianca blew him. "See? Maria likes you, too."

"I've got to find Marla," Jake said.

"You lost her again," Madigan said.

"You're in over your head," Reichard said.

"Give me back my ring!" Taggert rocked back and forth in his chair.

"That's it," Jake said as Bianca worked him over. He reached down for her head.

But Laurel pinned his arms behind his back. "Nothing's ever easy," she said.

Baldy slugged him in the gut. "Motherfucker!"

Dread snapped his head back and leaned so close that Jake saw the gold tooth in his mouth. "The Master wants to see you."

"I don't have a master," Jake said through clenched teeth.

Baldy slugged him in the stomach again. "*Motherfucker!*"

Groaning, Jake doubled over, his face inches from the crown of Bianca's head. She looked up at him, but everything about her had changed.

"You're not Bianca," he said, gasping.

"I'm better than her," Kira said. Then her forked tongue tickled his face.

"Motherfucker!" This time Baldy punched him in the face, knocking him to the ground.

Jake wiped blood from his nose.

AK kneeled beside him and held up a baggie filled with white powder. "You need some blow. I got some real good shit right here."

Jake shook his head. "You stabbed my eye."

"So? You killed me! That doesn't mean we can't help each other out now and then."

Katrina crouched beside them. "Put that away. What he really needs is Black Magic." She dangled the packet of black powder before Jake's face. "Don't you want to snort some Magic off my tits?"

Jake closed his hands into fists. "You killed Edgar."

"Don't exaggerate," Katrina said.

"She turned me into a raven," Edgar said. "You said so yourself."

"Freeze!" Maria said, aiming her Glock at Jake.

"I didn't do anything," Jake said.

"He was going to," Katrina said.

Maria gestured with her gun. "Get up."

Breathing heavy, Jake got to his feet.

Maria looked him up and down. "Put your dick back in your pants."

"Sorry." Turning red, he pushed his penis inside his pants and zipped his fly.

"Shoot him," Katrina said.

Maria wavered but she sure seemed angry.

"Eat him," Kira said.

"Suck him," Bianca said.

"Trust him," Laurel said.

"Depend on him," Marla said.

"Give him your love," Sheryl said.

Jake swallowed. "Give me a chance."

Maria's gun hand trembled, but she still managed to squeeze her Glock's trigger.

Damn, Jake thought.

Jake opened his eye in total darkness. He lay on one side, metal vibrating beneath him. Running his palms over the cold metal floor, his fingers touched long, parallel grooves. His head throbbed and his body felt like rubber, as if he had just come down from a three-day binge. The sound of an engine filled his ears, and gasoline fumes lingered in his nostrils.

Cargo van, he thought. *Or a truck.*

Moving.

Faces flickered in his mind: Sheryl. Kira. Laurel. Katrina. Maria.

Old Nick?

A dream or a hallucination brought on by the watcher's venom.

At least I'm alive.

His throat ached. He tried to sit up, but the task proved too difficult.

Paralyzed?

Perhaps the creatures' venom worked like a black widow's, immobilizing their victims. He raised his hands to his face and ran his fingers down to his chin, which caused his fingertips to tingle. His stomach clenched, and even as he worked his way up on his hands and knees, he vomited. So much for Angeline's cooking.

As an acidic smell rose to his nostrils, he stood, his knees wobbling, and stutter-stepped to the rear of the vehicle, his heavy footsteps echoing. The amount of headroom and the distance he covered told him he was in the back of a large truck. He slammed into steel doors and groaned. Sliding his hands along the doors, he determined there was no way to open them from the inside. His stomach still felt queasy. Bending his knees, he pressed his back against the doors and searched his pockets. They were empty: no wallet, no car keys, no Maglite. He patted his torso. They had removed his shoulder holster and Glock. He pulled at his fingers. The ring was gone.

Son of a bitch!

The truck rolled over a bump or a pothole, and a banging sound echoed through the compartment. The hair on the back of Jake's neck stood on end, and he examined the darkness for any trace of light, something he could use as a reference point to get his bearings. Pure blackness.

Bianca filled Jake's thoughts. Maybe she was in the truck, too. He addressed the darkness. "Hello? Is anyone else in here?"

No answer.

Where were they taking him?

To meet Avademe.

Despite the existence of the watchers, Jake refused to believe a giant sea monster had sunk the yacht with Governor Santucci aboard. He found his way to a corner and moved his right hand along the side of the truck. Tilting his head, he hoped to see a hatch in the ceiling, but darkness overwhelmed him.

With his back pressed against the truck's side, he inched toward the front end. The air grew thick, and he felt perspiration on his forehead and under his arms. His breathing came in short rasps, and when he tried to control it, his heart sped up.

Aftereffects of the venom or—

He smelled fish.

A low hiss sliced through the darkness ahead of him, causing him to jump back with his heart thudding in his chest.

A watcher!

He was locked in the truck with one of the creatures, without the protection afforded by the ring. Raising his fists in a defensive manner, he heard something scrape the metal floor to his left.

Claws.

An identical sound came from his right.

There are two of them!

Both of the "children" he had failed to kill. He prowled the darkness as he tried to determine the exact location of each creature. Had they been waiting for him to regain consciousness, or had he put them on defense by moving too close to them? Swallowing, he stepped back. One of the creatures hissed, then the other. The sounds reminded Jake of saliva gurgling through a breathing tube.

Wasting no time, he aimed a kick straight ahead and connected with one of the watchers. The creature let out a startled scream, and Jake heard it slam onto the floor. As he brought his foot down for balance and rotated his body to throw a punch at the second watcher, the left side of his face exploded with pain and he let out a cry. At first he thought the creature had shot him with its tongue, but when he felt his face, igniting a second wave of pain, three of his fingers slipped through a deep gash below his cheek and touched his gums and teeth. Jerking his hand back, the fingers came away sticky with blood. With a single swipe of its claw, the watcher had left four deep canyons in Jake's face. He felt warm blood flowing down his neck, and the sweat trickling down his temple caused the top gash to sting even more.

Driven by blind panic, he ducked low and passed the creature, turning in a circle where he estimated the center of the floor to be. He touched his face again and winced. It felt as if he had four new mouths below his missing eye.

He heard the creatures following him, the sound of their claws on the metal floor alerting him to their approximate positions. They seemed to have no trouble locating him.

They can see in the dark.

If they truly were amphibious, their eyes were developed to see in the dark water.

That's why they only come out at night—their eyes are too sensitive for sunlight.

Jake continued to turn in small circles, tracking the sounds of their movements. They seemed determined to face him from opposite sides, from the front and back. He reversed his direction and they hissed.

They're communicating. Strategizing.

Their sounds grew closer. He needed to seize control of the situation, or they would tear him to pieces. He stopped turning, and as they did the same, he jumped off the floor. Then he slammed his feet down on the metal so hard the sound reverberated around the walls. The creatures' hissing became louder, and then he heard a wet gurgling sound that he knew indicated they were about to shoot their tongues at him.

Have to time this just right.

If he moved too soon or too late, he would receive a double dose of the juice, which he imagined could easily kill him or destroy his mind.

Now!

Jake dropped to his knees and heard what sounded like water bursting from a garden hose. The watcher before him grunted, and Jake heard both creatures retract their tongues with slurping sounds. The watcher he had kicked to the floor returned there, and he heard it writhing around. Then it turned still.

Pivoting as he stood, Jake faced where he believed the remaining creature coiled to strike. At the gurgling sound, he tensed his body, ready to spring. The watcher drew the sound out, waiting. Then Jake heard the creature's tongue lash out, and he stepped to his left and swatted the space where he had just stood. The tongue wrapped around his left forearm several times, and he caught its tip with his right hand, causing the creature to shriek. He heard the venom strike the wall behind him.

Shifting the tongue's tip into his left hand, he jerked hard on the tongue, and the watcher staggered toward him with a high-pitched squeal. He punched the thing square in the face, burying his fist in the twitching feelers. The creature fell back, then sprang forward in an effort to protect its tongue. Jake groped for the feelers, but several tiny mouths sank their teeth into his hand and wrist. He charged into the watcher at full speed, driving the creature backwards into the opposite wall. When he felt the impact of it smashing against metal, he dropped low enough to ram his right shoulder into its chest and heard several ribs shatter, the creature bellowing in pain. Jake spun the watcher around so it faced the wall and drove the same shoulder into its back, which created more snaps.

Jake knew he could not let up his assault. In order to survive, he needed to stay within striking distance of the creature and give it no time to recover. Releasing its tongue, he hurled the monster to the floor with all his strength, and the watcher screeched. Jake followed the noise through the darkness. His prodding right foot touched the creature's back as it got to its hands and knees, and he slammed it back to the floor. He set one foot on the left side of the creature's head and the other on the right. Then he raised his right knee to his chest and drove his foot down as hard as he could. The watcher's skull collapsed, and Jake heard fluids squirting from both sides of its head. He stomped the soggy mass again and again.

With his chest heaving, Jake wrenched his foot free of the sticky mess on the floor and stumbled over to where the other creature had collapsed. Using his left foot for guidance, he located the watcher and kicked it. When the creature did not respond, he concluded that it was unconscious, stoned, or dead, but he didn't intend to take any chances. Further prodding confirmed this creature lay on its back, and Jake straddled the watcher's head. As he lifted his foot, he knew he was taking a chance: if the creature was playing possum, it could easily shoot its tongue straight up into his scrotum. He brought his foot down but felt powerful resistance as two claws seized his ankle and gave it a sharp twist. Jake turned in the same direction that the watcher twisted his ankle in, saving it, but he crashed face-first into the metal floor.

The watcher released Jake's ankle, and Jake rolled to his left just as the creature pounced where he had been. Jake attempted to get up, but the creature scrambled on top of him. The instant Jake felt the monster's claws touching his neck, he seized its scaly wrists and jerked the claws away before they could do to his throat what they had done to his face. In that moment, he realized he had left his face vulnerable to the watcher's tongue and venom.

When Jake heard the gurgling sound that prefaced each attack, he released the creature's wrists and reached up with both hands. In under two seconds, his left hand closed over the back of the creature's neck, and his right hand found what felt like a lower jaw. He was so close to the thing that its feelers slimed his face. He felt something in the undulating head open like a mouth, and he yanked its neck toward him while shoving its head back. The watcher's tongue hissed out above his head, at a different angle than the creature had intended, and he felt its neck snap. The tongue dropped over his face like a dying snake, and he threw the foul-smelling body on the floor.

Jake lay panting in the darkness, his throat and chest aching.

Thank God there were only two of them.

With great care, he felt along the wounds in his face. The gashes were at least four inches long. One stretched along his jawline, another ran from near his mouth to his ear, another from below his nose to his temple, and the top one ran from just below his glass eye almost to his hairline. He had always taken his good looks for granted but now knew he would never have that luxury again.

Sitting up with a groan, he crawled to the front of the truck and slumped with his back against the wall.

Who's driving this thing?

The truck rumbled to a stop, then proceeded at a slower speed.

We're passing through a security gate.

Thirty seconds later, the truck stopped again, turned around, and backed up. Jake got to his feet. When the truck stopped once more, he heard male voices outside but couldn't make out what they were saying. They grew faint, and he heard an automated garage door close—a big one, judging by how long it took. Then he listened to the sound of his own breathing.

What felt like ten minutes passed, and he sat back down. Then he heard clanging against the truck's doors and jumped to his feet, balling his hands into fists.

The doors groaned open and grimy light seeped inside. Jake squinted at a number of figures and sucked in his breath. At least two dozen watchers stood facing him, their feelers twitching in the air. He could only imagine how he looked to them, but he didn't have to use his imagination to picture the creatures he had killed. He saw them as plain as day, the floor smeared with oversized fish innards.

One of the watchers squealed like a pig, then the rest followed suit. As the creatures climbed into the truck, Jake sprinted across the metal. He kicked one watcher in the head, then another. A third creature managed to stand before him, and he kicked that one in the chest, sending it flying into the scaly crowd. He grabbed the edge of one door and slammed it shut on a watcher, producing a shriek that grew even louder when he planted his foot in its feelers and shoved it back. He reached for the other door, hoping to seal himself in the darkness again, and saw the bloody wounds all over his left hand where the feelers had bitten him in the darkness.

Two watchers clawed at his thighs and pulled him down to the oil-stained concrete floor. He tried to stand, but the creatures piled on top of him. One of them raked his back, and he heard the fabric of his jacket tearing before he felt his flesh do the same. Crying out, he couldn't move. Feelers slimed his face and neck, and tears filled his eye, the overpowering fishlike stench making him retch.

A gunshot rang out and the watchers froze.

"Get off him!" Jake recognized Weiskopf's voice.

The pressure on his back lessened as the watchers climbed off him. Claws seized his arms and hauled him to his feet.

Weiskopf leaned against Jake's Maxima with a cigar clenched in his mouth and Jake's Glock smoking in his hand.

They had brought the car rather than leave evidence of Jake's visit to Reichard's estate, Jake concluded.

"I know you're angry," Weiskopf said. "This man killed your brothers. Altogether he's killed eight of you."

The creatures started shrieking all over again, louder this time.

"He'll pay for that; I promise you. But he has to be judged first. Take him to Avademe!"

A cacophony of approving sounds rose from the watchers, who jerked Jake forward.

Struggling to break free, Jake looked over his shoulder at Weiskopf. "Don't do this! Let me go! Please, I'm begging you!"

Smiling, Weiskopf puffed on his cigar, and Jake screamed as the monsters dragged him away.

CHAPTER
22

The watchers hauled Jake through an enormous warehouse with ceilings as high as those of an aircraft hangar.

Reichard's shipyard, Jake thought. *We're in Brooklyn.*

They passed hundreds of wooden crates stacked on top of each other before reaching a steel door. A watcher pressed its hand on a scanner mounted on the wall, waited for the metallic click that followed, and opened the door. The others forced Jake through the door, with Weiskopf bringing up the rear.

The six other cabal members stood facing them on a wide indoor dock. Behind them, still, dark water reached fifty feet to the building's farthest wall. A small yacht could have fit in the space.

Or a submarine.

Jake noticed a vertical seam in the back wall. Glancing at the ceiling, he saw cables, wheels, and a large motor. A pair of enormous doors that could slide open to admit vessels comprised the wall. The watchers dragged him to within ten feet of the cabal members.

Reichard gazed at Jake's face, his features twisting in disgust. "What the hell happened to you? You look ghastly."

Jake felt hot, sticky sweat running down his back, then realized it was blood flowing from the wounds where a watcher had clawed him.

"He killed the watchers in the truck," Weiskopf said, closing the doors behind him.

Reichard's expression turned to stunned admiration. "How on earth did you manage that?"

Jake glared at the man. "Like you said, I'm resourceful."

"Yes, you are. But *why* did you kill them? They were only there to guard you. We were bringing them here for your judgment ceremony."

Jake felt claws pinching his biceps and forearms. "How flattering. But I couldn't very well know that, could I? These things don't talk. Maybe you should have taken those two in your limo."

"I think you realize how impractical that would be, even with tinted windows."

"You just don't want your car to stink like caviar. You also took my ring. I didn't feel safe without it."

"*Our* ring," Schlatter said with an air of triumph.

Reichard raised one hand in a placating gesture. "For now. Jake still has to be judged. Who knows? Avademe could approve him for membership after all."

Weiskopf laughed. "After killing eight of the children? I doubt it."

Reichard smiled. "I'm rooting for him. Look at everything he's accomplished."

Jake supposed it was good the cabal's leader wanted to see him succeed in becoming a member.

"In any case, we'll know soon enough." Reichard took a cell phone from his pocket and struck a button. A moment later, he spoke into the phone: "Bring them up."

Jake tried to free himself from the watchers who held him, but they sank their claws deeper into his arms, causing him to groan through clenched teeth.

Reichard clucked his tongue. "I like you, Jake. Please don't provoke them. They'll tear your arms off if you give them cause."

Jake relented. "I know we're in your shipping yard. How the hell do these things run around here without being seen?"

"It's a dedicated building. The children are generally restricted to this docking bay and the lower level. And the Atlantic Ocean, of course. They wear the robes just to be safe, in case they should be seen, though they hate them."

The Atlantic Ocean. They must frolic in this water and use it as a portal to get outside.

"I'm afraid Weiskopf is correct. Avademe will be most distraught that you killed eight of the children. That's one quarter of their number, and they're all sterile. They don't even possess sexual organs. I can't say that bodes well for you."

Twenty-four of these things left. Jake figured they all surrounded him at that moment.

A steel door set in the cinder-block wall thirty feet to Jake's left opened, and two women emerged. Jake's heart leapt in his chest at the sight of Bianca, followed by Marla. They were both alive! He recognized the muscular man who followed them: Lionel, the doorman from the brothel, who held a revolver aimed at the women's backs.

Marla's face appeared sheet white, her lips drawn tight. She looked ten years older without makeup. Bianca seemed to have recovered from whatever drug the cabal had given her. She moved sluggishly, but her eyes revealed panic. They walked along the dock's edge, their shoes clacking on metal, and Bianca cast a worrisome glance at the dark water, as if fearing the cabal intended to drown her like a witch.

Or maybe she prefers to drown herself, Jake thought.

The women stopped walking as they neared the waiting crowd. They stared at the watchers and held on to each other.

"Keep moving," Lionel said, prodding them with the gun.

They resumed walking, and Marla looked in Jake's direction, her eyes widening with disbelief.

"Jake?" she said as they joined the cabal members.

At the mention of his name, Bianca looked at him, too, and gasped.

Am I that unrecognizable? "Yeah, it's me."

Marla's lips quivered. "I'm so sorry I got you involved in this."

"Don't be."

"He thinks he's going to be one of us," Madigan said, lighting a cigar.

"Put that out," Weiskopf said. "Avademe doesn't like smoke."

"Sorry." Madigan pinched the end of the cigar, snuffing it.

"What does he mean?" Marla said.

Jake bit his lip, regretting it as the pain in his gums and jaw flared. He didn't want to disappoint Marla, but he had to maintain what remained of his cover in the hope of getting them out of the building alive.

"I mean that your knight in shining armor is no better than the other gnats you hired to spy on me," Madigan said, clearly relishing the opportunity to flaunt his power in Marla's face. "Oh, he did more than they did; I'll give you that. They all took the money and ran. Jake here is more of a big picture kind of guy. Aren't you, Jake?"

Jake held his tongue. *I'm going to be real disappointed if I don't get to kill you.*

"You never should have messed with me," Madigan said to his wife. "All you had to do was smile for the cameras whenever I gave a speech, take care of the kids, and open your legs for me once in a while."

"You repulse me," Marla said.

Madigan took a step forward. "You could have been wife of the governor of New York. You could have been the First Lady of the country."

"That's enough, Myron," Reichard said. "You're being deliberately cruel. I don't like it. And we don't discuss our plans in front of others."

Madigan huffed. "It's not like she can tell anyone."

Reichard gave Madigan a hard look that silenced the mayor.

Jake noticed Lionel remained behind the women. "What's wrong, Lionel? Are you uncomfortable around these kids? Don't worry. They don't bite. They just shoot you full of venom."

Lionel snorted. "Don't worry about me—worry about yourself. Half your face is about to fall off."

"Don't taunt him, Jake," Reichard said. "If you manage to impress Avademe as you have me, you and Lionel could end up working together one day."

Jake glanced at Weiskopf. "And you doubted *my* qualifications? This guy's nothing but a bouncer. Or a pimp."

Weiskopf gave Jake a crooked smile. "That's what you think, wise guy. Lionel is White River Security. Taggert was training him to be his successor. You whacked Taggert and took the ring that was meant to be Lionel's."

Now Jake understood the undercurrent of hostility he had sensed in Lionel at the brothel. That hostility was becoming more overt by the moment. He saw Lionel flexing his fingers on the revolver's grip.

"Take it easy, buddy. Yesterday you were in the sex trade. Now you're the head of a powerful mercenary corporation. You're welcome for the promotion."

Lionel didn't respond. Unlike Madigan, he knew when to keep his mouth shut.

A foamy cloud of bubbles burst to the water's surface, causing the women, Lionel, and Jake to flinch.

"Let's get on with it," Reichard said. "Avademe's heard everything."

There really is something down there, Jake thought.

The cabal members moved behind the watchers and stood with their backs to the wall. The watchers spread out, the two holding Jake remaining put. Lionel circled the women and turned them in the same direction, his broad back to Jake, so everyone faced the water.

More bubbles surfaced and the water grew choppy. Lionel stepped back. On either side of Jake, the watchers' feelers wiggled in the air, as if genuflecting.

This is not happening, Jake thought. *It* can't *be happening.*

The water churned and grew darker as a massive shape rose to just below the surface.

Jake's heart beat faster.

Bianca screamed.

A gray metal shape broke through the surface and ascended ten feet before the spectators.

A conning tower. I was right. Avademe is a submarine. Jake laughed despite the pain doing so inflicted on his lacerated face.

Lionel glanced over his shoulder at Jake with a stunned expression, as if Jake had lost his grip on sanity. Then Marla screamed, too, and Lionel returned his attention to the shape rising before them.

Jake blinked in confusion. Why were the women screaming? It was just a submarine, for Christ's sake!

But he knew better. His mind had somehow deceived him, refusing to accept anything this impossible. The thing in the water was dark gray but made of flesh, not metal. The great dome consisted of two halves, with a giant crevice running down the middle, and water poured off its lumpy, veined tissue.

Jake's knees shook. *Oh, my God.* He wanted to look away but couldn't. *It's a giant fucking brain.*

Avademe continued to rise, water raining down from its flesh. Four eyes the size of garbage cans appeared below the brain, two on either side of the thing's cone-like head. The eyes on the left turned in synchronization with each other, as did the eyes on the right, but each pair moved independently of the other. To Jake, they looked human despite their gargantuan size, with whites and irises and pupils rather than the black, indecipherable orbs of a whale or a shark. Below the brain, the monster's flesh was darker, almost black. The portion of Avademe that had surfaced was larger than a cement mixing truck.

Another creature split the water and then another after that: huge serpents shooting straight into the air, with suckers running their length. Then they curled and writhed, and Jake realized they were gigantic tentacles. Another pair surfaced, undulating like the arms of a belly dancer. Within seconds, their number doubled, with webs of translucent flesh connecting them. Waves struck the dock, and streams of water jetted high into the air. Avademe unleashed a deafening roar that shook the walls. Jake couldn't tell where the sound came from, as the monster had no mouth with which to bellow.

"Hail, Avademe!" the cabal members shouted in unison, their voices filled with wonder and terror and love.

Jake's knees gave out, and his two watchers jerked him back up. Marla and Bianca continued to scream, their voices puny in comparison to that of the great monster god. They broke free of Lionel and ran, but watchers caught them with ease. Glimpsing the terror in Marla's eyes, Jake struggled to escape from the creatures holding him, but he felt their claws cutting his biceps and stopped.

Left alone at the edge of the dock, Lionel turned rigid. Avademe grasped a beam in the ceiling and pulled itself closer. Jake could hardly blame Lionel for panicking and firing his revolver at the enormous creature, though he knew the bullets would cause little damage. He barely heard the gunshots over Avademe's roar, which reminded him of a foghorn.

"No, you fool!" Reichard waved his arms over his head. "Don't shoot!"

Too late: with blinding speed, one of the tentacles whipped through the air, disintegrating Lionel's head and torso in its wake. Blood spattered Jake, the women, and the watchers, and for a moment Lionel's legs and hips remained standing before they toppled to the dock, covered in loopy intestines. The tentacle returned to its former position, curling and uncurling with the others.

Jake felt a blast of agony on the side of his face and realized he'd joined the women in their screaming. With his fists balled and his arms trembling, he felt the muscles in his neck bulge.

To Jake's astonishment, Reichard crossed the dock and kneeled before the monster.

Avademe's four eyes focused on the old man.

"Mighty Avademe, we praise you and your deeds. Forgive us for presenting you with such an unworthy candidate for your church. We did not mean to offend you."

Reichard gestured at Jake. "We have another for you to judge."

Oh, God, no!

Avademe's eyes moved to Jake, and the watchers dragged him forward.

"No," Jake shouted. "*No!*"

Reichard screwed his face in anger. "Don't show fear, you idiot."

"Fuck you!"

The watchers threw Jake down on the dock, and for one terrifying moment he thought he would plunge straight into the water. His hands slapped metal, and the fresh wounds in his arms stung. Raising his head, he gaped at the monster.

"Stand up," Reichard said.

With much effort, Jake rose. The same tentacle that had annihilated Lionel maneuvered through the air in his direction. Its pointed tip stopped just short of his face, wavering between his real eye and glass eye. Feeling sweat and tears running down his facial wounds, Jake tried to control his shaking body. The tentacle's tip descended, and then he felt it encircling his waist like an anaconda. He glanced at Reichard, who offered him a reassuring nod. The tentacle tightened around him, and a sick feeling rose from his groin to his throat. Then his feet left the ground.

Jake set his hands on the tentacle for balance as Avademe lifted him from the dock. The touch of the monster's sandpapery flesh sent shudders rippling through his body.

Ten feet. Fifteen. Twenty.

Jake focused on the ceiling. Maybe he could escape onto one of those beams . . .

The tentacle descended with the speed of a roller coaster, bringing Jake to within ten feet of Avademe's eyes, which studied him with interest. Marla screamed again. Twisting his neck, he saw a tentacle had wrapped itself around her torso three times, pinning her arms to her sides. Its tip remained free and rose up her back and beneath her hair. Marla threw her head from side to side. Jake heard a loud crunch, then Marla turned silent and still. Her head tilted back, eyes wide and unblinking.

"No!" The word escaped Jake's throat as a scream.

Bianca screamed, too, and Jake jerked his head in her direction. A tentacle had wrapped around her as well, its tip producing a similar crunch from the back of her head.

Jake pounded his fists on the tentacle holding him.

Both dead, just like Sheryl and Carmen Rodriguez . . .

The tentacles unrolled from their victims, spinning them like human tops while holding them by their heads. They lifted the dead women like marionettes and dangled them in the air for Jake to see.

Marla's and Bianca's eyes had rolled up in their sockets with their eyelids twitching. Their mouths opened in unison, and they spoke in perfect synchronization. "We are Avademe." The women sounded as they had when they were alive but lacked emotion.

Jake yelled and kicked and thrashed around in the tentacle's grip.

"The earth is our dominion," the dead women said. "Will you serve us?"

Make this good. "Yes! I'll serve you!"

The tentacle brought him closer to one pair of Avademe's massive eyes, then moved him to the other pair. The monster's stench overwhelmed him. Then the tentacle raised Jake before the dead women again.

"You're a liar," the women said. "You killed eight of our children."

"Oh, Jesus God . . ."

"We judge you inadequate to serve us."

Jake saw no point in arguing with a giant mutant octopus.

"He still has Nicholas Tower's records," Reichard said somewhere below. "We sent a team to his office while he was in Albany, but his safe was empty. We didn't find them anywhere."

Avademe's dome-like body heaved and exhaled foul-smelling mist in Jake's direction, like an angry bull snorting. The mist soaked him.

"Where have you hidden Afterlife?" the dead women said.

That fucking file. "How do you know what it's called?"

"We know all about Nicholas's research project," Reichard said.

Avademe rotated Jake so he faced the old man.

"He initiated it while he still belonged in our circle," Reichard said. "We had numerous disagreements over it. As I told you, we serve Avademe. We don't worry about the afterlife, because we never face the consequences of our actions. We pledge our souls to our god knowing that the trade-off for a lifetime of immeasurable wealth and pleasure is that when we die, there will be no eternal reward—and no eternal suffering for our deeds in life. Nicholas got it into his head that he wanted eternity right here on earth. He betrayed Avademe."

"And I killed him," Jake said. "So I guess you owe me one."

"Did he suffer?"

"Greatly. One of his creatures chewed through his tonsils, and a broken skylight minced his body."

Reichard smiled, a twinkle in his eye. "I wish I could help you. I really do. But Avademe's word is final."

"You're parasites," Jake said.

"And you're nothing but a flea, hopping around to survive with nothing to show for your efforts."

"You worship a fish!"

The tentacle tightened around Jake's midsection, and he squirmed in its grasp.

Go ahead, kill me. Get it over with, damn you.

Reichard smiled. "Blasphemy. Avademe is no fish. Octopuses have extremely large brains that never fully develop because of their short life span. But Avademe has lived for centuries."

Avadame rotated Jake to face the dead women again.

"Afterlife," they said.

"Why should I tell you anything if you're going to kill me anyway?"

"You can die quickly or slowly," Marla's corpse said.

"We can end your suffering in an instant, as we did Lionel's," Bianca's corpse said, "or we can digest you over a period of several days, one layer of skin and muscle at a time."

While holding Jake in the same space, Avademe rocked its great body backwards, tipping its cone so it touched the sea doors, and lifted its underside to face Jake and everyone on the dock. The water slammed against the back wall, and a giant wave rushed toward the dock, dousing Reichard, who did not react.

The monster's underside was pale white and silver and covered with suckers except in the middle. There Jake saw two parallel slits, vertical from his viewpoint. The tentacle suspending Marla lowered her body to the slit on the left side. The lips of the slit peeled back, revealing tremulous layers of translucent membrane inside, and thick fluid gushed out. The stench that rose from the opening caused Jake to gag. The tentacle shoved Marla's corpse into the opening, snapping Marla's back and folding her in half so her head rested on her heels. Clear slime poured over her body, which disappeared into the hole. Jake watched in horror. The lips smacked shut and sucking sounds emitted from within. Jake squeezed his eyelids shut.

"Where is Afterlife?"

Dear God, give me strength. He opened his eye. Bianca dangled before him, close enough for him to touch. He found it impossible to fathom that her mouth had sucked him only the night before. "Go to hell, you bitch."

The tentacle squeezed Jake, forcing the air from his lungs. It furled up, winding itself around him with his body serving as its core, until he faced Avademe's eyes once more. Unable to breathe, he clawed at the monster's skin but only succeeded in scraping his fingertips raw. He heard his heart beating in his chest and prayed for a swift death.

"We will see you for breakfast," Avademe said through Bianca's mouth. "You will speak for us then."

The tentacle unfurled with blinding speed, spinning Jake so fast he experienced vertigo. The tentacle launched him through the air, and he struck the dock and moved across it like a rolling pin. The cabal members and the watchers scurried out of the way, and he crashed into the far wall and cried out.

"Take him below," Avademe said.

Watchers seized Jake and hauled him to his feet. Reichard gave him a sympathetic head shake. The watchers jerked Jake forward, and he swung his head close to Madigan's grinning face. "You killed her, you son of a bitch."

"She had it coming."

The watchers dragged Jake away. "You'll get what's coming to you, too."

As the watchers forced him toward the door through which Lionel had brought Marla and Bianca, Jake saw Avademe stuffing Bianca's corpse into its other slit. He closed his eye and stumbled, but the watchers held him upright. They pulled him through the doorway and into a stairwell with cinder-block walls, the sounds of his footsteps and their claws echoing on the steps.

CHAPTER
23

On a lower landing of the stairwell, Jake stopped to look at a viewing window set in the wall. Spotlights on the other side of the window illuminated the murky green water. One of Avademe's tentacles swept past the window, and the monster descended. One hate-filled eye blinked at Jake, who found himself paralyzed with fear. The body rotated so that another eye replaced the first in the window and continued to do so until each malevolent eye had scrutinized him.

The watchers led Jake downstairs. The lower level reeked of fish, and Jake noted clumps of seaweed strewn across the tiled floor. Many of the tiles had come off, and water had warped those that remained. The watchers took him around a corner, passing more crates stacked almost to the ceiling, then stopped at a gray metal door secured by three sliding bolts. One creature slid the metal bolts into the unlocked position and opened the door, and the others hurled Jake inside. Lying facedown on the floor, he heard the door slam shut and the bolts slide back into place one at a time.

Groaning, Jake got on his hands and knees and surveyed his surroundings: a stone floor, cinder-block walls, no windows or vents. Only one of the two fluorescent lights in the ceiling worked, and only one of the two tubes in that fixture functioned, and even that flickered and hummed. A toilet with no stall sat in the far corner next to a rusty sink. The LED light on a security camera in another corner glowed red, and he wondered if anyone actually manned the corresponding monitor.

Something did pique his curiosity, and he stood to see it better: a glass cylinder, three and a half feet wide and eight feet high, with hardware on the base and top connecting it to the floor and ceiling. Jake neared the cylinder, which appeared empty. He studied the base and top, determining the cylinder was hermetically sealed. Using caution, he pressed one palm against the curved glass surface, which caused it to hum. He removed his hand and the hum stopped.

Shaking his head, he walked over to the sink and studied his reflection in the dirty, cracked mirror above it, and a whimper escaped from his lips. The flesh framing the deep gashes had begun to sag, hanging off his face. Through the gaps in his skin, he saw exposed muscles and veins. The monsters had turned *him* into a monster. He wanted to cry but had already learned tears hurt these wounds. Taking a deep breath, he let out a tremulous sigh. Then he noticed something else in the mirror: shimmering gold light.

Spinning, he saw the light came from inside the cylinder. The light glittered in midair, intensifying and fading, then intensifying again. Jake approached the cylinder, wondering if the golden light was some unique power source. Standing before it, he felt a glow on his face that felt like sunshine, and he knew he had seen it before.

Jake's body relaxed for the first time in several hours. "Hello, Abel."

The shimmering light coalesced into a humanoid shape, and Jake heard a familiar voice inside his head. "Jake . . ."

The light faded again. Then it blossomed into a brighter form, and Jake discerned human features twisted in pain. He pressed both hands against the glass, provoking the hum, and stared into the light.

Abel materialized as Jake remembered him, with taut muscles and long blond hair. As the agent of Light assumed solid form, he absorbed the remaining light into him and stood nude before Jake, his face battered and trembling. He slapped his palms against the glass, opposite Jake's. Then he collapsed with a groan, and Jake saw his body was covered with red circles, similar to those the watchers had left on Jake's neck, only the size of saucers.

Suction marks from the suckers on Avademe's tentacles, Jake thought.

Abel attempted to rise but fell back, leaning his head and shoulders against the cylinder. He wrapped his hands around his raised knees and wept.

First Cain, now Abel.

Sliding his hands down the glass for balance, Jake crouched. "What the hell happened to you?"

Abel managed a smile. "You don't look so hot yourself."

"I don't understand. You manipulate your energy to suit however you want to appear. What's with the craters?"

Abel grimaced. "They tortured me. They absorbed some of my

energy . . . and destroyed it." His lips quivered. "They ate part of my soul and scarred me forever. I can't project any form without the damage showing."

Jake took a moment to register the implication in Abel's words. Not only was Avademe capable of devouring human souls but those of heavenly beings as well, just as Sheryl had feared. As the image of Sheryl popped into his head, Jake noticed the light in Abel's blue eyes intensify.

"Why can't you get out of there? Just dematerialize and jump onto cloud nine or wherever it is you go, like I've seen you do before."

"Isn't it obvious? I'm a prisoner. Avademe has made the energy around this glass cell nullify my energy. I'm powerless."

"How is that possible? You're from *heaven*."

Abel closed his eyes. "I thought I was."

Jake blinked. "What do you mean?"

When Abel opened his eyes, they filled with resignation. "Sit down. Let's talk."

"You mean, like the truth? Big answers? Or the evasive nonsense I usually get from you people on both sides of the aisle?"

"The truth." Abel seemed to swallow. "Big answers."

"Isn't that against the rules? Aren't you afraid you'll be consigned to the Dark Realm for singing like a bird?"

Abel smiled. "What difference does it really make? Avademe intends to devour me. What more harm can there be?"

"You sound like those old bastards upstairs."

"I'll take my chances. I've inhabited the Realm of Light longer than any other soul. Perhaps I need a change. Or perhaps my time has simply come."

"Self-pity is conduct unbecoming an angel."

"Don't you see? I've thought myself eternal for centuries. Now

I know I've been living a lie. I'm destructible. There are no guarantees that once attained, the Light is permanent."

Glancing at the security camera, Jake sat cross-legged on the floor. At least the hum stopped. "Enlighten my primitive mind."

Sliding higher up against the cylinder, Abel clung to his knees as if in pain. "Where do I start? My beginning or the beginning of this universe as you know it?"

Jake shifted his weight. "This is going to be a long story, isn't it?"

"I'll try not to ramble."

"I appreciate that."

Abel gazed at the ceiling. "I remember every moment of my existence from the time my brain developed in my mother's womb. I'm pure energy now, and memory is nothing but an electrical pattern. Once I ascended to the Realm of Light, those patterns became clearer. I had a twin sister, Aclima. We were very happy and emotionally connected, even inside our mother's belly. I was born first by six minutes. Cain and his twin sister, Myrwh, were our elder siblings by less than a year. As we grew older, Cain and Myrwh teased me and Aclima, but the four of us were still close. Myrwh was jealous of Aclima's beauty and grace. Cain enjoyed tormenting us and depended on Myrwh to side with him in all matters.

"Despite his bad behavior, Mother fretted over Cain. She did not favor him over the rest of us but always seemed more concerned that he might harm himself when engaging in the same activities we did. She and Father continued to procreate, and we had many brothers and sisters. The number never remained constant for more than one year during my entire life, and until I came of age, there was never a time I saw Mother when she was not either pregnant or nursing. Fortunately for her, we four eldest children were the only twins."

"I've done my research," Jake said. "According to the Bible, Adam lived almost a century and had close to eighty sons and daughters. That's a lot of labor, for both parents."

Abel smiled at Jake as though he were a child. "I don't know how much time we have, and if you question everything I say, I'll never reach the end."

"Sorry."

"We lived in a cave at first, which Father later built a clay house around. That house continued to expand as our family grew. Eventually, the cave became Father's place of worship. He worked hard in the fields, tending to our crops and livestock, which left Mother to care for us children. On Sundays, Father rested. He spent his mornings in the cave, where he professed to communicate with God. On numerous occasions, Mother chastised him for saying this. She said, 'You may speak to Him, but He hasn't spoken to *us* in years.' You see, our parents raised us to believe in God, but we never personally encountered Him. Father told us the earliest tales of what you know as Genesis, and Mother just shook her head. The stories constantly evolved, becoming more fantastical, but always with a lesson at the end. When Father told us God had created Mother from his rib, Mother laughed, which caused Father to grow sullen and retreat to his cave.

"We never saw any other people, except for some old Neanderthals hunting in the woods, so we had no reason to discount Father's stories, especially since Mother never offered us contradictory versions. Sometimes Mother and Father fought, and she referred to a woman named 'Lilith,' and he to 'that old serpent.' When we asked them who they meant, they refused to answer, though Father would say, 'Don't let that old serpent tempt you into misbehavior.' And Mother would warn, 'Watch out for Lilith.

She'll eat you up.'

"When we were old enough, Cain and I helped Father in the fields. We did so over Mother's objections; as always, she feared Cain would come to an unimaginable harm. Cain and I bickered so often that Father had to separate us. By that time, it was clear that Cain favored Aclima, my twin, for he teased her incessantly, which only added to Myrwh's insecurity and made her more jealous of Aclima. Because the animals loved me and grew skittish or showed outright panic around Cain, Father put me in charge of the livestock and Cain in charge of the crops.

"Myrwh got her first menstrual cycle, and Mother said, 'Thank God, now I can stop bearing children and you can take over. Good luck, girl.' Father instructed Cain to marry Myrwh, but Cain objected: 'I love my other sister, Aclima. I will marry her instead.' Father said, 'Aclima is not ready to marry and bear children, but Myrwh is. You and Myrwh were our firstborn, and your mother and I always intended for you to marry. Abel and Aclima are meant for each other.' I loved Aclima dearly, and she me, so I said to my brother, 'I will marry Aclima when she's old enough, as Father has said. It's the way it ought to be, since we love each other.' Cain grew angry and said, 'You are younger than me, so you have no say in this. I am the oldest child, and I will decide who I will marry.' Father said, 'I will go to the cave and ask the Lord to decide.'

"Father spent three days and three nights in his cave. During that time, a heat wave caused Cain's crops to whither, which made him even more bitter. Myrwh was equally impossible to deal with, partly because of her period, but also because Cain and I made it clear that neither of us wanted her. She argued with Aclima, who was innocent in the entire conflict, and Mother chastised her. I tended to the animals, while Cain tried to salvage his remaining crops. When we came home at sunset, it was unbearable to be around each other. Aclima reassured me with her beautiful smile, but Cain only grew difficult when Myrwh tried to soothe him, which made *her* even more difficult. They seemed perfect for each other to everyone but Cain.

"Aclima and I were greatly relieved when Father finally emerged from the cave. Mother taunted him, 'Well? Did He speak to you?' Father said, 'No, but I see He sent us a sign: Cain's crops have failed, and Abel's animals have survived this heat, so Cain has lost the argument. He shall marry Myrwh as planned.' This made everyone happy but Cain, who stormed off and did not return that night. The next morning, I found him at the bottom of the hill where I kept our sheep. He had butchered most of the animals with a stone tool and stood covered in their blood. We fought, and he hit me over the head with the tool. I remember lying there with the sun in my eyes, seeing this wild man with long hair and bloody features raising a rock above his head. I held up my hand to deflect the next blow, and I called out for Mother and Father, but my brother crushed my skull, ending my life on earth.

"It was painful; I'll tell you that. My skull caved in, lacerating my brain, and I felt my soul escaping from my body. I saw the world around me in all directions at once, including my own bloody body. I ascended to the Realm of Light and felt no more pain. My soul merged with a field of pure, white energy . . . energy that was sentient and wise. When I tell you it was like being born again, it's no exaggeration. But I raged at what Cain had done to me and cried out for vengeance. I also cried for Aclima. The Creator welcomed me into His kingdom. Although He did not speak to me directly, I felt His presence, and I knew that Father's stories were at least partially true, in the only way that his primitive mind had been able to interpret the cosmos. And as the Realm of Light replaced my anger and loss, I became part of it.

"God created this universe and everything in it, including the formation of the planets and the evolution of man. Father was the first Cro-Magnon man, but Mother was not the first woman; Lilith was, and she gave birth to my father's first daughter, Eve, my mother. Father tried to subjugate Lilith to his will, but Lilith demanded equality in all things and mocked Father when he demanded her obedience. So he drove her off, and when Eve was old enough, Father married her. It was this act that displeased the Creator and caused Him to stop communicating with Father. Lilith returned to the land one day, and when she discovered that Father had married their daughter, she cursed Eve: 'Your firstborn son will suffer for your sin.' When Father ordered Lilith to leave again, Lilith laughed and kissed him, causing Eve to become jealous and flee.

"Mother came across a man in the woods, the first man she had ever seen besides Father. The man was charming and handsome and wiped away Mother's tears and soothed her sorrow. He explained that he knew Lilith and that Lilith belonged with Father, and he seduced her. They made love in the foliage, and when they were finished, the man transformed into a giant serpent and Mother screamed. Lilith seduced Father as well, and when they were finished fornicating, she transformed into a raven and flew away. Lilith had met the serpent during her long absence and had made a pact with him and had become his unholy vassal. The serpent was the master of the Dark Realm, and Lilith became the mother of all black magic. Father and Lilith evolved from two separate bloodlines, and when Father procreated with his own daughter, the resulting generations had increasingly shorter life spans until the gene pool had sufficiently thinned out.

"In the Realm of Light, I learned to observe happenings on earth. Cain buried my body in the ground, then cleaned himself up and returned home. When I failed to return the next day, Aclima went looking for me and discovered the butchered flock. Father confronted Cain, who denied having anything to do with my disappearance or the animals' slaughter. Mother joined the interrogation, and eventually Cain broke down into tears and confessed. Father drove him off, as he had driven off Lilith, which upset both Mother and Myrwh. Mother had always dreaded that something terrible would befall Cain because of Lilith's curse, but his terrible fate turned out to be enduring banishment for slaying me and for committing his soul to the Dark Realm. Father told Myrwh, 'You shall marry your brother Seth, for he is next oldest.'

"Father was the first man, but he was not the *only* man. The Creator caused the evolution of men and women on all of the continents, spread out to avoid conflict. Eventually, after years of wandering, Cain encountered other people, and he settled down and married. In fact, he married our half sister, born by Lilith with Father's seed. When Cain died, after siring sons and daughters of his own, his soul descended to the Dark Realm, where the serpent appointed him its champion and emissary.

"As I once explained to you, the Realm of Light and the Dark Realm are polar opposites, drawn to each other and repelled like magnets at the same time. We agents of Light are content to leave the Dark Agents alone, but the Dark wants nothing more than to see us all destroyed. We must constantly be on guard, which is why we continue to monitor the activities of mankind."

Jake arranged the components of Abel's story in his mind. "I once asked you if God existed . . ."

"And I told you I did not know. What I should have said was,

'I don't know if He *still* exists.' For a time, every soul that ascended to the Realm of Light experienced His glory and light. Then, for reasons none of us understands, He decided to walk on earth among his creations, *as one of them*. During that brief period, we still sensed His power. Then He allowed Himself to be executed by men, and we lost connection to Him. He simply ceased to exist in our world—and in yours."

"I've never bought the Bible as being anything more than a collection of morality tales written by different authors, but in the New Testament, Jesus was resurrected three days after His murder."

"We have our religious beliefs as well—our different theories and fantasies about what happened to our Creator. But they're all speculation. Many of us believe He came from a dimension more evolved than our own to which He ultimately returned. We're not angels or cherubs. Prior to His crucifixion, we observed the beings that humans have described as angels, and we sensed His presence in them but were unable to interact with them. We believe that they are of a higher order, that one day we will ascend again, this time to a greater plane, where we shall be rejoined with Him, and that we inhabit the Sphere only until we attain perfection."

Jake massaged his right temple. Both of them ached, but he knew better than to touch the left side of his head. "Okay . . ."

"After He failed to return to our Sphere, the first blind spot formed on earth. We could not see anything that transpired within it and believed this to be an aftereffect of His disappearance, a weakening of our Sphere's combined energy. Then human souls started vanishing, never to be sensed again. At first, the souls belonged to American Indians, then European explorers, German settlers, and British soldiers. All of them disappeared near the same body of water."

"Lake Erie," Jake said.

"In 1929, after your stock market crash, the disappearances stopped for one decade. In 1939, they resumed near a second blind spot in Brooklyn, New York."

Jake looked at the ceiling and walls.

"During the decades that followed, more blind spots formed in the United States. The radiance of each one extends for miles and contains a pulse that repels us and the Dark Agents. We're dealing with an unknown quantity that threatens the Light and the Dark. Over half a million souls have vanished, which has had a dramatic impact on the intensity of both Realms. As Sheryl informed you, we call this predator the Destroyer of Souls."

Jake bristled at the mention of Sheryl's name.

"I'm sorry," Abel said. "You can never understand the bonds that form when a soul ascends to the Sphere."

"Let's stick to business."

Abel nodded. "As the chief of martyred souls and the oldest agent of Light, I took it upon myself to investigate the disappearances. The mystery became an obsession with me, but I came no closer to solving it. The blind spots multiplied around the globe. Then Nicholas Tower created a blind spot of his own, as others have done, further complicating my efforts."

"The Tower."

"I knew it was Old Nick and his Tower because he *only* protected that building. The souls you freed were critical to the war between the Light and the Dark because so many other souls had already ceased to exist before them. After Tower's death, I resumed my investigation. I narrowed the blind spots down to a number of locations around New York."

"This warehouse, Reichard's estate, the Dream Castle . . ."

"I remained just outside the perimeter of this area. I guess you could say I was on stakeout. Then one day, the blind spot diminished enough for me to enter it. Even though I sensed a trap, I had to press on."

"I know the feeling."

"Too much was at stake to pass up the opportunity. I entered the shipyard, located this building, and discovered Avademe. That confrontation was the single most horrifying experience of my existence."

"Avademe's one ugly mother."

Staring at Jake, Abel raised his eyebrows. Then he burst into laughter, which in turn caused him to wince.

"Was it something I said?"

"Oh yes. Yes, it was. I spent centuries investigating Avademe, and you practically solved the mystery with an offhand remark."

"I did?" Jake furrowed his eyebrows, which sent a spasm of pain through his face.

Abel pressed one hand against the cylinder, level with Jake's face. He wiped the glass with his palm, leaving behind a trail of golden light that spelled out *Avademe* as a child would write with his fingers in condensation left on a car window. "Avademe is an anagram."

Narrowing his eye at the glowing word, Jake rearranged the letters in his mind. *Oh, my God.*

He swallowed. "Adam. Eve. Adam and Eve."

"My parents."

Jake pictured the enormous brain that formed the octopus's cone, which appeared to be two giant brains attached to each other, and the monster's four eyes. *"Avadiim* was an Indian word . . ."

"No, Avadiim was an Indian *pronunciation* of an anagram based on an English *translation* of the Hebrew Old Testament."

"Lake Erie is a long way from Eden."

"Father and Mother damned their souls by becoming lovers. They damned them further by committing the sexual acts they performed with Lilith and the serpent. There were other infractions and atrocities throughout their lifetime, including suicide, and more still when their souls reached the Dark Realm."

"How do you know what happened in the Dark Realm?"

"They told me after they took me prisoner. We spoke at length. They enjoy tormenting me. Because they had lived such long lives, they achieved high status in the Realm. But even there, they could not stay out of trouble. Angry that they had not reached the Realm of Light, they plotted to escape the Dark Realm. They failed spectacularly, and the serpent stripped them of their rank. So they schemed to overthrow the serpent, much as the Bible claims that Satan schemed to overthrow God in heaven. Similarly, the serpent banished my parents from the Realm. He sentenced them to serve out eternity here on earth and restored them to human form. As a joke, he fused their hips together and abandoned them at the northernmost part of Canada, and he cursed them with immortality so their suffering would know no end. Reduced to freaks, they attempted to commit suicide many times during their southward trek, but nothing worked. Their efforts resulted in broken bones, which healed into obscene shapes; their flesh cracked and became infected; their clothing grafted onto their running sores.

"By the time they reached Lake Erie, they resembled a hideous creature more than two broken human beings. At the cliffs overlooking Lake Erie, they hurled themselves into the water. The fall smashed their bones but did not kill them. They sank deep into the water, which did not drown them. And they mutated into a monstrous creature that inhabited the lake. Their limbs became tentacles and their brains became one. They learned to manipulate the curse that the serpent had placed on them, subverting its power for their own purposes. They formed the first blind spot to shelter themselves from the serpent's eye.

"Slowly, they crossed Erie. Upon their arrival on the shore of Western New York, they fed on the Seneca and the Iroquois Indians. Absorbing the human souls, they became even more powerful. When the Europeans arrived, my parents took great delight in learning about the Bible, which, as you say, was written and rewritten by many men. They took the name Avademe as a joke and conveyed it to a tribe of Senecas who worshipped and fed them.

"Over the years, they made several humans their liaisons. They dreamed of turning the earth into their own realm, and as technology advanced, they saw their opportunity. They forged an alliance with Stephen Reichard, Karlin's grandfather. They instructed him to design and construct this building and arranged for him to transport them. During their ten years of inactivity, they created the Order of Avademe with Stephen and laid the foundation for their plans. They involved the United States in World War II and salvaged the nation's economy. Stephen and the first order reaped the benefits of the war, establishing the pattern the order would follow for the next century. Stephen's son, Rudolph, succeeded him as spokesperson for the order, and Karlin succeeded him. Because of the importance of this facility, a Reichard has always led the order."

"Those creatures that brought me in here. The watchers . . ."

"They are my brothers and sisters, though they are clearly of a different species. They are mutant offspring. Though they live, they lack souls."

Jake's fingers and toes tingled. "Can't you do anything to stop this?"

Abel gestured at the cylinder. "Does it look like I can?"

Leaning on the cylinder, Jake ignored the hum and got to his feet. He dug his thumb and forefinger into the eye socket on the injured side of his face and plucked out his glass eye. "Then I guess we'd better call in reinforcements."

He threw the glass eye on the floor, shattering it.

"Cain!"

CHAPTER
24

The fragments of the shattered glass eye glowed like drops of lava on the floor. As smoke rose from the tiles, the fragments vibrated, then wiggled, then slid. They raced across the floor toward each other, resembling pollywogs and fireflies at the same time. When they met, a single spark ignited a fiery explosion. Jake shielded his eyes, and a jagged fissure, like a horizontal lightning bolt, zigzagged in the air. Glowing black liquid spewed out of the fissure, struck the floor, then poured upward, defying gravity, and formed a dense statue.

When Cain had fully formed and electricity crackled around his transparent bones and organs, the fissure closed behind him.

The demon's lungs seemed to fill with oxygen, enabling the flames inside his powerful body to burn. He took in the room, the pinpricks of light in his eye sockets flashing at the sight of Abel.

"*Qayin*," Abel said as he rose inside the cylinder.

Cain strode past Jake, who felt a blast of heat in the demon's wake, and stood before the cylinder. "*HEVEL*."

"How—?"

"THE DARK REALM IS BLIND TO THIS SHIPYARD, SO I GAVE THIS TALKING INSECT A PIECE OF MY HEART TO CARRY."

"I think this talking insect did pretty well," Jake said. "Better than either of you and with none of your powers."

Abel flattened both hands against the glass. "Mother and Father—"

"I HEARD EVERYTHING. IN THE DARK, WE ALWAYS KNEW MOTHER-FATHER WERE BEHIND THE BLIND SPOTS AND THE MISSING SOULS. MY MASTER PROVIDED THEM WITH THE POWER THAT ENABLED THEM TO SURVIVE, AND THEY TURNED THAT POWER AGAINST HIM. WE REALIZED TOO LATE HOW DANGEROUS THEY HAD BECOME."

"We have to stop them."

"*I* HAVE TO STOP THEM."

"You can't do it alone. They can destroy your soul just as easily as they can mine."

Cain turned to Jake, who took an instinctive step backwards. "I HAVE HIM TO HELP ME."

Jake grunted. "I don't remember volunteering for this particular mission. You said to locate Abel and you would handle everything else."

"He deceived you," Abel said. "That's what he does. I keep telling you not to trust him."

"I don't trust him."

"But you will help me."

"I want those old fuckers to pay for what they did to Abby, Marla, and Bianca. For what they did to *me*. Especially Madigan. Promise you'll leave him to me."

"If that's what it takes."

"You still need me," Abel said.

Cain looked him over. "What use could you possibly be? You're even weaker than usual."

"I can handle myself and anything else that comes along. Mother-Father must be punished. That will take both of us."

Cain emitted a booming sound, like thunder. It took Jake a moment to recognize the sound as howling laughter. "How will *you* punish them? With the milk of kindness?"

Abel eyed his brother. "They must be destroyed. No mercy can be shown."

"I say we let him come," Jake said.

Cain aimed a burning finger in Jake's direction. "You have no say in this."

Jake raised his hands. "Right, whatever you say."

Returning his gaze to Abel, Cain rubbed his chin. "I suppose you *could* help this insect."

"You know damned well I can do more than him," Abel said.

Cain opened and closed his hands into fists. "All right. I've waited centuries for this."

"As have I."

Cain wound up his arm and delivered a powerful blow to the cylinder that shattered it. A deafening alarm rang out before the first shard of glass struck the floor.

Abel collapsed in a heap, and Jake helped him to his feet. As soon as he stepped free of the base and top that had sealed the cylinder, Abel clenched his fists, and the clothing he had worn once before—cowboy boots, jeans, a button-down shirt, and a Western duster—materialized on him.

Cain doesn't share your modesty, Jake thought.

Cain held out one hand. Storms raged within his fingers. "HEAVEN AND HELL—TOGETHER AGAIN."

Abel grasped the hand. "For the first and only time."

Their bodies rippled, and Jake felt himself being pushed back by an invisible force.

"This is touching," he said over the alarm. "I love family reunions. Now let's take it to the next level, since they already know we're coming."

Turning his back on Abel, Cain stormed straight for the steel door and smashed it off its hinges. The door crashed against the opposite cinder-block wall and fell to the floor.

"Let's go," Abel said to Jake, and they hurried after Cain.

✳

In the corridor, Jake and Abel watched Cain take long strides away from them.

"He knows exactly where he's going," Abel said.

"Because he saw everything through my head," Jake said.

Four watchers appeared around the corner ahead and shrieked at the same time. In this lower basement, they wore no robes and looked even less human.

Cain stood and flexed his arms, giving Jake a perfect view of his glowing ass. "NICE OF YOU TO GREET US, BRETHREN."

The watchers charged at Cain, who met them head-on. He

moved with blinding speed, leaving trails of fiery light in his wake. His knuckles exploded a watcher's head in a shower that painted cinder blocks green and black. Swinging his arm sideways, the flat of his fist pulverized another head into a mess that resembled moss and seaweed.

Without hesitation, the other two watchers leapt upon him. One attacked him with its feelers: the ends opened into mouths with tiny teeth that fastened onto Cain's left collar. The demon roared in pain, and that roar metamorphosed into laughter. The watcher squealed, its feelers releasing their grip. Black blood poured from the mouths, then smoke. The feelers danced in the air, flames rupturing their sides. The watcher clawed at its wiggling appendages, then unleashed a wail as its reptilian hands melted like butter. It fell to the floor and writhed, smoke pouring out of the suckers on its stumpy arms.

Cain jerked the remaining watcher off the floor. He buried his face in its feelers and pivoted so Jake and Abel saw his grinning face emerge through the back of the creature's melted head. The smoking husk joined the others on the floor.

I'm glad we're on the same side, Jake thought.

Then he heard the scrabble of claws on the floor behind him and turned to see four more watchers closing in on him and Abel. Two of the creatures pounced on Abel, taking him down to the floor. They seized his limbs, the suckers on their hands clinging to his clothing. But Abel's clothing was no different than his flesh, made up of the exact same energy, and the agent of Light screamed.

Jake stood still as the other two watchers came for him, then turned sideways and jumped between them. The creatures ran straight into Cain. Jake did not need to see what Cain did to them. He heard their screams as he ran down the hall where the second group of watchers had come from. His shoes slapped the cement floor, and when he reached the wall, where a recessed compartment contained a fire hose and extinguisher, he lifted a long-handled ax from metal prongs. He raced back the way he had come, both hands clutching the ax's handle.

Cain had caught two more watchers by their heads, smoke billowing from between their feelers. He lifted them off the floor, spread his arms wide, and slammed their heads together, smashing them into mush. Jake had seen him do the exact same thing to Laddock and Birch, two security guards under his supervision at the Tower.

Abel thrashed around on the floor, his head weaving from side to side to avoid the feelers of the watchers assaulting him.

Jake raised the ax high in the air and buried its stout blade in one watcher's head. The creature shook in a violent spasm. Unable to wrest the ax free, Jake waited for the watcher's body to drop, then set one foot on its back and gave the handle a mighty pull. The blade came free with a ripping sound.

Abel managed to get on top of the remaining watcher and pounded it with his fists, his face a mask of wild fury. He punched the center of the creature's head over and over until the feelers stopped moving and green slime coated his knuckles. Then he rose, gasping.

Cain grinned at his brother. "IT FEELS GOOD, DOESN'T IT?" Abel looked Jake in the eye. "Yes."

Jake gestured at the opposite end of the corridor. "Let's move." *Best to let Cain lead the way.*

They hurried down the corridor, which reeked of burning fish. As they rounded the corner, a small army of watchers charged in their direction.

There should be fourteen of them left.

Cain threw himself into the nearest watchers, tackling them. Others piled on top of him. Smoke rose from the bottom of the pile.

Jake passed the demon, closely followed by Abel, and felt heat radiating from the mass of wiggling arms and legs. A watcher shrieked behind him, and before he could react, a sword appeared in Abel's hands, golden flames dancing along its gleaming blade. Jake almost dropped his ax in surprise. Abel buried the sword in the creature's head, the impact driving it to its knees. Abel pulled the sword free of its mushy target just as two more watchers fell on him and Jake. Their tongues lashed out, and Abel halved them with a single parry. The creatures screamed, venom streaming from their damaged organs. Jake buried his ax in the head of one creature, and Abel did the same with his sword in the other.

Setting his ax down, Jake grabbed a fire hose out of another recessed compartment and twisted its pressure valve. The high-pressure jet of water knocked back two watchers closing in on him, and Abel proceeded to dismember them with brutal efficiency, flames trailing in his wake.

Jake continued to drive watchers back with the powerful spray, and Abel charged the remaining creatures, swinging his burning sword as water ricocheting off the watchers doused him. He struck one at knee level, then another in the neck. As the first watcher collapsed on its hobbled leg, Abel swung the sword overhead and chopped off the creature's feelers, which spewed green fluid. The creature's wail sounded almost human. The other watcher fell against him, spraying slime from the gaping wound in its neck. Abel shoved the creature to the floor, then plunged the sword deep into its wound, separating its head from its shoulders.

Another watcher leapt at Abel, but Jake forced it back with the jet spray. Still another watcher came at Abel, who slammed the sword's pommel into the thing's face, driving it against a wall. Then he swung the sword into the head of a watcher Jake had pinned to the wall with the water. As the creature sank to its knees and pitched forward, Abel swung the sword like a baseball bat, decapitating the other watcher.

Jake felt movement above his left knee and looked down to see the feelers of a wounded watcher crawling up his leg like eight snakes. The feelers opened their jaws, which snapped at his groin. Jake aimed the hose at the center of the thing's head, and the water blasted the watcher's feelers from its face. The force of the water striking at close range also slammed Jake against the wall. He managed to drive the nozzle closer to the creature's head, which flattened out and gushed in several directions at once.

When the muscles in Jake's arms gave out, he dropped the hose on the floor, allowing the water to strike the wall near Abel, who stood with his sword raised, all of his foes vanquished. With his chest rising and falling, Jake realized they had wiped out the watchers: genocide.

Cain rose from the scorched remains of several of the creatures, and the unmanned fire hose blasted fish guts across the floor. Cain also grasped a sword in one hand. The flames on his black blade crackled deep red.

"I don't suppose I can have one of those?" Jake said.

Cain and Abel shook their heads in unison.

Jake returned to the recessed case and fumbled with the valve, shutting off the pressure. The corridor stank like the Fulton Street Fish Market in Chinatown.

We make a pretty good team, he thought as he retrieved his ax. It felt good to have backup again. "Let's go get the generals."

They walked side by side along the corridor. The flaming

swords distracted Jake, but he certainly did not object to them. At least he had the ax. The trio reached the stacked crates. Jake took one down and split its nailed lid open with his ax, which he then tossed aside. Pulling the broken wood apart, he removed the packing materials and revealed a score of shiny black metal machine guns.

"*Now* I get one." He snatched one of the high-tech weapons: compact, with a thick body, unlike any weapon he'd seen before. Rummaging through the crate, he found a thick clip, which he slapped into place ahead of the gun's trigger. Then he examined the device beneath the weapon's barrel.

"Bullets will do no good against Mother-Father," Abel said.

Moving the guns in the crate aside, Jake took out what appeared to be a hand grenade with a hole bored through its center. He slid the grenade over the secondary barrel and snapped it into place. Then he flipped off the safety switch and switched on the laser sight. "You were saying?"

"You'd need an army equipped with those to do any good."

"We'll see."

Glancing at Cain, Jake led the way up the stairs. On the mid-level landing, they stopped at the viewing window and glimpsed a single tentacle uncurling, its suckers opening and closing in a nervous pattern.

"Let's rock this joint."

The three of them emerged from the stairwell onto the dock. Avademe's great cone remained above the water's surface, its eyes aimed in their direction. The seven cabal members stood facing

Cain, Abel, and Jake, who marched forward with the machine gun in his hands.

Portions of Avademe's tentacles broke the water's surface and sank from view again, like the humps of whales. They continued doing this as the monster watched its enemies approach. For the first time since Jake had met them, the cabal members looked frightened. Weiskopf still held his Glock.

"I suggest you stop right there," Reichard said, his attention drawn to Cain.

Jake slowed to a stop and Abel did the same. Cain strode past them, but the sight of Avademe brought him to a standstill. The fires in his body traveled along his muscles at a faster rate. He glanced over his shoulder at Jake and Abel, steam hissing from his body, then faced the cabal members.

Avademe's body rose, undulated, and sank halfway into the water. One set of eyes stared at Abel, the other at Cain. The cabal members gaped at Jake's comrades and their flaming swords.

"You've proven to be even more troublesome than I'd feared," Reichard said to Jake. "Are all the children dead?"

Avademe's four eyes settled on Jake, who felt vulnerable despite his backup.

"Very," Jake said.

Reichard looked at his god for guidance, then turned to Jake. "I'm afraid that's not going to—" His body turned rigid, his eyes widening. Avademe's tentacle impaled the old man's skull and lifted him off the dock, twenty feet in the air.

The six remaining cabal members gawked as their nominal leader turned dead cold. Jake's Glock shook in Weiskopf's trembling hand.

"You're in charge now," Avademe said to Weiskopf through Reichard's mouth. "Karlin bungled things badly. The children were his primary responsibility. Settle this."

Weiskopf's wrinkled face contorted with newfound power. "Drop your weapons," he said, but he aimed the Glock only at Jake.

Glancing at Cain and Abel, Jake hesitated. Their swords did not waver. He looked at the barrel of his own gun. "My Glock won't do any good against these guys."

"Maybe not, but it will do a number on you. Do you see the irony?"

Jake raised the machine gun's stock to his shoulder, training the laser sight on Weiskopf's forehead. "You'll kill me anyway."

He triggered a burst from the gun and through its muzzle flash saw Weiskopf's head explode in a shower of gore that spattered the other cabal members, who flinched. The headless body dropped the Glock and fell into the water with an unceremonious splash.

Cain turned to Jake. "I *LIKE* THAT!"

"You'll like this even more." Jake cocked the gun's grenade launcher.

"Stop him!" Avademe said through the mouth of its flesh puppet.

The five remaining cabal members stared at Jake.

"Bring it on," Jake said, gesturing at them with the gun.

Instead, all but Madigan ran for the door behind Jake. In a flurry of motion, four enormous tentacles rocketed from the water, extending straight out from Avademe. Jake dropped to the dock, and a tentacle just missed decapitating him. Flat on the ground, he saw Cain and Abel had dropped as well.

Hearing screams behind him, Jake ran in a half crouch across the dock and scooped up his fallen Glock, which he shoved into his waistband. The tentacles dragged Bradley, Browning, Coffer, and Schaltter screaming across the dock. The old men clawed at the floor as the appendages pulled them into the water and out of sight, the water churning in their wake.

His tattered face burning with rage, Jake charged at Madigan, whose eyes and mouth opened wide. He had almost reached his target when something snared his feet and he slammed facedown on the dock. As he felt himself being dragged, he glimpsed Madigan, smiling now. He managed to roll over onto his back as Avademe pulled him toward the dock's edge. "Abel! Cain!"

Avademe raised four of its tentacles into the air, suspending its four latest victims level with Reichard's corpse. None of the cabal members moved except for their fluttering eyelids, which revealed the whites of their upturned eyes.

Jake clawed at the dock with the fingers of his left hand, the machine gun still gripped in his right hand. His ass slid off the dock's edge, and just as he expected his body to smack the water, the tentacle jerked him upside down into the air, dangling him like a doll, and turned him around. He saw Cain and Abel standing side by side on the dock, Madigan rooted closer to the edge. Avademe's tentacles curled and uncurled, the five corpses and Jake rising and falling.

"You're now the most powerful man in the world," Avademe said to Madigan in five different voices. "Do not fail us as these fools did."

Madigan nodded so fast Jake thought his neck would snap. "I swear it. I *swear* it!"

"You'll lead a new order," Avademe said, its voices echoing each other. "We will provide you with the names of the next generation."

Jake struggled in Avademe's grip. It wasn't fair for Madigan to be rewarded for killing Marla.

The tentacle turned him right side up and lowered him to face Avademe's four eyes. "Your death would have been swift had you provided us with Afterlife. After killing all our children, that is impossible."

Jake gripped the machine gun in both hands, ready to fire.

Avademe rocked back, angling its cone away from him even as it raised the two slits on its bottom above the water's surface. The slits opened and closed, like giant gills.

Abel stepped forward. "The power you offer mankind is short-lived, Mother-Father."

Cain seized Madigan, who screamed. "*Very* short-lived."

Cain flattened his palms against the sides of Madigan's head. A moment later, his hands pressed together in prayer, dripping the man's brains and fragments of his crushed skull. An eyeball dangled on its stem from one of his thumbs. The headless body fell and a dark soul rose. Cain's body shuddered as it absorbed the darkness.

Yes! Although Jake had wanted to kill Madigan himself and Cain had reneged on his promise to allow him to do so, at least the man was dead and had left a disgusting corpse.

Avademe spoke through two of its puppets, Reichard and Schlatter: "*Qayin, Hevel*, why must you disappoint us so? Leave this plane and never return. Your mother and I would rather be childless than suffer your betrayal."

Abel held his sword at the ready. "Leave this world to your brand of evil, Father? You know that's impossible."

"You've robbed us of many souls. What parents steal food from the mouths of their children?"

Avademe spoke through the other three corpse puppets. "Your father is right. I regret ever giving birth to you miserable little monsters."

"You have your kingdoms," Avademe said through Reichard and Schlatter. "Leave us to ours. 'Honor thy mother and thy father.'"

"I serve a greater master than either of you can ever hope to be," Abel said.

"Your invincibility originated in the Dark Realm.

Now that I'm in your presence at last, I reclaim that power for my master."

Reichard screamed in rage. So did Schlatter. And Bradley. One by one, each corpse puppet joined the chorus.

Jake aimed the gun between Avademe's eyes, then raised it to the center of the cone, the laser sight tracing the crevice that separated the two halves of the giant brain. He squeezed the trigger. Nothing happened.

Avademe's body shook, and the corpse puppets burst into laughter. As Jake examined the controls on the weapon, the tentacle squeezed him, cutting off his oxygen and pressing his rib cage to the point of rupture. Pressure built up in his head until he no longer heard the laughter.

Flipping a safety switch he had missed, he aimed the gun again and squeezed its trigger. This time he heard a piercing sound, like a cannonball fired through a giant silencer, and a trail of concentrated smoke streaked toward the cone. A moment later, a concussion of hot, wet air blasted him, followed by a downpour of sticky flesh. The last thing he saw before the tentacle released him was an enormous fissure forming in the cone, splitting it almost in half.

Then Jake plunged into the cold, dark water. Chunks of flesh the size of traffic cones sank beside him, followed by the puppets. A tentacle jerked through the water like a shark, just missing him. He saw the old men staring facedown at him with unblinking eyes as he swam to the surface; he felt the water passing between his torn flesh and exposed muscles.

The tentacles moved about, stirring great waves, the monster far from dead. One tentacle crashed down on the surface beside him, like a tree trunk falling into a river, and the impact slammed him against the dock.

Clawing at the side, Jake pulled himself up and swung one leg over, his soaking wet clothes weighing him down. He had lost the machine gun and had only his Glock for self-defense. The tentacles flopped on the dock with tremendous noise, and he jumped to avoid them.

Where the hell were Cain and Abel? Turning, he saw the brothers racing across the slick, pale surface of Avademe's upturned bottom side. With their swords raised, they stopped at the slits and hacked their way inside the orifices, fluid gushing over them. Within seconds, they vanished into the membrane.

Avademe convulsed and roared. One tentacle whipped along the dock at Jake, who dove over it and rolled across the floor. The fissure that had formed in Avademe's cone finally split all the way open, and the monster used its tentacles to tear its body in two, each half still controlling four tentacles. One half of the monster sank beneath the surface, creating a whirlpool, and the other half hauled itself onto the dock and fell over on its side. One of its two eyes had ruptured and filled with blood, but the other one zeroed in on Jake, who stepped back. The thing dragged itself forward, bearing down on him. Even separated from his better half, Adam loomed large and threatening.

A tentacle swept Jake's feet out from under him, and he crashed to the dock. Another climbed into the air, high enough to touch the ceiling, and came crashing down.

Jake rolled to one side, and water from the impact splashed him. He struggled to his feet and a third tentacle snared him, pinning his arms to his sides so tight he could not wrest his Glock free. The tentacle coiled around him, pulling him close to the monster's remaining eye. Jake saw unbridled hatred in the massive orb. In the water, a single tentacle of Eve's rose from the surface and thrashed around. Then it stiffened and sank from view. Jake knew the two halves of Avademe were dying, and Adam was determined to snuff him out first.

As long as he doesn't turn me into one of those puppets, he thought.

The tentacle squeezed him tighter, crushing his helpless body.

Closing his eye, he accepted his fate and thought of the one person who could bring him peace.

Sheryl.

His chest burned with fire, then turned numb, and a tingling sensation gave way to a soothing warmth. He felt his soul departing his body.

No, not my soul . . .

Opening his eye, he saw golden energy in the air beside him solidify into a human figure.

Sheryl!

Like Abel, she brandished a sword burning with golden flames. Avademe's eye bulged in its socket, and Jake recognized fear in the dying god. Sheryl raised her sword in both hands and brought it down in a clean arc that chopped into the tentacle, separating the half that held Jake from the half attached to the body.

A shriek emitted from somewhere inside Adam, and Jake fell back. Loosening the tentacle from around his waist, he got to his knees and saw Sheryl drive her sword straight into Adam's remaining pupil. Opaque yellow fluid gushed out of the wound, drenching her. The monster turned spastic, its three remaining tentacles slapping the dock. Then they quivered and stilled.

Sucking in his breath, Jake stood. Beyond Adam's immense corpse, the water grew calm. A black shape rose from Adam's shell. For a moment, it resembled a man. Then it compacted on itself, forming a dark sphere, and faded.

"You saved my life again," Jake said.

Sheryl's sword glowed bright with golden energy and melted into her arm.

"I used the portion of my soul that I left inside you like a homing beacon." She spread her hands apart. "I feel whole again."

Abel materialized beside her, without his sword. Before he could say anything, she embraced him. For an instant, their bodies melded together, as surely as Adam and Eve's had. Jake knew there was no denying they belonged to each other now.

Cain materialized as well, a triumphant smile on his skull-like features, and Abel and Sheryl separated. The fire within him burned brighter and hotter than ever. He glanced at the dead monster on the dock. "I KILLED MOTHER AND RETURNED BOTH THEIR SOULS TO THE DARK REALM." He faced Jake. "A PITY I COULD NOT CLAIM THE SOULS OF THE ENTIRE CABAL, BUT AT LEAST I GOT MADIGAN'S."

"Make him suffer."

"HE ALREADY IS."

Jake thought of Marla. "What about the souls Avademe devoured?"

"They're gone," Abel said. "Mother-Father destroyed them. And a part of me."

Sheryl grasped Abel's hand.

Cain set his hands on his father's corpse. Jake thought the demon was about to show remorse. Instead, Cain sank his fingers into the dead flesh. The entire carcass vibrated, then disappeared.

Jake looked for the severed tentacle, but it had vanished as well. He walked to the edge of the dock and looked down at the water. Five of the six corpses floating facedown had holes in the back of their heads through which crushed brains were visible. The sixth corpse had no head.

"If you're getting rid of the evidence, I'd like to see what you intend to do with these."

"I CANNOT REMOVE THOSE BODIES, BUT THE WATCHERS ARE GONE."

"The watchers never should have existed on this earth," Abel said. "But these men . . ."

Jake grunted. "The authorities will have their hands full. As long as I don't get blamed."

"You won't." Abel held out a plastic bag containing Jake's wallet, cell phone, and keys. "Weiskopf had these as well as your gun. My brother neglected to retrieve them for you."

Jake eyed Cain, who glared at Abel. "GOODY TWO-SHOES."

Abel extended one hand. "We did it, Brother."

Cain looked at the hand, then shook it. "YES, WE DID. THOUGH YOU DESERVE LITTLE OF THE CREDIT. THIS TALKING INSECT DID AS MUCH AS YOU."

"You'll never change."

"YOU'RE RIGHT."

Cain squeezed Abel's hand, crushing it. Abel cried out, going down on his knees. Cain seized his brother by the throat, straddled him, and smashed his head on the floor.

Sheryl stepped forward with alarm on her face. "Stop it!"

Abel grabbed Cain's wrists, but Cain still pounded his brother's head on the floor repeatedly.

Here we go again, Jake thought.

Abel's eyes rolled up in their sockets, and the back of his head caved in. Cain laughed, a sound like a garbage compactor in action. Abel's hands fell away, but Cain continued to smash the broken head on the floor. Then they both disappeared.

Jake turned to Sheryl, but she had vanished as well.

322

Shit, he thought.

Drawing his breath, he sighed and looked around. The entire dock glistened with water. No sign of Avademe remained. Whatever blood Weiskopf had spilled had washed away. The bodies floated on the water, and Jake spotted at least one ring glinting in the light.

CHAPTER
25

Jake turned the Maxima around and drove it alongside the truck that had transported him to the building. The clock on the car radio flashed 3:17 at him. Leaving his door open, he drew his Glock and walked over to the metal gate. A control box hung off to one side, supported by an electrical coil. Two buttons were set in the box: one red and the other black. He thumbed the red button, and as the gate rumbled open, he ran back to the car and got in. His body ached all over, which at least defused the pain in his face.

Rain pelted the shipyard. Recalling the armed guards he had seen patrolling the grounds during the daytime, he prepared himself for another fight. When the gate had risen halfway, he pulled out. Floodlights illuminated the sheets of rain that struck the buildings and driveways, and he saw city lights far in the distance beyond the fence. Proceeding at a slow pace, he approached the security booth at the front gate. The guard watched him approach, then threw whatever switch opened the gate.

He must have been on duty when they brought the car in.

Waving to the guard without looking at him, so as to conceal his wounds, Jake drove through the gate and gunned the engine.

Half an hour later, he parked outside his building and knocked on Laurel's parlor door.

When Laurel opened her door, her eyes heavy with sleep, she gasped. "What the hell happened to your *face?*"

Jake moved past her and she locked the door. "It's a long story." He gave her a full view of the damage. "Can you do anything about it?"

Laurel stepped closer, and Jake disliked the way the blood drained from her face. "No. It's too late for that, and the wounds look infected. You stink, too. Go upstairs and take a shower, then come back and I'll see what I can do."

Jake didn't argue. Upstairs, he gazed at his reflection in his bathroom mirror. Half of his face resembled a monster from an old horror movie, like *Mr. Sardonicus* or *I Was a Teenage Frankenstein.*

Moving into his office, he glanced at the open safe door and the silver metal particles all over the floor. He had done the right thing leaving Afterlife with Laurel; if Reichard's men had gotten their hands on the program, Avademe would have devoured him on sight.

He showered, the hot water and steam stinging the wounds on his face, arms, and back and causing him to flinch. After changing into dry clothes and inserting his glass eye, he went downstairs, where Laurel had set up disinfectant and bandages on the round table.

"Sit down and tip your head back," Laurel said. "This is going to hurt a lot."

Jake sat back and looked at the ceiling. Laurel raised the bottle above his head and tipped it. He saw the clear disinfectant pouring down toward him and closed his eyelids. Fire consumed his face, and he dug his fingers into the chair's armrests and bared his clenched teeth at her. Still she continued to pour the disinfectant on his wounds, and he jerked his shoulders from side to side. Finally he screamed and she stopped. He opened his eyelids, and through the tears he saw Laurel waving a roll of gauze.

"This should hold you together long enough for you to see that shady doctor of yours."

Lawrence Metivier treated special clients for cash and left no paper trail.

She positioned a wide gauze strip over one of the lacerations. "I take it you've saved the world and punished the wicked, or you wouldn't be here."

Jake sighed. "I guess so." *For now.*

Three days later, Martin sat feeding Edgar in Jake's office. Jake's chest swelled with emotion at the sight of father and son reunited in such a strange manner. He and Martin had shot some baskets, then came to the office dripping sweat.

"He likes me," Martin said.

"He sure does," Jake said.

"What's his name?"

Jake hesitated. He couldn't tell Martin that the raven on his desk shared a name with his father. "Just call him buddy."

Martin stroked Edgar's back. "Good boy, buddy."

Edgar cawed, then pecked at Martin's face with his beak, which elicited laughter from the boy.

A cell phone chimed and Martin answered it. "Hi, Mom." He paused. "Okay, I'll be right down." He shut the phone. "Time for me to go."

Jake guided the boy through the suite to the door. "How about next Saturday?"

"You got it."

Jake watched Martin board the elevator, then closed the door and locked it.

Returning to his office, he stopped in his tracks. A woman sat in the chair facing his desk. Edgar perched on the arm she held upright for him.

"I've really got to upgrade my security. It doesn't do much good against you cosmic types."

Sheryl rose and faced him. Edgar remained on her arm.

Jake moved closer to her. "Edgar seems to trust you."

"Don't you?" Her hair appeared short, the way she liked it.

"I have my doubts."

"Your face looks better."

"I look like a jigsaw puzzle. Eighty stitches. My doctor recommends plastic surgery."

"That sounds like a good idea."

"Maybe I'll wait to see what the scars look like before I decide. Is this a social visit? I thought you and Abel would be honeymooning in the clouds by now."

"Don't sulk."

"I'm not sulking. I'm disfigured. Thanks for getting me

involved in all this."

"Marla Madigan got you involved before I came to you, and so did Joyce."

"Why did you add your two cents?"

"I wanted to make sure you were properly motivated and had a sense of the bigger picture if you stumbled on Avademe."

"Your new in-laws. I hope to God you aren't here to enlist me in another cause. I need a break from this heaven and hell stuff."

"I didn't come here to ask you for any favors. I doubt you'll see me—or anyone else from the Realm of Light—again. We're busy getting our house in order."

"Then why are you here?"

"I came to say good-bye, for one thing. I didn't get a chance to back at Reichard's shipyard."

"You did take off kind of fast."

"I also came to thank you . . . and to reward you."

Jake raised his eyebrows. "With a kiss? Does Abel know you're here?"

She smiled. "I came to give you something you desire much more than a kiss from me."

"Don't be so sure about that."

Sheryl turned to Edgar. "Part of my soul resided inside you for almost a year and a half. I was aware of everything you did during that time, except whenever you entered that psychic business downstairs. That was the first blind spot I encountered after the Tower. And ever since then, your mind has acted as a blind spot to me, too. I've been unable to observe you in that parlor and unable to read your thoughts where the psychic's involved."

Holding Sheryl's gaze, Jake said nothing. Instead, he visualized that brick wall, just to be safe.

"She must be a very powerful witch."

It had occurred to Jake that Laurel was more than a psychic. After all, Kira Thorn had created the shield for Old Nick, and she had studied witchcraft with a coven in Massachusetts. "Who said my psychic connection is a she?"

Sheryl's eyes twinkled. "Call it a woman's intuition. Or maybe this psychic never thought to create a blind spot within Edgar."

Jake glanced at the raven, his heart beating faster.

"But that doesn't really matter. What does matter is this: she told you Katrina was the only person who could reverse the spell that turned Edgar into a raven, and that isn't true. A reversal spell can be performed by someone else from Katrina's bloodline."

Jake stared at Sheryl. "Katrina was an orphan. Drug dealers killed her parents."

"She had other relatives."

"Her grandmother was her guardian. She drowned in New Orleans."

"You're a private eye. Start snooping. There's a solution to Edgar's predicament, but you'd better hurry: he loses a little more of his humanity every day he remains in this form, and he's aging twice as fast as a human."

"Can't you just tell me who I should look for?"

"Don't push your luck."

"Abel told me a lot more—"

Sheryl cocked one eyebrow, which Jake took as a warning. She tapped Edgar's beak. "Thanks for everything, Jake. I mean that. I hope you find happiness." She waved her arm and Edgar flapped his wings, settling on Jake's shoulder.

As the bird turned around, Jake frowned. Sheryl had disappeared. Jake walked to the window and gazed out at the Tower. It seemed like any other building now. The day's commotion over the murders of the cabal members, including the mayor of New York City, awaited him. Looking at Edgar, he wondered if Laurel had simply not known there was a chance Edgar could still be returned to his normal self or if she had deliberately withheld the information.

"So much for putting this supernatural shit behind us."

Edgar croaked.

Staring at the raven, Jake recalled that his partner had admired the poetry of Emily Dickinson.

"'Parting is all we know of heaven, and all we need of hell.'"

The Jake Helman files
TORTURED SPIRITS
OCTOBER 2012

THE JAKE HELMAN FILES
PERSONAL DEMONS
BY GREGORY LAMBERSON

Jake Helman, an elite member of the New York Special Homicide Task Force, faces what every cop dreads—an elusive serial killer. While investigating a series of bloodletting sacrifice rituals executed by an ominous perpetrator known as The Cipher, Jake refuses to submit to a drug test and resigns from the police department. Tower International, a controversial genetic engineering company, employs him as their director of security.

While battling an addiction to cocaine, Jake enters his new high-pressure position in the private sector. What he encounters behind the closed doors of this sinister operation is beyond the realm of human imagination. Too horrible to contemplate, the experimentation is pure madness, the outcome a hell where only pain and terror reside. Nicholas Tower is not the hero flaunted on the cover of Time magazine. Beneath the polished exterior of this frontiersman on the cutting edge of science is a corporate executive surrounded by the creations of his deranged mind.

As Jake delves deeper into the hidden sphere of this frightening laboratory, his discoveries elicit more than condemnation for unethical practices performed for the good of mankind. Sequestered in rooms veiled in secrecy is the worst crime the world will ever see—the theft of the human soul.

ISBN# 978-160542072-1
Mass Market Paperback / Horror
US $7.95 / CDN $8.95
AVAILABLE NOW
www.slimeguy.com

THE JAKE HELMAN FILES
DESPERATE
BY GREGORY LAMBERSON SOULS

They're not breathing. That's why they're so still. But that's not possible . . .

Eleven months after battling Nicholas Tower and the demon Cain, Jake Helman has set up shop as a private investigator in Lower Manhattan. When a woman hires Jake to prove that her dead grandson is dealing a deadly new drug called "Black Magic" on a Brooklyn street corner, Jake uncovers a vicious drug lord's plot to use voodoo to seize control of the city.

While panic grips New York City, Jake Helman battles gun-wielding zombie assassins, hallucinations, and betrayal at every corner. But voodoo creates more terrors than zombies, and Jake finds himself poised on the edge of insanity as he fights to restore the soul of the one person he trusts.

ISBN# 978-160542170-4
Mass Market Paperback / Horror
US $7.95 / CDN $8.95
AVAILABLE NOW
w w w . s l i m e g u y . c o m

Also By  GREGORY LAMBERSON

THE FRENZY WAY

ISBN# 9781605421070
Trade Paperback / Horror
US $15.95 / CDN $17.95
AVAILABLE NOW

THE FRENZY WAR

ISBN# 9781605424538
Trade Paperback / Horror
US $14.95 / JUNE 2012

MEDALLION
P R E S S

Be in the know on the latest
Medallion Press news by becoming a
Medallion Press Insider!

<u>As an Insider you'll receive:</u>

• Our FREE expanded monthly newsletter, giving you
more insight into Medallion Press

• Advanced press releases and breaking news

• Greater access to all your favorite Medallion authors

Joining is easy. Just visit our website at
<u>www.medallionpress.com</u> and click on the Medallion
Press Insider tab.

1215

MEDALLION

P   R   E   S   S